HER ODDS AGAINST HAPPINESS
WERE TWO AGAINST ONE

There were three men in Caroline Hanscombe's life.

One was her father, the angrily imperious Sir Alfred, who ordered her to wed for the wealth he desperately needed, and threatened to blight her beloved sister's chances for happiness if Caroline refused.

One was Jason Kincaid, the devastatingly handsome Baron Radford, who made her an offer of marriage for reasons she did not know but could only fear, since he clearly loved another far more fervently than he could love her.

And the third was the honorable Captain Richard Davenport, who would never dream of stealing another man's intended bride, no matter how much he wanted her . . . or how much she wanted him to. . . .

The Diabolical Baron

Mary Jo Putney

AN ONYX BOOK

ONYX
Published by New American Library, a division of
Penguin Putnam Inc., 375 Hudson Street,
New York, New York 10014, U.S.A.
Penguin Books Ltd, 27 Wrights Lane,
London W8 5TZ, England
Penguin Books Australia Ltd,
Ringwood, Victoria, Australia
Penguin Books Canada Ltd, 10 Alcorn Avenue,
Toronto, Ontario, Canada M4V 3B2
Penguin Books (N.Z.) Ltd, 182–190 Wairau Road,
Auckland 10, New Zealand

Penguin Books Ltd, Registered Offices:
Harmondsworth, Middlesex, England

Published by ONYX, an imprint of New American Library,
a division of Penguin Putnam Inc. Previously published in a Signet edition.

First ONYX Printing, August 1999
10 9 8 7 6 5 4 3 2

*To Eileen Nauman,
for generous professional guidance
and to
my fishy friend, John,
for total warmth and support*

Chapter 1

"Lord Radford," announced the butler in a voice whose chilly perfection exactly matched the elegant salon his lordship was entering. Indeed, Jason Kincaid, nineteenth Baron Radford, could have also been characterized by the term "chilly perfection." Certainly his appearance came as near as humanly possible to that state. His tall, broad-shouldered frame was admirably suited by flawless tailoring. Everything about him, from his mirror-bright top boots to his artfully styled black hair, proclaimed the man of fashion.

A closer study would have also revealed an athlete's muscles beneath the coat of blue superfine. The chill lay in his dark cynical eyes; a naturally passionate disposition had been warped by too many people who sought his fortune and influence. There had been few indeed who had more interest in "Jason" than in "Lord Radford."

On this occasion, a certain uneasiness lay behind his impassive face. Since Honoria, the dowager Lady Edgeware, had been intimidating people since the reign of George II, discomfort was not surprising. In addition, Lord Radford suspected he knew the cause of his aunt's imperious summons, and her temper would not have improved during the three days he had kept her waiting for his appearance.

Disdaining preliminaries, Lady Edgeware fixed her target with snapping black eyes and attacked with a directness Napoleon might have envied. "It was your birthday last week, Radford."

"Indeed, Aunt Honoria. Since it is April, I am not entirely surprised by the news. All of my birthdays have fallen in April, I believe."

"I'll have none of your insolence! By my calculations, you now have thirty-five years in your dish. What are your plans for securing the succession?"

Lord Radford permitted himself a wry inward smile. The Honorable Honoria Kincaid's marriage to Lord Edgeware fifty-some years ago had not made her forgo allegiance to the Kincaids; on the contrary, her persecuted relations unanimously agreed that she delighted in bullying two families. Considering the importance she placed on the Radford title, it was surprising she had held off so long before choosing to dress him down.

It would have surprised him more to know he was the only member of her two families that she felt any hesitation about interfering with. Other relatives would have understood: Lord Radford and Lady Edgeware were generally acknowledged to be the spit and image of each other, from their unyielding dispositions to the darkly sardonic eyes and tight lines around the mouths that marred the classical regularity of their faces.

"The family is a long way from running out of Kincaids, Aunt. Surely Cousin Oliver has two or three potential heirs amongst his brood?"

"Bah, they stink of the shop!" Lady Edgeware spat

out, dismissing the whole branch for her nephew Oliver's crime of marrying a young lady whose grandfather had made his fortune in trade. It was of no consequence that Oliver and his growing family showed every sign of being happier than any of her more toplofty relatives.

"Of course you weren't the elder son, but your brother Robert has been dead more than five years now. You are perfectly aware of your obligation to your name, but I have yet to hear you've paid the least attention to any eligible female. Keep as many married mistresses as you like, but it's high time you found yourself a wife and got an heir on her."

"Such plain speaking, Aunt Honoria! Almost I regret to tell you I have been thinking along similar lines myself," Lord Radford drawled.

"Indeed? Who's the gel?" Honoria demanded.

"I've no one in mind," Jason said indifferently, "but I don't think a suitable wife should be hard to find. After all, the title is one of the oldest in England. More important, the Radford estates are known to be extensive and prospering."

"Aye, I can't quarrel with how much you've increased the annual property yields," the dowager said grudgingly.

If so, it's the first time I've heard of something you couldn't quarrel with! his lordship thought.

"But I'll never understand," she continued irascibly, "why you felt it necessary to waste such money on schools for the tenants' children and on rebuilding cottages."

"Would you believe I did it from Christian charity?" he inquired. Taking her ladyship's snort for an answer, he continued, "The money I 'wasted' is actually the cause of the improved yields you so admire. Tenants who don't suffer rheumatism from damp houses and who have a modicum of education prove to be vastly more productive farmers. My father seldom invested a groat in Wildehaven, and the smaller properties were in even worse case. My dear brother could never even remember his bailiff's name. Land will not prosper without proper care, and only a fool will kill his golden goose."

Lady Edgeware gave a bark of cynical laughter. "There are plenty of such around. I hear that you are interested in acquiring some lands from one of your foolish neighbors."

"Your sources of information never cease to amaze me. My distinguished neighbor the Earl of Wargrave managed to alienate every friend and relative he ever had before he died last year. The lawyers are trying to determine the heir. If there is no one left in the direct line, that wastrel Reggie Davenport will inherit. I believe he's the late earl's nephew. He may be happy to sell the unentailed property to finance his extravagances. The lands would make a nice addition to Wildehaven."

"It was typical of that old screw Wargrave that he would lose track of his own youngest son," Lady Edgeware said maliciously.

"Shocking language, Aunt. In fairness to Wargrave, it was logical to assume that one of the two older brothers would inherit. If I recall correctly, the youngest son left the country a good few years ago amidst some kind of scandal."

"He ran off with Randall's young sister. She was betrothed to some rich old lecher, and young Julius thought to rescue her. I never heard anything after that, but I suppose they ended up pinching pennies somewhere on the Continent. No doubt she eventually regretted her romantic escape. Love is poor compensation for poverty. Still, Julius would be the sixth Earl of Wargrave now. Or if he had a son, the son might be. If the lawyers can ever find him," Lady Edgeware said thoughtfully.

"If there is even a 'him' to find," Radford said dryly. "Meanwhile, there is a pack of cousins slavering for the title, with Reggie in the lead. A fortune like that won't go begging if the Crown decides there are no males left in the direct line."

"To return to our original discussion, may I assume that I will see you betrothed before this Season is over?"

"You may."

"Very well, you know what is due to your name. Let me know when you've chosen her so that I may hold a dinner to introduce the gel to her new family."

"You shall be one of the very first to know, Aunt. It only remains for me to make my choice, then inform the lucky lady."

The atmosphere that evening was rather different when the question of Lord Radford's marriage rose again. He and his boon companion, the Honorable George Fitzwilliam, had been lingering over their port for quite some time, and while they weren't precisely bosky, they were certainly past the point where discretion and judgment operate normally; in fact, they were ripe for becoming outrageous.

"Fine color this wine has, George," said Radford as he held the glass up to the candlelight. "I'm glad I laid in several cases' worth. By the way, I believe I'll be getting married."

"I say, Jason, perhaps we've had enough to drink. It sounded distinctly like you said you were going to marry, and when one starts hearing voices it's time to lay off the wine. Otherwise, I'll have a headache that would flatten a plow horse on the morrow," said Mr. Fitzwilliam with owl-like solemnity.

The friends did not much resemble each other. Lord Radford associated with the sporting Corinthian set and affected an elegantly simple mode of dress which perfectly suited his athletic form. Shorter, fair-haired, and slighter in build, the Honorable George Fitzwilliam looked much younger than Radford, though in fact only three years separated them. While he was described by some as a "fashionable fribble," it was an unjust accusation that would have wounded his sensibilities. Certainly he enjoyed following, and occasionally creating, the very latest fashions, and he wasn't above wearing quite daring waistcoats. However, he avoided extravagances such as overpadded shoulders, lilac pantaloons, and neckcloths so high as to prevent the wearer from turning his head. Charming and correct in his manners, hostesses always welcomed him for his willingness to dance with even the most regrettable female guest with never a loss of good nature.

"You heard me correctly, George. As my Aunt Honoria has kindly pointed out, it is time I married. So I shall do the deed."

"How splendid! What lovely lady has consented to be your bride?"

"None yet. That's why I wanted to talk to you.

You're much more *au courant* with the fashionable world than I. What is the selection this Season?"

"Do you just mean to choose one, like a horse at Tattersall's?"

"George, you do me an injustice! I spend considerably more thought on selecting my horses."

"But . . . but what about love?" The Honorable George was something of an authority on the subject since he succumbed to the emotion at least half a dozen times a year. However, while his tender feelings had yet to show much longevity, they were undoubtedly sincere while they lasted. In fact, his own marriage would certainly follow the discovery of a lady for whom he could maintain a *tendre* for a twelvemonth.

"Bah, love is an illusion of the young and feckless, an illusion maintained by lady novelists for their own enrichment. How many couples of our order have you known to stay 'in love' for any length of time?"

"Well . . . there are the Grovelands . . . no, he's taken to keeping opera dancers again. Lord and Lady Wilberton . . . no, I heard they had a flaming row at a ball last month and haven't spoken since. And . . . well, my own parents are dashed fond of each other. You see?"

"On the contrary, you confirm my point. Surely theirs was an arranged marriage? A system that has gone out of style, but which had much to commend it. A rational analysis of family background, fortune, and station in life is surely the best foundation for a successful union."

"I very much doubt it," George said boldly. "And even if *you* don't believe in love, young ladies do."

Lord Radford's mouth crooked cynically. "I'm sure

any young lady will find it easy to fall in love with my title and fortune even if my person fails to please. I have been defending myself from matchmaking mamas and ambitious debutantes for years. Now that I am ready to throw down my handkerchief, I should have my pick of the available fillies."

"Jason, hasn't there ever been anyone that you wished to marry?"

"Well . . . once when I was very young," Lord Radford said with a softening of his eyes. He gently swirled the wine in his crystal goblet, divining the past from its burgundy depths. "I was just down from Cambridge, and was hunting in the shires when I met her. I thought she was the most dazzling female I'd ever laid eyes on. Rode like Diana, hair like flame, and a figure that would keep a Cyprian wrapped in jewels for the rest of her life. It appeared to be love at first sight, but when I offered her my hand, my not inconsiderable fortune, and my honorable name, she threw them back in my face."

"You actually made an offer for her, and she turned you down?" George gasped. Having seen women languish after his friend for years, he was hard put to imagine so firm a rejection. "Was she attached to someone else?"

"She gave every evidence of returning my feelings," Radford said, then stopped in mid-sentence at an unexpectedly vivid stab of long-buried pain. A gentleman could not talk about it, but he had never forgotten those forbidden kisses stolen in the garden one magic night. Such sweetness, and such fire. . . . He had searched in many places for their equal, but without success. And finally, of course, he had ceased searching.

He shook off the memory and continued, "And one would have thought she would welcome the match. Her birth was unexceptionable, but her father had gambled away his fortune and they were living in reduced circumstances. She was due to be presented the next Season, but it's doubtful the family could have afforded to have done the thing in style. It would be hard to catch a duke if looking shabby genteel."

"Do you think she would have accepted you if you'd been Lord Radford instead of a younger son?"

"I have to say she probably wasn't hanging out for a title. I'm not even sure she knew my father was Lord Radford; it all happened so quickly. I later heard she married a military man and went off to India. No doubt she has long since succumbed to fat and freckles, if what I hear about the Indian cuisine and climate is true."

"But surely that proves that not all women are mercenary."

"It proves women are incomprehensible. At least the mercenary ones are easy to understand. Since they are the vast majority, I shouldn't have any trouble selecting the future Lady Radford. To get back to my earlier question, who is available this Season who would be suitable? You are much more in touch with the Marriage Mart than I—choose the future Lady Radford for me."

"Jason, do you seriously think that any girl you offer for will accept you?"

"In a word, yes. Or to be more accurate, she'll accept my fortune and title."

"Would you care to wager on that—staking your team of grays on it?"

Radford considered for a moment, then drawled, "It

depends. What is your stake, and what are the conditions?"

"Let's see . . . what if I bet a season of salmon fishing at my Scottish uncle's estate? He allows only a dozen guests a year, and I'll give you my position if you win." George made the offer with a touch of guilt. He wasn't overfond of fishing himself, but since Jason was addicted to all forms of sport, the incomparable Craigmore waters would make a desirable prize. And if Jason lost the wager, his magnificent team of grays would allow the Honorable George to cut a considerable dash at the fashionable park promenades.

"As to conditions," he continued, "give me a list of your requirements in a wife, and I will write down the name of every eligible lady who fits them. Then we'll put the names in a bowl and you can draw one out. You must take the chosen lady to the altar within six months to win the wager."

"Done! It is as good a way of choosing a wife as any other. Now, my requirements: she must be of good birth, naturally, and with no madness, serious health problems, or really offensive behavior in her family."

"You've just eliminated half of the *ton!*" George chuckled. "Still, not an unreasonable requirement. What else?"

"She must be passably good-looking—no sour-faced antidotes. After all, I shall have to see her in the daylight sometimes. And I don't want any spoiled, petulant Beauties who are used to having odes written to their eyebrows and who expect men to languish at their feet."

"Right, no Beauties. Is there anything else you particularly want? Think carefully, you are choosing your life's companion here, Jason."

"No need to make a great drama of this—any well-brought-up, docile maiden of average looks will do. How many can you come up with?"

The next half-hour was punctuated by the scratching of a pen and George's muttering of such phrases as, "No, Miss Emerson-Smythe won't do, she has a distinct squint," and, "Hamilton's run off his legs and would demand some ridiculous settlement for that frumpy daughter of his." A bottle of wine later, he had twenty-some names ready for the drawing.

"There you are, Jason, a careful selection of the most eligible young ladies the polite world can offer. Choose your future!" Mr. Fitzwilliam dropped the slips of paper in a bowl, first dumping the nuts it contained on the table, then swirled the bowl ceremoniously and held it well above his head.

Lord Radford also stood, carefully adjusted his cuffs, and reached into the bowl. A moment's fumbling, then he pulled a slip out, opened it, and stared at the name.

"Well, who is she?" George said eagerly.

"Caroline Hanscombe. The name is unfamiliar to me. What can you tell me about her?"

His friend looked a bit disappointed as possession of the coveted team of grays became unlikely. "She shouldn't be too much of a challenge. She's a quiet little thing with no conversation. Not unattractive, but two or three years older than the average debutante. Almost on the shelf. Her parents kept her back to present her with a younger sister. Her father, Sir Alfred Hanscombe, is a bit of an oaf but wellborn enough. The sister, Gina, is a jolly strapping wench, much livelier—but she's nearly betrothed. Still, I'm sure Miss

Hanscombe will make you a fine, tractable wife, or I shouldn't have entered her name."

"Caroline Kincaid, Lady Radford. It sounds well enough. I suppose she'll be at Almack's tomorrow night with the rest of the husband-hunting maidens. Lord, I haven't been to one of those stuffy assemblies in years—courting has hazards I hadn't anticipated. Shall we drink to my future wife?"

Raising their glasses, they solemnly clinked them together. "To Lady Radford!"

"Aunt Jessica, can you give me one good reason why I should go to Almack's tonight?"

Jessica Sterling raised her auburn head from her mending and smiled sympathetically at her favorite visitor. "Well, your stepmama will insist on it, for one."

"That's a compelling reason but not a *good* one. Truly, Jess, isn't there some way I can get off this marriage-go-round?" Caroline Hanscombe raised her tawny head from the lute she was tuning, her deep blue eyes shaded with humorous pleading. While her proportions were pleasing and her movements graceful, she was characterized as "a mere dab of a girl" by more than one critical elder. She forgot her shyness only with close friends or when she was absorbed in music; then her delicate face relaxed to a dreamy, ethereal loveliness.

More often, her considerable intelligence and humor were concealed behind the anxious look produced by her stepmother's continual criticism. Her small stature and dark blond coloring gave her a chameleonlike ability to fade into the background on the numerous occasions when she wished to avoid notice. On this early-morning visit to the aunt who was also her best friend, she could speak her mind in a way impossible under her parents' roof.

"Oh, Caro, I do wish you enjoyed the parties more. They can be quite fun—I enjoyed my own come-out tremendously."

"Confess, Aunt: you haven't a shy bone in your body. And beautiful as you are, half the men in London must have been languishing for a single look from your glorious green eyes."

Jessica chuckled engagingly. "It wasn't quite like that. While I attracted some attention—including, my girl, sixteen sonnets and no fewer than *three* odes—I was considered too headstrong by the high sticklers. And indeed, they were right. I really wouldn't want you to follow my social example too closely. Although," she said parenthetically, "I do believe I would have attracted less censure had I not had red hair. It was *very* hard to pass unnoticed! You are much better at rendering yourself invisible than I. But it would be nice if you could see the Season as something other than torture."

"It *is* torture. I feel paralyzed by shyness whenever I meet someone new. And when one of the dragons looks me over and so clearly finds me wanting . . . ! Almack's is the worst of all. The patronesses are positively panting to find something wrong with us trembling mortals. I shrink to think of it."

"Still, it is a young woman's best opportunity to meet a future husband. Much of aristocratic Britain gathers in London to mingle. It gives you the opportunity to meet people you would never discover buried on your father's estate in Wiltshire."

Caroline sighed. "But since the purpose of it all is to

catch a husband, I still cannot become enthusiastic. I don't want to marry; I want to move in here with you. Apart from Signore Ferrante's house, this is the only place I have ever been comfortable. And while he has been the best and kindest of music masters, I can't imagine that he would want me to live with him."

Jessica's gaze softened as she looked at her niece. "You know I would love to have you. But you are too young to bury yourself with a widowed aunt and her daughter in an unfashionable neighborhood. Marriage is what you make of it—you can see it as a trap or as a girl's main chance to change her life. If you didn't like the way you were raised, attach a man in a different mold from your father. It's something of a gamble, of course, but it makes life more interesting."

Caroline giggled mischievously. "Jessica, you're incorrigible. You look and sound exactly the way you did when you were breaking all those hearts at seventeen. I was only eight then, but I remember clearly. It's all very well for you to say 'attach a man' as if it were just a matter of making your choice. That may have been true for you, but I have no such magical power over the opposite sex. And I wouldn't want such power! I can truly think of no happier life than to move in here with you and Linda and your admirable pianoforte."

Jessica sighed and applied herself to her sewing for a few moments. While complimentary gentlemen were fond of saying that she looked no more than a girl, she felt the weight of her experiences if not her years. The life of an officer's wife had been exciting, but also full of fears and constant change. She was thirty years old, had borne a child and buried a husband, and would never be truly young again.

"Things change, love. It may seem like the ideal life for you now, but nothing remains the same. Linda will grow up and marry, you might start longing for a nursery of your own—I might even marry myself. One can't choose a way of life and say, 'It will stay like this.'"

"Do you really think you might marry again? It is the first time I have ever heard you mention the possibility."

"While I have accepted the idea of remarriage in principle, it may never happen in practice. My income is not great, but it is adequate, and I do enjoy my freedom. It would take someone very special to make me wish to marry again, and that is unlikely to happen a third time."

"A third time? Was there someone besides John?" Caroline looked up in surprise from the now-tuned lute.

"Oh, just one of those calf-love affairs." Her aunt shrugged dismissively. "I ruined it through my foolish temper, though I'm sure it was doomed anyway because we were both so young. Still, it was very . . . intense. And one doesn't meet too many kindred spirits in a lifetime."

Caroline's curiosity was aroused, but since her aunt had closed the subject, she struck a chord on the lute and said, "Shall we return once more to the dread topic of Almack's? Tell me what I should wear, then I shall play you some of the new Elizabethan dances I have learned." She underlined her last words with several toe-tapping measures.

"Minx! I know perfectly well you have been dressing as unbecomingly as possible to repel potential suitors. And though it is unkind of me to admit it, all that has been required is wearing what your stepmother bids- you. Her taste is adequate for herself and her high-colored daughters, but does nothing for you, as well you know. When you meet a man you fancy, you'll start wearing clothes that do you justice. So choose whatever gown least becomes you, and let us hear your new dances."

The law firm of Chelmsford and Marlin, Solicitors, resembled any other such office in the City of London. Bland and impenetrable, it sat on its secrets. Inside, the young man climbing the stairs to Josiah Chelmsford, senior partner, moved with a hesitation beyond the physical limp of his right leg. His face was worn with an accumulation of fatigue and pain—a familiar look on soldiers who had fought for England and were no longer needed in the aftermath of Waterloo.

The man known as Richard Dalton was glad to have closed the book on that chapter of his life. Waterloo lay ten months in the past, and much of that interval had been spent learning to walk again. He approached what the doctors thought an impossible task with the silent determination that was one of his chief characteristics. That same iron will had kept his command nearly intact while fighting across four countries, and inspired his troops with a loyalty and respect bordering on reverence. Yet though he still wore his faded uniform, in his heart he was a captain no longer.

Like most people, he regarded lawyers warily, but a chance glimpse of a small advertisement had brought him here today.

ANYONE KNOWING THE WHEREABOUTS OF JULIUS DAVENPORT OR ANY OF HIS HEIRS IS ASKED TO CON-

TACT CHELMSFORD AND MARLIN, HOLBORN, TO LEARN
SOMETHING OF BENEFIT TO SAID JULIUS DAVENPORT
AND HEIRS.

The advertisement had been running in the *Gazette*
for months, though Richard had been in no position to
see it. When it did catch his eye, he very nearly did
not respond. But curiosity outweighed lethargy, and
now he was being announced by the surly law clerk.
"Captain Richard Dalton to see you."

"Come in, come in!" Josiah Chelmsford's brusque
voice carried easily across the cluttered office. The rotund lawyer glanced up impatiently from his paper-
covered desk, then paused with an arrested expression
on his face. Surveying his visitor carefully, he saw a
young man of medium height and wiry build, with a
gaunt face that would have been handsome were it
less tired. Needs fattening up, the lawyer thought. The
thick brown hair was fashionably casual, but through
nature, not artifice. Changeable hazel eyes with a crin-
kle of laughter lines looked from a face browned by
years in a harsher sun than England's.

The lawyer stood up slowly, extending his hand
over the desk. "Don't tell me you are anyone other
than Julius Davenport's son, because I won't believe
you."

The smile that lit Richard's face as he shook Chelmsford's hand made him look younger than his twenty-
eight years. "You knew my father, sir? I am said to
resemble him greatly."

"You do indeed. The features show some of your
mother, but the build and coloring and overall impression are Julius to the life. Where is your father now?"

"Dead these last three years."

Chelmsford sighed and shook his head as he settled back into his chair. "Have a seat, boy. It is what I feared. I'd heard from him now and again over the years—not much, just an occasional note. But it has been too long since last he wrote. What happened, if you'll pardon my asking?"

"He and my mother were sailing a small boat in the Greek Isles. A sudden squall came up—they had no chance." Richard's voice was tight; he paused a moment, then continued. "It was what they would have wanted, to go together. Few people get the chance to die doing what they love, with the one they love most."

He stopped abruptly, having said more than he intended. He had spoken to no one of the tragedy since the village priest's letter reporting the accident had reached him in Spain. First he couldn't talk about it, and then there had been no one who had known his family. Living in a world where the friend one breakfasted with might be dead by nightfall, it had seemed wrong to burden another with his private grief. Speaking of his parents now brought a sense of release, a loosening of the knot of tension he had carried for years.

Deliberately lightening his tone, Richard said, "What is this talk of 'benefit' in your advertisement? My father was heir to a chest of diamonds, perhaps?"

"Not precisely," the lawyer said seriously. "Tell me, how much do you know of your parents' background?"

"Almost nothing, really," Richard replied. "I know they left England abruptly at the time of their marriage, and they never talked of earlier times. I do know my father's real name was Davenport, but we always used the name Dalton."

"And you never knew the reason why?" Chelmsford persisted.

"One doesn't spend too much time speculating about a parent's unlawful conduct," Richard said dryly. "I suspect my father killed someone in a duel— a matter concerning my mother, perhaps. He was lethal with both sword and pistol, and would not have hesitated to use them if necessary.

"As a child I just accepted the name change—only later did I wonder. I think my parents wanted to forget the past. They lived very much in the present, wasting no time on regrets or worries about the future."

"Your guess is correct. There was indeed a duel." The lawyer gave a short bark of laughter. "It was no great loss to the world. Lord Barford was a filthy old *roué*, and had been living on borrowed time for years. He was betrothed to your mother against her will. She and your father were childhood playmates and sweethearts, but both sets of parents objected to the match since neither of them had any real fortune. Julius fought and killed Barford. His father disowned him over the scandal—they had never gotten on well. After that, it was not surprising your parents preferred the Continent. Do you have any idea who your paternal grandfather was?"

"Some gentleman named Davenport, I assume."

"Not 'some gentleman.' Your grandfather was the fifth Earl of Wargrave. And with your father dead, you are the sixth earl."

A heavy silence hung in the dusty office. A nearby church bell could be heard striking the noon hour. Richard felt a chaotic whirl of emotions, but the predominant one was anger. His eyes narrowed and his voice was clipped as he said, "I want no part of it. That damned old man rejected my mother and father, and I want nothing of his. Nothing!"

He stood and stalked to the window, tension in every line of his body. As he looked across the sweep of London, his irritation ebbed, leaving amusement in its wake. It was a strange reaction to what most people would consider a honeyfall. Anger aimed at an unknown grandfather was a waste. Being cut off from their families hadn't ruined his parents' lives; on the contrary, he had never known two happier people.

When he was relaxed again, he turned back to Josiah and said steadily, "Quite apart from how my father was treated, I have no wish to be an earl. Great wealth is a great burden. I want nothing more from life now than my freedom."

"Since when has responsibility been a question of choice?" the solicitor asked. "Your grandfather was an evil-tempered old tyrant who did little for the land or the people he controlled. The heir after you is an extravagant rake who will complete the destruction of Wargrave in no time at all. Do you have any idea how many families depend on the estates you now own?"

"No, nor do I care. It is nothing to me. I lived the first half of my life out of England. I was schooled here, but spent the next seven years fighting this country's battles under conditions that would cause convicts to riot. Do not speak to me of responsibility. I have paid any debt I owe England a dozen times over."

The hazel eyes were unflinching, and Chelmsford was forcibly reminded of Julius Davenport thirty years before, declaring family and fortune of no importance when weighed against the woman he loved.

"I have no desire to force you into anything. I was far too fond of your father to coerce his son. But I think he hoped you would come back here someday."

"Why do you say that?"

"Because he sent notarized copies of his wedding lines and your birth certificate as those events occurred. He was the youngest son but life is uncertain. There was always a chance you would inherit, and he must have wanted to make it easy for you to prove your identity. Don't you think you owe it to yourself and him to look at what you are throwing away? You may find a feeling for your heritage that goes beyond the burdens involved. Or is there some other part of the world that calls you?"

"No, there is nowhere else I wish to go," Richard said slowly. His anger had passed, leaving weariness in its wake. With his parents dead he no longer had a home. The handful of military friends who had survived the wars were closer than brothers, but they were scattered to their own lives now. There was no place or person he owed any special loyalty. And only a fool would cast aside even an unwanted fortune without investigating it first. "What is this legacy you are so anxious to foist on me?"

Content to have captured the captain's attention, Josiah Chelmsford started to explain what it meant to be the Earl of Wargrave.

Chapter 2

Caroline Hanscombe carefully checked her appearance in the mirror. Success! She definitely looked a dowd. Not only that, a short, easily overlooked dowd—certainly so insignificant that no gentleman at Almack's would look across the crowded room and decide his life would be incomplete if he did not meet her. The white muslin dress, so suitable for a young miss in her first Season, made Caroline look pale and wispy. Its shapeless cut did a good job of concealing her slender figure, and the neckline was too high for fashion. She abjured the maidenly trick of pinching her cheeks for heightened color, and her dark blond curls drooped around her face to obscure her features.

"Are you ready yet, Caro? Do I look all right? Do you suppose that Mr. Fallsworthy will be there? I do so hope he likes my dress." The buxom maiden who bounced into the room clearly did not share her half-sister's desire for concealment. Her rose-pink gown did not show her ruddy coloring to complete advantage, but it was a pretty and distinctive shade, and cut as low as she dared without being utterly beyond the line for a girl in her first Season. Her elaborate garnet necklace drew attention to her abundant charms, should someone have missed them.

Caroline smiled affectionately at Gina. They managed to be friends in spite of different tastes and temperaments, and Lady Hanscombe's unconcealed preference for her first-born daughter over the undersize child she had acquired with her marriage to Sir Alfred.

"As ready as I'll ever be, Gina. You look quite delightful, and of course Gideon Fallsworthy will be there. He has never missed an occasion when he knew you would be present, and I don't believe he will start tonight. I certainly wish I could share your enthusiasm for this evening's treats."

"I will never get over enjoying Almack's. I still can't believe that Mama managed to procure vouchers for the most exclusive gatherings in the fashionable world. I expect it was because your mother was related to two of the patronesses, and they had to take me along with you," Gina said shrewdly.

Caroline nodded in agreement; the first Lady Hanscombe was much better connected than the second. Louisa Hicks was thought to have made a good catch when she persuaded Sir Alfred Hanscombe to let her soothe his broken heart after his first wife's death. Critics said he had let himself be soothed with indecent speed.

The two young ladies left Caroline's room and headed down the stairs where Lady Hanscombe waited. Her ladyship nodded in approval of their appearances; quite right that her own daughter outshone her half-sister. Louisa Hanscombe was not actively hostile to Caroline and would have indignantly rejected any suggestion that she had not done her duty by her stepdaughter. Still, there was her own hopeful brood of three daughters and two sons to be provided

for, and she wanted Caroline taken care of in a way
that would not reduce her own children's prospects.

"Come along now, we don't want to keep the horses
waiting," she boomed in a voice ill-suited to a drawing
room. A tall, heavyset woman with iron-gray curls,
Lady Hanscombe was possessed of a limited understanding that kept her from any appreciation of her
stepdaughter's talents or sensitivities. Their relationship was based on duty; without love it didn't prosper.
Caroline's dreamy absentmindedness drove Louisa to
distraction, while the older woman's abrasive voice
and criticisms reduced the girl to silence or fearful
stammering.

Gina could cheerfully ignore her mother's dogmatic
opinions, or bellow back if needful; Caroline coped by
disappearing until the storms subsided. Unfortunately
it was harder to hide in London. With the younger
children home in Wiltshire, Lady Hanscombe was free
to concentrate on making sure the girls didn't waste
their social opportunities.

The Hanscombes' rental town house was on Adam
Street—not the first stare of fashion, but a respectable-
enough address, and only a short ride to King Street.
The small party entered Almack's at the perfect time—
not so early as to appear anxious, nor so late as to appear blasé. The vast entry hall was clearly designed to
impress on the fainthearted that the pinnacle of Polite
Society had been attained. Since most guests were sen-
sible of the honor of receiving vouchers to the sub-
scription balls, the patronesses felt it unnecessary to
waste money on high-quality refreshments or musicians. The stale cakes and insipid drinks were notorious, and the orchestra occasionally made Caroline

shudder—one of the violinists seemed incapable of keeping his instruments in tune.

This evening started like the other half-dozen assemblies they had attended here: dowagers and unclaimed young ladies chatting in chairs around the walls of the main salon, couples dancing, and dozens of sharp eyes watching to see what interesting connections might occur.

Also on schedule, Gideon Fallsworthy hurried up to claim Gina's hand for the country dance now forming, and to beg the honor of a waltz later in the evening. Since he would be allowed only two dances with the lady of his choice, he definitely wanted one to be the exciting and erotic new Austrian dance that had taken London by storm. Traditionalists considered the waltz very daring, but young lovers were delighted to hold each other close publicly.

"You are in rare good looks this evening, Miss Gina. Will you join me for this dance? And pray save a dance for me, Miss Hanscombe," he added to Caroline with a friendly smile. Gideon was a pleasant-looking young man with a slight tendency to beefiness. His intelligence was not profound, but he had a kind heart and a smile of great sweetness. He had endeared himself to Gina by his obvious belief that she was the handsomest and most amusing female he had ever met, and to Lady Hanscombe by being heir to a fine property in Lincolnshire. The match might not be a brilliant one but it was respectable, and her ladyship daily expected Gideon to call on Sir Alfred to request Gina's hand.

As the happy couple moved onto the floor, Caroline sat next to Lady Hanscombe and absently watched the elegantly garbed people dipping and turning in the figures of the dance. She could amuse herself indefinitely this way, withdrawing into the world of her imagination and mentally playing variations on the music. With her highly developed talent for invisibility, she should be left alone most of the evening. She had been very successful at discouraging possible suitors; the few men who asked her to dance seldom troubled to do so a second time. There had been one regrettable young man with rabbity front teeth who had been disposed to admire her, but she had discouraged him with references to her father's violent temper and his oft-expressed wish to keep his eldest daughter as a Comfort in his Old Age, a view that would have much surprised that gentleman, since he barely troubled to tell his daughters apart and frequently said he looked forward to getting them off his hands.

The evening was well advanced when she noticed purposeful movement in her direction. She recognized George Fitzwilliam, who had partnered her on several occasions when hostesses prevailed on him to help with the wallflowers. George was pleasant, unthreatening company, but she frowned slightly at the sight of his companion, a tall, darkly impressive man who radiated arrogance and power.

Mr. Fitzwilliam arrived and swept his most graceful bow. "Lady Hanscombe, Miss Hanscombe, my friend Lord Radford has begged me for the pleasure of an introduction to you."

Lady Hanscombe bridled happily. "The pleasure is ours, Lord Radford. My other daughter is about, and I'm sure she would also be delighted to make your acquaintance."

While Lady Hanscombe and the Honorable George exchanged polite nothings, Caroline looked up at his lordship's dark eyes and froze under his piercing gaze. This must be how a rabbit feels while it waits for a ferret to strike, she thought wildly. She had no idea what he was looking for, but the dark stare under the ferocious brows was anything but casual.

"Will you do me the honor of accepting this dance, Miss Hanscombe?" His deep voice was abrupt, projecting the same sense of power that his appearance did.

Caroline nodded mutely; what else could she do? She rose and went onto the floor with him. Unfortunately the orchestra was striking up the first notes of a waltz. "Have you been given permission to dance the waltz here, Miss Hanscombe? . . . No? Then let us get it for you."

Looking across the room, Radford caught the roving eye of Lady Jersey. He gestured expressively at his partner, Lady Jersey nodded, and then Caroline was swept into his arms. She was startled at his speed of action. Her lack of permission to dance the waltz would have been a good excuse to cry off from the dance; before she could even voice her thought, the objection had been overcome.

Looking down at the fair curly head, Jason didn't know whether to be amused or irritated at her shyness. Certainly there was no lack of maidenly modesty. Pity she wasn't taller; she seemed determined to spend the dance examining the buttons on his waistcoat rather than strain her neck to look in his face. The chit wasn't at all bad-looking, he decided; dress her properly, get her hair out of her face, and he would not be ashamed to have her by his side.

For her part, Caroline felt like she was in a particularly bad dream. She didn't know that Radford's appearance at Almack's was so unusual as to be noteworthy, but she felt instinctively that eyes all over the room were watching them. She concentrated on dancing presentably since her only previous waltz experience had been with her brothers and the dancing master. Being held so close by a man of rather overpowering masculinity was quite a different matter. Why on earth had he asked her? There was no social connection between them, and there could be nothing in her appearance to attract a fashionable gentleman who could have his choice of partners anywhere he went.

"And what do you think of your first London Season, Miss Hanscombe?" Radford asked urbanely.

"It is very . . . interesting, my lord." The words were muffled by the downturned head.

"Has Almack's lived up to your expectations? Some find the reality a letdown from its reputation," he continued.

"I had no expectations, my lord."

Fitzwilliam certainly hadn't exaggerated about her lack of conversation. Still, Jason persevered with polite commonplaces. It was heavy going, but a gentleman known for his address could converse well enough for two. As he returned her to Lady Hanscombe, he said, "I hope you would not object to my calling on you soon, Miss Hanscombe."

She stared at him blankly for a moment, then murmured almost inaudibly, "Of course not, my lord."

Lord Radford moved away, pleased that his campaign was under way. Complicated tactics should not be required; the mother had clearly been dazzled to have the chit distinguished by his attention. Lady Hanscombe seemed to be a bit of a toadeater, but that

would work in his favor. Now that they had been formally introduced, he could call on the girl and further
the acquaintance. He would not rush things by dancing with her again tonight; that he had singled her out
was enough. It was just a matter of time. Boringly easy,
really.

While Lord Radford was searching for his friend Mr.
Fitzwilliam to call this portion of the evening to an
end, Caroline was being interrogated by Lady
Hanscombe. Unsure whether to be pleased that Caroline had been sought out, or insulted that Lord Radford had no interest in meeting Gina, her ladyship was
relentlessly extracting every iota of information.

"And then what did he say? . . . And you
replied? . . . And I myself heard him say he wished to
call on you. Straighten up, Caroline, don't slouch! Perhaps he has decided it is time to start hanging out for a
wife. Past time, really, the man has been on the town
this age! Well, I'm very sure he must be pleased with
you, there is no substitute for breeding and manners,
and you are a very pretty-behaved girl."

At this point her ladyship interrupted her monologue to look dubiously at Caroline. While the girl had
a well-bred air, it was difficult to imagine why someone like Radford would pay such distinguishing attention. Well, if he did call, it would give him a chance to
meet Gina and note her superior charms. If his lordship was ready for a wife, Gina was just as well-bred,
and more attractive as well. Here Lady Hanscombe
conveniently forgot that her own forebears could in no
way compare with those of Caroline's mother. At least,
not in the eyes of those who used the same standards
for judging people as they used for horseflesh.

Gina's enthusiasm was more generous but no easier to bear. Throughout the ride home she talked ceaselessly about Lord Radford's darkly handsome countenance, his superb tailoring, and his well-known fortune. "They say, Caro, that he *never* comes to Almack's, *or* dances with girls making their come-out. They say he has kept some of the most dashing high fliers—!"

"Gina, how dare you refer to such things!" Lady Hanscombe interjected. "It is not at all proper for you to know how gentlemen amuse themselves."

"But, Mama, everyone *does* know," Gina said irrepressibly. "He must have seen Caroline at a ball or in the park and decided he must make her acquaintance. It is so romantic!" Loyal to her older sister, Gina was quite willing to believe a gentleman would be struck instantly by Caroline's sweetness and charm. Content with her Gideon, she felt not a shred of jealousy. "It will quite make Caro socially. Everyone will wish to meet the girl who took Lord Radford's fancy."

Surrounded by such avid speculations, it was unnecessary for Caroline to say a word. And she could not discuss the most important fact about Lord Radford: that she didn't like him and had no desire to see him again. She knew it was irrational but she had felt deeply uncomfortable in his presence. Silent and unhappy, she had a throbbing headache when they returned to the Adam Street town house.

"Excuse me, Mama, I am very fatigued and wish to retire directly," Caroline said in a thin voice.

"Yes, yes, my dear, we must keep you in looks for Lord Radford's call," Lady Hanscombe said magnanimously.

Caroline's bedchamber had the slightly drab air

common to rental properties, but tonight it represented safety. She tossed her cloak across the shield-back chair, then walked slowly to the window and leaned her aching forehead against the cool glass. Logically, it made no sense to read so much into a single dance; even a wallflower such as herself had stood up with a number of men during the Season. But she had never been singled out in quite this way. Moreover, she felt in her bones that the encounter with Radford was significant. She had a mental image of herself as a twig that had been slowly drifting down a lazy creek. Now abruptly she had been seized by a current that could sweep her away from the life of music and peace she longed for.

Caroline suddenly chuckled. Such a to-do over nothing! Jessica always said she had too much imagination. Time to put her worries in perspective. Taking a worn instrument case from the wardrobe, she perched on the bed and carefully removed her lute. It was a very old instrument, dating back to the time when the lute was fashionable and widely played. She stroked the silky cedarwood of its sound box lovingly for a moment, then tuned it and started to play an air by John Dowland.

The lute had been a gift from her beloved teacher Signore Ferrante when she came to London earlier in the spring. Both of them had known matters would never be the same again; she would marry or stay in London with her aunt, and the closeness of master and student would change in the future. He had chosen the perfect gift. Whenever she played it she thought of him and the happiness they had shared in exploring ancient and modern music. While the pianoforte was her first love, the gentle lute was easily carried and could be played without disturbing the rest of the household. After plucking several Elizabethan tunes, Caroline rippled out an Italian lullaby, singing softly in her sweet true voice. Half an hour later she was ready for sleep.

Rising earlier than the rest of the family, Caroline had a quick breakfast and set out for her Aunt Jessica's house with a young maid trailing behind for propriety's sake. The housemaids took turns at chaperoning her, and debated among themselves whether it was easier to scrub steps or keep up with Caroline's brisk pace. For all her fragile appearance, she was a vigorous walker and much preferred it to riding. Today she was to give her cousin Linda a lesson on the pianoforte, and she blessed the excuse to be out early.

A late night rain had left the streets bright-washed as a new-minted coin, and Caroline felt her natural serenity return as she mentally translated the street rhythms to music. Irrepressibly social sparrows chattering overhead, peddlers making their rounds with fresh bread and early strawberries, a grave child on a pony headed toward Hyde Park with his proud papa—it would make a splendid concerto, or better still, an overture. As she softly whistled a melody, it was impossible to take seriously her anxieties of the night before.

As an Army wife, Jessica had learned to keep early hours and her household was fully awake when Caroline arrived glowing with color from the fresh air. She looked around the small entry hall with pleasure. The house was not large, needing only three servants to be comfortably staffed. Still, it had a welcoming air and was possibly her favorite place in the world. The walls were light-colored and the uncluttered rooms free of crocodile-footed sofas and other such fashionable monstrosities. The furniture had the graceful lines of the middle eighteenth century, with some foreign accents Jessica had acquired while traveling with her husband.

Being able to visit Jessica whenever she chose was Caroline's compensation for the rigors of the Season. They had corresponded regularly ever since Caroline was old enough to write, but they seldom saw each other in person while Major Sterling was posted in India, Portugal, and Spain. After her husband's death in the Battle of Salamanca, Jessica brought her daughter back to England and they took up residence in the small London town house she had inherited.

Although she liked having her own household and independence, Jessica frequently took Linda to visit the child's paternal grandparents in Wiltshire. Jessica had grown up in the area and had many friends there, and since the Sterlings lived within five miles of the Hanscombes, she could visit Caroline at the same time. Nonetheless, being within a few minutes' walk of each other was a new and pleasant experience for both of them.

Caroline entered the breakfast parlor but she had no time to greet her aunt before a small figure squealed and whizzed into her arms. "Caro! A kitten wandered into the kitchen and Mama says I can keep it!"

Caroline laughed and gave her nine-year-old cousin a hug. "And how did this creature happen to 'wander in'? In your pocket, perchance?"

Linda wiggled a bit and ground a toe into the carpet. "Well . . . "

"Never mind, poppet. I'm sure your mother was no

more deceived than I am. Bless you, Jessica," she said, reaching for the cup of coffee her aunt had just poured. "What did they ever do before coffee was discovered?" In the Hanscombe household, tea was the hot beverage, since it was her stepmother's preference; having coffee as well would have been wasteful. "I assume this undernourished scrap of orange fluff is your new friend?"

Reaching under the table, she scooped the fur ball onto her lap. The kitten was a ginger tom with startlingly green eyes, and he seemed to find the Sterling residence much to his taste. Now he was content to purr in delight as Caroline expertly scratched under his small chin. "And what is this peerless pussy's name?"

"Wellesley. For the Iron Duke, you know," Linda said seriously.

"A fine name. He even looks as if he has the famous Wellington hooked nose. At least, as much as a cat is able." Having duly admired the new member of the household, she said, "Jessica, the oddest thing happened at Almack's last night."

"Does that mean you had a better time than expected?"

"Not really," Caroline said ruefully. "I was sought out by a rather elderly lord who insisted on waltzing and who threatens to call on me."

"Goodness! Who was this ancient gentleman?"

"Well, he wasn't really ancient—perhaps around forty. About old enough to be my father. His name is Lord Radford, and he looks like the devil in fancy dress. All dark hair, frown lines, and glowering looks. He stared at me as if I were a filly ready for market. I was so nervous I'm sure he thinks me witless. Which is all to the good. I have no desire to further the acquaintance."

"Lord Radford. . . . The name is familiar. I believe there is a family seat in Gloucestershire. He is mentioned in the papers regularly—a famous horseman and hunter. Cuts quite a dash. You have found yourself a very eligible *parti*, little one!"

"Please don't laugh at me, Jess! This is serious. What if he *is* interested in me? The man terrifies me!"

"Isn't that putting it a bit strongly?"

Caroline frowned and twisted a lock of tawny hair around her finger. "I'm not sure if I can explain it. He is not really unattractive, though rather old for me. I just felt . . . overpowered by his presence. As if he were a bomb waiting to go off, or a fire that would consume me."

"I think I understand," Jessica replied. "The Duke of Wellington is something like that. No one could be more affable on a social occasion, but one can always feel the power in him. He could never be mistaken for an ordinary man, even when he was plain Arthur Wellesley. Perhaps that is why he is called the Iron Duke."

"Well, Lord Radford is certainly no ordinary man. I would like him much better if he were."

Jessica shrugged. "A man like that will add greatly to your consequence. If you fall in love with each other and make a match of it, you would be established for life. Certainly his attentions can't hurt. No one can force you to marry him."

"That's the problem, Jess. Mama and Papa *could* force me. When they start shouting, and talking about my filial duty . . ." Her voice trailed off as she examined the ribbon she had twisted past any future use.

"I shan't let him have you!" Linda said. "I will say that you are promised to us here."

"It shouldn't come to that, Linda." Jessica chuckled

and drew her daughter close to her side. They shared
the same fiery auburn hair and glowing vitality, but
the child had inherited her father's brown eyes rather
than her mother's green ones. Laughing together in
the breakfast parlor, they were perfect subjects for one
of the livelier master painters—Rubens, perhaps, had
he preferred a slimmer sort of female.

"I expect you are right and I am worrying about
nothing. I'll probably never see the Diabolical Baron
again, except in the distance at some crowded affair. In
the meantime, poppet, it's high time you and I got
started with your music lesson. I must be home early
to go shopping with Gina. She needs some ribbon to
refurbish a gown before the Cavendish ball tomorrow
night."

"I think I am too old to be a poppet, Caro," Linda
announced. "I am almost ten, you know."

"Indeed, I am very sorry to have made such a mistake. If Miss Sterling is ready for the pianoforte, may
we begin? And if Miss Sterling has done her practice
faithfully and performs well, there may just be some
fresh gingerbread for her."

With a squeak of delight, Linda abandoned her newfound maturity to dash to the music room, her cousin
following with more decorum. Jessica looked after the
figures a little sadly. Indeed, her little girl was not
going to be a little girl much longer, and the niece that
was almost a daughter was being forced into womanhood before she was ready. The hardest part of being a
mother, she thought, was knowing that growth was
painful. And that there was no way she could spare
them those pains.

Chapter 3

Caroline returned to the Hanscombe town house later than intended; the few minutes spent on a Mozart concerto became a full-scale composing session after Linda left munching her gingerbread. Even at best she could be absentminded, and when she got involved in music, time lost any meaning. It was a family joke that Caro must be kept from the pianoforte if there were any important engagements. Once she had settled down for a few minutes' playing after lunch, and had been forcibly dragged away by Gina six hours later to dress in time for dinner. She had been in a creative daze all that evening, but it had been worthwhile; it was the first time she had composed a concerto worthy of the name.

In London, Caroline took pains to avoid getting over-absorbed in her music. The many distractions of town, coupled with the inferior performance of the pianoforte in the rented town house, kept her in touch with the normal world. Today, however, she had been seduced away from her good intentions by the fine instrument Jessica owned. Gina was doubtless waiting impatiently.

She was breathless and flushed from hurrying when she burst into the sitting room to find Gina. She took two steps into the room and stopped in shock. The Diabolical Baron was there.

Jason did not miss her gasp at seeing him. Clearly Miss Hanscombe must learn that when he said he would do something, it was as good as done. Not for him the casual social promise; he said he would call, and was here at the earliest acceptable hour. He was pleased to see her, having endured a quarter-hour of Lady Hanscombe's intrusive chatter as well as the forcible introduction of Miss Gina. A good-enough girl, but not one he could envision as Lady Radford; that jolly country squire from Almack's would suit her very well. Caroline at least had possibilities. Thank heaven she wasn't a talker like her mother.

"Good day, Miss Hanscombe," he said smoothly as he rose and made his bow. "The morning air suits you admirably. I have come to beg the honor of taking you for a turn in the park."

Caroline blushed and looked at the carpet. "It would be a great pleasure, my lord, but . . . but I am engaged to my sister."

"Oh, that is quite all right, Caro," Gina said helpfully. "We can go tomorrow. I shouldn't wish to interfere with your enjoyment." She cast a roguish look in Lord Radford's direction. "Besides, Gideon will be here soon and we are also going for a drive."

"Indeed, Caroline, it was very bad of you to keep his lordship waiting," said her stepmother sternly.

"She did not know when I was coming, Lady Hanscombe. But I do hope you are now free to accept my invitation," he said to her.

"Of course, Lord Radford," she said, still studying the carpet. "If you will but give me a few moments to freshen up, I will be with you directly." With that, she turned and left the room quickly enough to qualify it as flight.

She hurried up the stairs in confusion. What was the man doing here? Surely he had better things to do. She entered her room and took a quick inventory of her wardrobe. The gray morning dress with dark blue trim should do; she always looked as if she were succumbing to a minor illness when she wore it. She changed quickly, and spent a moment combing her hair over her brow to conceal her face more. To complete the effect, she took her least favorite bonnet, one of her stepmother's castoffs. It had been unimpressive even in its salad days, and age had not improved it. She drew a deep breath to calm herself, then proceeded downstairs to meet her fate.

Lord Radford studied her as she entered the salon. He gave her several points for the speed with which she had made ready, but had to subtract them for the poor results. Really, the girl dressed a fright. She had looked quite pretty when she came in from outside; now she looked like a nondescript governess. Her wardrobe must certainly be altered as soon as they were betrothed.

Even a young woman·as inattentive to fashion as Caroline could not fail to notice Lord Radford's high-perch phaeton. It was magnificently black, with accents in silver. The superbly matched black horses were clearly of superior lineage, and their harness continued the black-and-silver theme.

Jason watched Caroline's eyes widen and asked, "Do you approve?"

"It is not for me to approve or disapprove, your lordship."

"Nonsense. You are entitled to an opinion, and I'm

sure you have one, even if you are not in the habit of
stating it," he said as he helped her up into the vehicle.

"Well, it is very dramatic," she said hesitantly as she
settled herself against the black velvet squabs. "But
perhaps a little . . . ominous." She certainly couldn't
tell him it exactly confirmed her naming him the Diabolical Baron.

"Your mother likes it. Before you returned, she told
me it was most handsome."

"Stepmother."

"Ah, we are making progress, Miss Hanscombe!
That is the first comment you have made that goes beyond the minimum necessary to answer my remarks,"
Jason said genially. He was pleased to learn that the
girl was no blood relation to Lady Hanscombe; he
would rather not have a wife from that mold.

"I . . . I'm sorry, Lord Radford." She flushed and
looked at the glossy horses before her. "I did not mean
to be uncivil."

Jason cursed his misstep. He wasn't sure whether
she took his remark as a criticism, or merely had no
sense of humor; in either event, he had lost any
ground he had made. Glancing sideways, he guessed
the lovely porcelain skin would always betray her feelings in easy blushes. Unfortunate for her, perhaps, but
convenient for him.

"I am sure you have never been uncivil in your life.
Is this your first visit to London?" Back to the neutrali-
ties of their first meeting at Almack's; it seemed safer.
English weather was always good for extended conversation, so Jason spent the drive through Hyde Park
discussing it while she replied in monosyllables. Yes, it
was unusually warm for late April. Indeed, it was very
pleasant; yes, rain would soon be needed for the crops.

They tooled elegantly about during this scintillating discussion, attracting considerable attention from those fashionable folk in the park this early. No one could ever remember Radford taking a drive with a female who could be safely introduced in mixed company. And a marriageable miss just out of the schoolroom? It must be serious!

Sublimely unaware of the speculations, Caroline was slowly starting to relax. While she would have preferred to be almost anywhere other than this conspicuous vehicle with its even more conspicuous driver, at least she was in no immediate danger. She was still unclear about what kind of danger Lord Radford represented, but she couldn't shake that disturbing sense of unknown forces around her.

They were starting to head back when a familiar voice hailed them. George Fitzwilliam trotted his horse over and gave a cheerful smile even though he saw his chances of owning Jason's grays rapidly diminishing. "Good day to you, Miss Hanscombe, Jason. A splendid morning to be taking the air." As he chatted easily, he studied Caroline. The chit didn't seem best pleased; the most positive thing one could say about her expression was "resigned." Perhaps his wager wasn't quite so hopeless after all.

After George had moved on to greet others, Jason expertly gathered the reins and made a tricky turn around a badly driven barouche. "Tell me, Miss Hanscombe, do you have any special interests that you would like to discuss? I am exhausting my store of commonplaces, and it is your turn to suggest a topic."

Caroline glanced at him hesitantly. "I am . . . very fond of music, my lord."

Jason managed to avoid groaning, "Spare me!" but

she saw in his face the look of a man who had heard too many painful concerts by conscientious, untalented maidens. So many weeping harps! Pounded pianofortes! Voices either inaudible or all too easily heard in the next street. In a society where music was a necessary "accomplishment" for a young lady, great crimes against the human ear were perpetrated. She flushed again and looked across the park at a group of horsemen. "Of course it is of no importance," she said stiffly.

Jason sensed her withdrawal and felt a pang of regret. She was so vulnerable. Was he going to have to watch every word for the next forty years? He suddenly realized he was almost old enough to be her father. His mind digressed—about fourteen years' difference in age? He grinned as he remembered Lizzie, the so-friendly dairy maid. Yes, technically he could have been her father. . . .

His off-leader shied slightly at another carriage, bringing him back to the present. Assuming a properly sober expression, he said, "I do wish, Miss Hanscombe, you were not quite so nervous in my presence. I am really not an ogre about to eat you."

"Are you not?" she said in an unexpectedly dry voice, slanting a quick glance up at him. Jason was startled both by her tone and by her surprisingly deep blue eyes. He realized it was the first time she had looked directly at him, and he had the uncomfortable feeling she might have seen more than he intended. Perhaps there was more to the girl than he thought. He smoothly retreated to safe topics and his quarry resumed studying the surrounding traffic.

As they headed back to Adam Street, neither was pleased with the way matters were progressing.

* * *

While Jason and Caroline were circling the park, Sir Alfred had summoned his wife to his study to discuss their finances. A burly, choleric man, the baronet was a breathtaking example of selfishness. While he did have a modicum of interest in his fifteen-year-old heir, Master Colin, and he quite enjoyed fighting with his wife, he had an almost total lack of interest in the welfare or comfort of anyone other than himself. The handsome fortune he had inherited was seriously depleted by years of self-indulgence and poor investments. While he had wisely refrained from mortgaging his estate, he had been financially embarrassed for some time now, and was ready to check on the progress of his other "investments."

"Well, Louisa, you promised that spending all of this money launching the oldest girls would pay a handsome return as well as getting them off our hands. How do matters stand?"

"Quite well, Alfred. In fact there is a surprising development taking place at this very moment. I have already informed you of Gideon Fallsworthy's interest in Gina. I am sure he is on the verge of offering for her, and he seems so besotted he will probably take her without a portion."

"Yes, yes, I know all about him," Sir Alfred said impatiently. "But I do not scruple to say our financial situation has worsened. The East India trading ship I invested in is far overdue, and almost certainly lost. I had counted on the profit of that to pay for . . . never mind what. Is there any chance a richer man may offer for Gina? If so, I'll refuse to let Fallsworthy have her."

Lady Hanscombe was revolted by her husband's casual greed, but she knew better than to argue the issue on romantic grounds. "I really do not think that is possible. She and Gideon have been so absorbed in each other that her other suitors have looked elsewhere. Besides," she said reluctantly, "even if there were someone else, I fear she would elope rather than give Gideon up."

"What kind of doxies have you been raising, madam?" Sir Alfred bellowed. Like many men of casual morals, he demanded that his daughters behave with a propriety that he would have abhorred in a potential mistress.

"Watch your language about your daughter, sir! She is no doxy, she just knows what she wants. Fallsworthy is a very amiable young man, and I'm quite sure the minx would be able to persuade him to run off," her proud mother said. "If you disliked the match, you should have said so when they first met. You approved at the time, you might recall."

"Aye, I was not at a standstill then."

"I had hoped the substantial portion Caroline will inherit from her mother will make her more marriageable—"

"Don't be counting on that," Sir Alfred interrupted.

"You haven't spent the money? That would be embezzlement! It was left in trust for her."

"Don't be so anxious to send me to jail," he snapped. "I invested it in a surefire canal scheme, but the company was bankrupted when the director ran off with the funds. It was a legitimate investment for her trust money," he added defensively in the face of his wife's glare. While she had her share of faults, Lady Hanscombe was scrupulously honest, and her husband's actions appalled her.

After collecting herself, Louisa said coldly, "Then it is just as well Caroline never knew the size of her inheritance. The other news I have for you could not be better timed. I had begun to despair of finding someone for her—she has no countenance or vivacity, and seems quite uninterested in attaching anyone. But it is the most amazing thing—Lord Radford has taken a marked interest in her. He sought her out at Almack's last night, danced only with her, and called for her this morning for a drive. Hard as it may be to understand, he seems quite smitten with her."

"Lord Radford? The man has had some of the most dashing mistresses in London. What interest could he have in a milk-and-water miss like Caroline?"

"Mysterious are the ways of love," Lady Hanscombe said sententiously. "He probably wants a well-brought-up young lady who will bear him a son and not curb his pleasures. Caroline should suit him very well. And she won't present any problems if he comes up to scratch. She's always been a most obedient girl."

"Well, see she stays that way!" her loving husband barked as he ended the interview by leaving the room for his club.

Chapter 4

Richard Davenport's leg was aching badly by the time he reached the legal offices of Chelmsford and Marlin, but since that was common nowadays, he ignored it. He was taking long daily walks to rebuild the damaged leg as much as possible; on difficult days, like this one, he carried a cane and distracted himself by whistling complicated musical themes.

He had always been a whistler, and often maddened and intrigued his fellow officers with his habit of whistling tunes that were comments or footnotes to what was being discussed. When other amusements were in short supply, as was often the case in the Peninsular campaigns, it was considered a good game to guess what chain of unconscious logic led Captain Dalton to whistle his current choice. It was not hard to understand why mentioning London brought forth "Oranges and Lemons," or a lament on the lack of decent drink a chorus of "John Barleycorn." But sometimes the references were more obscure, and numerous energetic discussions had resulted on why "A-Rovin'" or "Jack the Jolly Tar" had been heard. Richard was no help; when questioned, he would just smile and whistle a Spanish phrase that translated as "Who knows?"

More than a week had passed since his initial discussion with Josiah Chelmsford, and he was still uncertain whether the life of an earl was worth considering. Josiah had invited him back with the bait of more information on his parents' early years. He entered the office and was received by the clerk with much more civility than on his first visit. He smiled wryly. Such toadeating would doubtless be a principal side effect of becoming a peer of the realm.

Josiah greeted Richard with a handshake and a jovial "Good day, my boy. You are looking very much more the thing than when we last met. Are you coming to terms with your unexpected fortune?"

"Good day, sir. I am sorry to disappoint you, but I have no more idea what to do now than last week."

"I don't want to press you, but I should explain the rather unusual way your grandfather tied up the estate. It has been almost exactly a year since he died. Under the terms of the will, I was to administer the estate for eighteen months while a search was made for Julius Davenport or his heir. The earl was estranged from your father for much longer than the seven years it takes to declare a missing person dead, but when he revised his will after the death of your second uncle, I told him of the letters I had received from Julius. The last had been years before, but it seemed quite possible that he might have left an heir even if he had passed on.

"After all, he had notified me of your birth, and in the absence of evidence to the contrary, I preferred to assume you were alive. Unfortunately I had no idea where to look for you. Your father's letters were remarkably unforthcoming. He was determined that no one should trace him.

"At any rate, if no direct heir is found after eighteen months, the estate will pass to the heir presumptive,

your father's cousin Reginald Davenport. He is the son
of the earl's younger brother, but closer in age to you
than to your father."

Chelmsford paused and fiddled with the pipe he had
been puffing. "Your grandfather did not like many people, but he particularly disliked Reginald. Your cousin
has quite a reputation as a gamester, fighter, and all-
around rake. He was forbidden entry to his lordship's
presence for the last ten years. Nonetheless, he assumes
himself to be the next earl and has all but painted a
crest on his carriage. He is pressing me to wind this
business up as quickly as possible, and I suspect he has
been living on his expectations for some time."

"You haven't told anyone about me, have you?"

"No, no, I will respect your wishes on that point. The
only one who knows is my senior clerk, Wilkes, and he
is discretion personified. I would like to suggest something to you. Why not go to Gloucestershire with me
and visit the estate unofficially? You could stay there as
Richard Dalton. We can find some pretext to justify
your presence to the staff. Perhaps you could be taking
inventory for me, preparatory to winding up the trust.
The country air would be good for you, and the
Cotswold scenery is some of the finest in Britain."

Richard bit his lip reflectively. "I certainly wouldn't
mind getting out of London, and the surgeons are
about ready to release me. But will Wargrave Park be
full of old family retainers who will instantly recognize
me as a Davenport?"

"No, I think it unlikely. While you greatly resemble
your father, his resemblance was to his mother. He did
not look at all like a Davenport."

The solicitor smiled nostalgically. "Your grandmother was a remarkable woman. Not a great beauty,

but with a sweetness of temper that softened even your grandfather. She brought fresh blood and common sense to the family—had she been alive, the rift between the earl and your father would never have occurred."

"What kind of men were my uncles?" Richard asked.

"Rodrick, the eldest brother, was wild and extravagant. Several fortunes went to covering his debts. When he was of an age when he could no longer avoid settling down and taking an interest in his inheritance, he succumbed to lung fever. I sometimes wonder if he died rather than do an honest day's work."

"And the middle brother?"

"Henry was an unhappy man. He felt, rightly, that Rodrick was his father's favorite, while Julius was very much his mother's son. Instead of becoming his own man, he turned his back on his family. He . . . didn't like women. He would not marry even after he became heir to the estate. I believe it pleased him to frustrate his father."

"A delightful pair. More and more I can understand why my father felt no desire to stay in contact with his family."

At this point a fracas outside the office distracted Josiah from his account. The clerk Wilkes could be heard saying, "You can't go in there. Mr. Chelmsford is with a client."

The reply was muffled but peremptory. The door flew open and a tall, contemptuous-looking gentleman strode in. He looked to be near forty, but the lines of dissipation in his face may have aged him prematurely. Dark hair and a sallow face contrasted oddly with eyes of a pale, cold aquamarine blue. While his clothing was expensive, he wore it with a damn-your-eyes carelessness that lacked the immaculate neatness Brummell had made fashionable. His glance passed indifferently over Richard to fasten on Josiah.

"How much longer must this farce go on?" he said in a scornful voice. "Your delay in settling the estate is seriously discommoding me, and I've a strong mind to find a judge who agrees the trust should be wound up immediately."

Chelmsford looked back coldly. The cheerfully rotund solicitor had been replaced by the hard-eyed man of law. "Do not waste idle threats on me, Mr. Davenport. Getting the Chancery involved in this would only result in considerably more delay. There is not a lawyer born who cannot stall a case for four or five times the natural length, and I promise you that is what will happen if you interfere with your uncle's will. The trust will end normally in six months. I would suggest you attempt to live within your means until then."

The intruder's mouth tightened. "Then perhaps you could advance me some monies from the estate? It is, after all, my own."

"That remains to be seen. In the meantime, I am responsible for the Wargrave lands and fortune, and not a penny will be spent except on legitimate expenses. If the property ever comes to you, it will be intact to that point."

"You realize that the day I assume the title, you will cease to be employed by the Wargrave estate?"

"Believe me, if you do become the next earl, I should resign your employ the moment you inherit."

"Then it seems we understand each other perfectly, Chelmsford." The tall rawboned figure turned in a flurry of driving capes and stormed out, closing the door with a slam.

"And that, Richard, is your cousin Reginald," the lawyer said dryly. "In case you hadn't guessed."

Richard had been watching the scene with a half-smile on his face. "He is a poor inducement to declare myself an official Davenport. Would I acquire many relatives like him?"

"They aren't all such a set of dirty dishes. Even Reginald has his better moments. This is the first time he has lost control and railed at me; I expect it means a particularly bad run of cards or horses. Or both. Certainly he is a selfish care-for-nobody, though he has a reputation for courage. They say he has fought several duels and is a dangerous man to cross. Do you find him alarming?"

"Having a regiment of Napoleon's crack cavalry charge when you are outnumbered three to one is 'alarming.' My cousin I merely find rag-mannered. Is he a 'typical Davenport'?"

"That he is. However, since you were raised away from the traditional mold, you have the perfect opportunity to change the definition."

The lawyer paused, then continued, "Now is the time to tell you the other drawbacks. The Wargrave properties are potentially among the richest in England, but they were badly neglected in your grandfather's later years. In addition, much of the property was mortgaged to cover your uncle's debts. The estate can provide a comfortable income as it stands, but years of care and good management will be required for Wargrave to yield its full potential. It may not be a task to your liking."

"What would the income be if Wargrave were free and clear?"

"In the neighborhood of thirty thousand pounds a year."

"Thirty thousand pounds!" Richard jerked upright in his chair, his calm at last disturbed.

Chelmsford shrugged. "About that. More if some capital were invested in the Yorkshire moorlands you own. There's coal under them, and mining would provide some badly needed jobs in the area, as well as being a good investment. Mind you, the estate is producing nothing like that now, and it would take years to pay off the outstanding mortgages."

Richard swallowed. "Back on the Peninsula when our pay was months in arrears, we joked about having fifty pounds to call our own. I have trouble comprehending thirty thousand pounds."

"Your Uncle Rodrick could not only imagine it—he could spend it," the lawyer said with a faint smile.

"No wonder this country is having so much social unrest. It is abominable that a few have so much, and the rest so little."

Chelmsford shot him a startled look. "I thought you were fighting republican ideals, not learning to espouse them."

Richard shook off his seriousness with a laugh. "The problem was not that the French were republicans. After all, Boney crowned himself emperor. We fought because the Corsican wanted more than he was entitled to—far, far more. I don't know that I am precisely a republican, but controlling the kind of fortune you speak of seems more a burden than a blessing. Are there any alternatives?"

"You can take on the earldom with all its problems, learn management, and make the estate productive with perhaps five years of hard work. You can accept the title, sell the unencumbered property, and have a comfortable income for the rest of your life. Or you can walk away and let Reggie inherit. He will almost certainly sell out to Lord Radford, who owns the adjoining estate. I would be sorry to see Wargrave broken up, but perhaps it would be the best solution. Lord Radford is said to be an exemplary landlord."

"I have trouble seeing myself as a landed gentleman," Richard said. "A soldier's experience of agriculture is limited to foraging for food when the supply trains are lost."

"There is nothing beyond your ability to learn," Chelmsford replied. "I think a stay at Wargrave Park would be quite an education. Will you come with me on my next visit there?"

Richard hesitated. Clearly Josiah was playing spider to his fly, trying to entangle him with a web of possibilities and obligations. He had no desire for the complication of the title and estate, but further study wouldn't hurt. And it would be heaven to get out of the noise and dust of London.

"I'm willing to visit Wargrave with you, though I won't promise to stay there. When is your next visit?"

"Splendid, splendid! It will be in about three weeks, though I can rearrange my schedule—"

"No need for that," the captain interrupted. "I have business to take care of at the Horse Guards. My commission needs to be sold, and there are some friends I want to trace. The end of the month will be fine."

Chelmsford beamed, the very image of a satisfied spider. "You won't regret this, my boy."

"Let us hope not."

* * *

"Caroline, Caroline, it's happened! He's talking to Papa and been accepted! It's all set! It's wonderful! Hello, Jessica! I am the happiest woman in the world!" Gina hurtled into her sister's bedroom with a velocity that gravely threatened the cheval glass mirror, two china shepherdesses, and a coal-scuttle bonnet on the bed. Caroline rose from the floor where she was pinning an embroidered band around her aunt's hemline and threw her arms around Gina when that young lady slowed down.

"That's marvelous! Not unexpected, but still marvelous. I assume Gideon had spoken to you privately? You've been looking like the cat in the cream pot for the last several days. Have you made any wedding plans yet?"

"Yes, you and Mama and I are to visit the Fallsworthys in Lincolnshire at the end of this month. Gideon wants his parents to meet me, and we can work out the details then. We thought perhaps an August wedding at the church back home in Great Chisbury. Lots of summer flowers, and you of course my maid of honor. It is so fortunate you are here, Jessica. Will you help me decide on my wedding gown? Something to make me look slim and elegant for once in my life."

Gina looked enviously at the sarcenet morning dress Caroline and her aunt were working on. It was an unusual shade of russet that complemented Jessica's rich auburn hair, and its simple lines and exquisite cut showed her magnificent figure to perfection. The mameluke sleeves were tied with dark brown ribbons, and the embroidered wrist frills matched the band Caroline was pinning to the hem. Perfect for Jessica, but no lesser woman could have done it such justice. Jess had a flair for fashion and always designed and made her own clothes. Fortunately she was happy to share her talent. She smiled her own congratulations at Gina and said, "I'd be delighted to help. May I be one of the first to wish you happy? Mr. Fallsworthy is an estimable young man, and I am sure you will deal extremely well with each other."

Gina bounced over to her honorary aunt and gave her a hug. "Thank you so much. You will come to the wedding, won't you? Since you spend part of each summer with the Sterlings, it shouldn't be inconvenient. I will need your fine hand to help keep Mama in check." She smiled roguishly. "Of course, you may be needed to help with Caroline's wedding plans, too."

Caroline finished her pinning, then stood and went to the wardrobe for her lute. "Don't be silly. Why would I be getting married?" She took the instrument out of its case, tuned it a bit, and started strumming snatches of music.

"What would you like for a wedding march, Ginny? Something dramatic like this?" Heavy chords rumbled through the room. "Or something light and waltzlike?" Lyrical streams of music. "Or perhaps this." She moved into a famous song commemorating the end of a successful hunt.

Gina laughed and said, "Spare my blushes in the hour of my victory. No well-brought-up young lady would admit to being the hunter rather than the quarry, and I usually try to look proper.

"And don't think you can change the subject so easily. Why shouldn't you be thinking wedding thoughts? Lord Radford has been so very particular in his attentions. I think he must be ready to make an offer."

"Don't be silly, Gina. He isn't really interested in me."

"No? Then why has he called almost every day for the last few weeks? And why does he ask you to stand up at every ball you've been to? I swear the man must be bribing one of the maids to find out where we'll be."

Acutely distressed, Caroline started tracing the inlaid patterns around the lute's sound hole. The deeper her feelings, the more difficult it became to discuss them, and Lord Radford's continuing attentions were affecting her in ways she found impossible to describe. She had developed a sense of fatality about him. At every affair they attended, eventually his dark, elegant form would appear and he would claim her for dancing or conversation. His inexplicable attentions had increased her popularity as half the bucks and dandies in London sought to discover her mysterious charms. It had been a deeply uncomfortable period, continually meeting strangers, feeling the speculative eyes, hearing murmured conversations stop when she entered the ladies' retiring rooms.

"I don't know what he wants of me, Gina. But think: can you not feel Gideon's love for you? Isn't there a . . . a warmth, a sense of caring coming from him?"

Gina had to think about that for a moment. Then a soft smile slowly spread across her face. "Of course. I know exactly what you mean. It's like his arms are around me even when he is across the room."

"Well, I don't feel that from Lord Radford. I don't even think he likes me particularly. I feel like some kind of . . . of chore he must accomplish."

Jessica listened to the conversation with a small frown between her brows. "Perhaps it is just that he is unlike any other man you have known. Fashionable gentlemen don't display their feelings, but why else would he court you except for love?"

"Perhaps he is using her to make one of his mistresses jealous," Gina said helpfully. "It certainly isn't for our money! And there are plenty of experienced women around for more rewarding flirtations."

Caroline laughed, her worried mood broken. "If you mean what I think you mean, you have no delicacy of mind whatsoever. But I must admit, that theory makes more sense than any other. It may even be true, because several ladies have been at great pains to inform me, in the most considerate way, that I am not at all his lordship's type. It is my one solace."

Her sister shook her head mournfully. "I really cannot understand you. Three-quarters of the women in London would give their family jewels to be in your position, and you act as if you have been singled out for deliberate persecution. He is always most charming, he is wonderfully handsome, and such a fortune! And you, my bird-witted sister, are not even flattered by the attention. What is it about him that bothers you?"

"It is difficult to explain," Caroline said hesitantly. "It is not what he *does*, but what he *is*—a man used to effortlessly controlling everything around him. I can feel the leashed force in him. He dominates me without even trying. And I do not wish to be dominated. Being ignored is much more comfortable." She laughed a trifle nervously. She was trying to make light of it, but what she said was true: Lord Radford did not have to do anything to make her shrink; his mere presence was enough.

Jessica was uneasy about Caroline's remark, but uncertain how to reply. She could understand how a forceful, arrogant man would make her shy niece unhappy. She was reminded of a Spanish exhibit she had seen of a lion and a lamb living together in a cage. It was an impressive sight, but she rather thought the lamb had to be replaced regularly.

While she knew very little of Lord Radford, the picture she was getting was very lionlike. She sighed to herself; if she had gone out in society these last years she might have met him and been better able to counsel her niece. Caroline had little experience of men; perhaps she was overreacting. If he were a good person who truly loved her, he might be a wonderful husband.

"He may be somewhat alarming now, Caro," her aunt said carefully. "But he must truly care for you or he would not be courting you so assiduously. With a basis of affection, even two very different people may live in harmony. Indeed, my darling John and I were quite unlike, and yet that difference was a pleasure to both of us."

"There are degrees of difference," Caroline said gloomily. "Wine and water may mix with ease, but fire and water will never blend." With a visible effort she shook off her misgivings and added with a smile, "Enough of worrying about the dire possibility of becoming a rich, pampered lady. It is time to talk of Gina's bride clothes."

Chapter 5

Jason Kincaid and his friend George Fitzwilliam had reached the after-dinner port before conversation turned to Radford's courtship. George was resigned to losing the wager, and accepted the loss of his salmon-fishing privileges with fortitude. Still, he felt a few qualms about his part in the situation.

"Y'know, Jason, it was a silly bet we made about your marriage. Would you like to call it off? Most improper. Not at all a suitable topic for gambling."

"Back out of a wager!" Radford said in mock outrage. "What kind of a maw-worm do you take me for? Or do you fear losing?"

Fitzwilliam snorted indignantly. "Those would be fighting words if I were a fighting man, which of course I ain't. It's just that when I see the two of you together, you both look like you're coming from the funeral of your favorite uncle, and you found out he hasn't left you anything to boot. I'm willing to concede you my fishing rights. I just don't want to see you unhappy the rest of your life because of a foolish bet. Marriage is a serious matter."

"Indeed it is, George, and I am deadly serious about it. Even if we did call off the wager, I would still have my Aunt Honoria to answer to. I promised her a bride by the end of the Season." Jason paused, then added slowly, "It has occurred to me that perhaps I should have given you a few more guidelines for the selection. Miss Hanscombe is a pleasant-enough young lady but very hard to know, and there is a want of spirit in her . . ."

His voice trailed off; then he resumed in a more vigorous tone. "Nonetheless, I'm sure she will discharge her duties well. I could not in conscience draw back now in any case. I mean to call on her father tomorrow, and I foresee no problems. As she and I become better acquainted, I trust we will rub along tolerably well. Now I think on it, I believe I'll invite her and her family to Wildehaven right away. The Season will be ending soon and it will give her a chance to become relaxed with me before the wedding. If we left at the end of next week, there would be time enough to improve her wardrobe before we leave. Yes," he said decisively, "that will do very well. Now, if you will excuse me for not lingering over my port, I must intercept my soon-to-be-betrothed at Lady Beechwood's musicale."

"I think I'll go with you," George said. "I'm sure I have a card for it around here somewhere, and I'd like to be present for the final act of your little drama."

Lady Beechwood's house was only a few minutes away. It was obvious when they entered and gave their hats to a footman that the musicale was in full swing, or perhaps full voice was a more appropriate term. There was a distinct caterwauling coming from the reception rooms that could be identified by the *cognoscenti* as one of Miss Smythe-Foot's infamous assaults on Mozart. Jason twitched visibly, while George put on his blandest social face. In a stirring example of British grit in action, they headed manfully toward the source of the wailing.

Their valor was rewarded by the song's end and the beginning of an intermission. Leaving George to his own devices, Jason scanned the rooms for some time before sighting his intended. Really, the girl was amazingly easy to overlook; for the first time he wondered if it was a deliberate effort on her part. With this intriguing thought in mind, he headed toward the small figure he located in an alcove at the far end from the performers. She seemed absorbed in her reticule and started when he spoke to her.

"Are you enjoying the evening, Miss Hanscombe? I recall you said that you are very fond of music."

Caroline gave a slight shudder and replied, "Not when the performances are as inferior as this. It is a blessing that Herr Mozart is not alive to hear what is done to his genius."

Jason gave a broad smile; the girl was capable of a strong opinion. It was a very good sign. "I see we are in accord on the subject. I assume you prefer a different type of music?"

Caroline looked scandalized. "To dignify this drivel as music debases the meaning of the real thing. Music is, or should be, the truest language of the heart. It can express feeling far beyond the power of words to move us. It can create harmony from anger, impose order on the chaotic, and carry us to realms beyond imagination. It . . ." She stopped abruptly and colored in confusion. "I'm sorry. It was very rude to carry on like that." With a glimmer of a smile she added, "Music is many things to many people, and I trust even Miss Smythe-Foot finds pleasure in her endeavors."

Jason watched her transformation with fascinated eyes. She had become a whole different person for a moment, with a flash of real beauty. He had little interest in music, but he was delighted to see she was capable of passion. It gave him an unexpected hope for the future.

"You are more tolerant than she deserves," he said as he offered her his arm. "Would you care for some refreshments?"

Caroline smiled and took his arm, pleased that he felt as he ought when music was abused. For the first time, they were in charity with one another.

Caroline was humming as she sat at her writing desk the next morning. She felt more relaxed than at any time since she had met Lord Radford. She still had no idea why he sought her out, but she thought it possible they might become friends.

She was writing an overdue letter to Signore Ferrante, her music teacher in Wiltshire. She had not written for weeks, to avoid distressing him; he could always sense her moods, and she cared far too much for the old gentleman to wish him unhappy on her behalf. Caroline gnawed on the end of the pen and thought back to their first meeting.

She had been eight years old, and a new student at the day school in Chippenham, where the *signore* was music master. For weeks she had heard fascinating sounds coming from the music room; indeed, it was the only thing in the school she enjoyed. Shy and tongue-tied, she was a butt for the older girls' jokes.

On this particular day the music-room door was open and she slipped in when she saw the room was empty. First she had looked around in wonder; there was a golden harp in one corner and an elaborate pianoforte in the center of the room. Lying on top of the instrument were sheafs of music; she had never seen written music before, and felt frustrated at not understanding it. She felt she *ought* to be able to read it; the meaning seemed to lie just beyond the edge of her memory.

After gently striking the center keys, she started to pick out the tune of "Greensleeves," her favorite of the old country songs her nurse sang when she was a child. Signore Ferrante was unnoticed when he came in several minutes later. Wordlessly he had watched the small figure faultlessly playing the song by ear, singing the words in a clear true voice. He had crossed to the instrument and said softly so as not to frighten her, "So, little miss, would you like to learn music?"

She had lifted her deep blue eyes to his and said gravely, "I want to learn more than anything on earth."

The *signore* let the headmistress know of the child's interest, and a message went to Lady Hanscombe. She disliked wasting money on educational extras but playing the pianoforte was undeniably necessary to a well-bred young lady. Besides, for the first time in her life Caroline cared enough for something to wage a campaign for it. Her ladyship became reconciled to the expenditure after she conceived the happy thought that Caroline could instruct her younger sisters, thus eliminating further expenditures.

The happiest hours of her childhood belonged to Signore Ferrante's cluttered parlor, for he was soon giving her private lessons in his home. It was obvious that Caroline had an extraordinary talent; her ear was faultless, she had an amazing memory for both technique and musical literature, and she learned instruments as if she already knew how to play them and just needed reminding. By the age of twelve it was also clear she had a gift for composition that exceeded even her performing skills.

Signore Ferrante had sometimes wondered what cruel fate sent him as a political exile from sunny Italy to this land of cold rain and cold people, but he wondered no longer after meeting Caroline. A deeply religious man, he felt God had sent him to the *bambina*, to be her teacher and guide. He and his placid wife always had their door open to her, and they found in her a child to replace those grown and gone from home. The *signore* would sigh when he thought of God's oversight in making Caroline a female and from a high rank of society; a man would have won acclaim throughout Europe. Even a woman could have been accepted as a performer if she came from a class that permitted such a scandalous career.

Still, he believed such talent as Caroline had was its own justification. By the time she had been taken off to the Marriage Mart, she was a skilled performer on all the keyboard instruments, plus the lute, violin, harp, recorder, and flute. Her fine singing voice had much more range and power than would have been expected from her soft speech. And she left behind her a handful of carefully copied musical compositions that could stand comparison with the best of Europe's young musical geniuses. Caroline had resisted all suggestions of publishing her work; she felt she would be forbidden her music if anyone discovered her in so unladylike a pursuit as composition. Signore Ferrante didn't press her; he knew her time would come.

* * *

Caroline's reverie was interrupted by a knock on her door. Turning, she saw one of the housemaids timidly saying, "Please, miss, you're wanted in your father's study right away."

She felt a shock of fear. Her father never wanted to

talk to her. It could only be . . . she refused to speculate further. Drawing a deep breath, she laid her pen down and rose slowly. "Thank you, Elsie. I'll go down directly."

It took all her courage to enter the room euphemistically called her father's study. He had never been known to read a book or write an unnecessary letter in his life; the room served mainly as his escape from his family. Going inside, she saw that her stepmother was also present, giving her a cool smile of approval. It could mean only one thing.

Sir Alfred came toward her, beaming with self-satisfaction, and said in what was meant to be a fond tone, "Congratulations, my clever little puss. Lord Radford has been here to ask permission to pay his addresses to you, and you will soon be Lady Radford. He wishes for a speedy wedding." This was accompanied by a lascivious wink.

With a sick feeling in the pit of her stomach, Caroline stared at her father in dismay. She was just beginning to feel less threatened by his lordship, and now this! Stammering and almost incoherent, she embarked on her first attempt to defy her parents' will. "But . . . but I do not wish to marry him. And if . . . wh-when he asks me, I shall refuse him."

His good nature instantly transformed into anger, the baronet started turning red while he yelled, "We'll have none of your missish airs! You're damned lucky to have such an offer, and you'll accept him with no shilly-shallying!"

Trembling, a white-faced Caroline said desperately, "I *won't*! I turned twenty-one at the end of February, and you can't make me. I'll leave home and teach music. . . . "

Purpled with anger, Sir Alfred took two quick strides across the room and grabbed her shoulders, shaking her violently. Raising one hand to strike her, he bellowed, "Oh, can't I now? If you don't agree immediately, you'll be begging me—"

"Stop that this instant, Alfred!" Lady Hanscombe moved forward and seized his upraised hand before he could complete the blow. "There is no call to behave like a wild beast. Let me talk to Caroline. She will come around when she understands what is involved."

Breathing heavily, Sir Alfred backed off. "See that you make it good, then, because if she isn't ready to accept Radford when he calls tomorrow, she'll be sorry she was ever born." He strode across the room and slammed the study door with a force that rattled the windows.

Left with a sobbing Caroline, Louisa hesitated before starting to address her. She was not a perceptive woman, but she knew that only the most acute distress could have caused her stepdaughter to defy her parents' wishes. However, Caroline's compliance was essential to the family. Since Louisa genuinely believed Radford would make a good husband, she had no qualms about using any method necessary to bring the marriage off.

"Sit down and calm yourself, Caroline. Here is my handkerchief." She gave the girl a few moments to collect herself before saying, "You have formed no other attachment, have you?"

Her sobs subsiding somewhat, Caroline shook her head and made a muffled noise that must have been "No."

"Why is it such a surprise to you that Lord Radford

has declared himself? I'm told that in the clubs they have been betting on the outcome for weeks."

At this Caroline raised her head in pure shock, saying, "How *could* they?" in a dazed tone.

Realizing that it was a mistake to mention the matter, Lady Hanscombe said hurriedly, "His attentions have been of the most flattering. Admittedly there is something of an age difference, but he is a very well-looking man, and what is of particular importance, a very wealthy one." Here she paused, wondering how best to phrase the nub of the argument, then continued firmly, "I have always attempted to shield my children from unpleasantness, but it is an unfortunate fact that our financial situation is very difficult. In fact, I do not scruple to tell you it is desperate. Surely you must have wondered why only you and Gina came to London while the children remained in Great Chisbury?"

Her unwilling attention caught, Caroline said, "You talked about their educational needs being more important . . ."

"The real reason was to reduce our costs. Every penny we had went into making it possible for you and your sister to be presented creditably. It is essential that one or both of you make very good marriages. Your younger brothers and sisters are depending on that fact."

"Isn't there money to come to me from my mother? I am of age now. I do not mind giving it to help them."

"It is not enough to signify," Louisa said quickly. Far better to leave that stone unturned!

"Gina is making a good marriage. Everyone says so. Can't I be released from this one?"

Ignoring the girl's pleading blue eyes, Lady Hanscombe said, "It is a respectable alliance, but of little

use at present. Gideon will eventually have a good
property and income, but his parents are still alive,
healthy, and relatively young. He does not have the personal fortune to help his wife's family. The best we can
hope for is that he accept Gina without a portion, as indeed he has done. And"—playing her trump card—
"were it not that Lord Radford's offer was imminent,
we would have been forced to refuse young Fallsworthy's suit. You remember Sir Wilbur Hatchett? He was
willing to make a very good offer for your sister, and
could still be brought up to scratch should we indicate
that she is available. I am reluctant to do that. The man
is in Trade, and personally unattractive as well. Certainly Gina showed no partiality for him."

Caroline could only blink at the understatement;
Gina detested the man and referred to him as "the toad"
when her mother was not around.

"Lord Radford has offered a generous settlement,
very generous indeed. If you persist in refusing him, we
will have to force your sister to cry off from the engagement. Unlike you, she is not yet of age and must do as
her parents bid her." Even though Louisa was sure the
headstrong chit would have her Gideon in the face of
any opposition, she did not hesitate to play on Caroline's affection to gain her cooperation.

Caroline bowed her head in defeat. She remembered
her sister's joyful proclamation of her marriage, and
Gideon's tender adoration whenever he was near his
beloved. How could she make the two of them so unhappy, as well as blighting the chances of the younger
children? There was no way out. "Very well, then," she
said in a dead voice. "I will accept him."

Lady Hanscombe nodded her head approvingly. "I
was sure you would know your duty." She paused,

then added awkwardly, "Do not be unhappy. Radford is a fine man with an impeccable reputation. I am sure he will treat you with all kindness and consideration, and soon you will look back at these megrims and laugh."

There was no way under the heavens Caroline could have explained why the prospect of marriage to his lordship was so distressing. She didn't even try; her temples throbbing with pain, she whispered huskily, "May I go now, Mama?" Without waiting for an answer, she stood and went blindly to the door. Her stepmother made no attempt to stop her.

It was late that evening when Jessica entered the Adam Street town house, drawn by Gina's hastily scribbled note: *Please come at once. Caroline needs you.*

As the footman took her cloak, Gina hastened down the stairs, motioning her into the small ground-floor salon with gestures to keep silence. The door safely closed behind them, Jessica demanded, "What is going on here? What is wrong with Caroline?"

Gina shook her head, her round face drawn and worried. "It has been the most dreadful day! Apparently Lord Radford offered for Caroline. There was terrible yelling from my father's study, then Caro went to her room and cried for hours. I asked what was wrong, but she would only say she is to marry Radford. But why would she accept him if it makes her so miserable? She has only to say no, after all. She hasn't talked or eaten all day. I've never seen her like this. Usually if she is unhappy she just wanders off or plays the piano or some such. This time she looks like she is under sentence of death. Please, Jessica, see if you can do something for her!"

Jessica's lips tightened; she had suspected something

of the sort. Much better than Gina, she could understand how Caroline could be forced against her will. "I'll go up to her room immediately."

She tapped softly on her niece's door, then entered without waiting for an answer. In the low light of a single lamp, the crumpled child-size figure lay unmoving. "Caro, are you all right?" She walked quietly across the room and sat on the edge of the bed. Her lips parted in silent shock; Gina had not exaggerated. Caroline looked barely alive, her blue-white lips contrasting sharply with the swollen red eyes, the skin drawn tight to the bone, and her eyes staring blankly. A bowl of water and a cloth sat on the bedside table; Jessica picked up the cloth and wrung it out, smelling lavender as she did so. She carefully spread the cloth over her niece's forehead and asked, "Can you hear me?"

Caroline blinked and stared at her aunt, slowly bringing her into focus. "Jess." She half-rolled into her aunt's lap, wrapping her arms around her as if there were no other security in the world. Jessica stroked her hair for a few moments, then said gently, "Gina told me you are to marry Lord Radford. Why have you consented if it distresses you so? You know you can come to me if you are forced to leave your parents' house." No matter how much trouble would be caused in the family and in Wiltshire, Jessica was prepared to stand by her word.

Caroline replied in a flat, lifeless voice, "There is no help for it. Money is the problem. Lord Radford is willing to pay a ridiculously high price for me. If I refuse him, Gina will be forbidden to marry Gideon."

Jessica swore softly to herself. She had never had much opinion of her brother-in-law's judgment, but she had had no idea matters were in such bad case. They had found the perfect emotional blackmail to persuade Caroline.

Her niece added after a moment, "Apparently he will help the younger children as it becomes necessary. He is certainly getting a poor bargain for his money!" She ended with a half-hysterical bubble of laughter.

Continuing the gentle massage from her niece's head down to the neck and shoulders, Jessica asked, "Since you have decided to marry him, we must find why you dislike him so. What has he done to you?"

There was a long silence before Caroline answered, "He has not really done anything to me. I would not dislike him if I did not have to marry him."

Probing gently, her aunt continued, "Then what is the problem?"

There was a long, long pause, then the painful words, "He . . . reminds me of my father."

What Jessica had heard about the elegant, sardonic lord sounded very unlike Sir Alfred, but there had to be a reason for the reply. "In what way is he like your father?"

"He . . . frightens me. I always feel there is anger just behind those black eyes."

"And that is how your father has always seemed to you?"

"Yes . . . you know how Papa was never much around? I was always glad . . . I think he dislikes me as much as I dislike him. When I was little, sometimes he would want to play, but one could never tell when he would lose his temper. He would scream at me . . . hit me . . . and I never knew what it was that would cause him to behave as he did. I never knew!" She ended on a shuddering sob, close to breaking down entirely.

Under Jessica's hands, she struggled to regain control, then said more calmly, "I do not mean he was always beating me. Indeed, he was more violent with the boys. Gina would yell back at him—she had so much more courage than I. What made it so hard for me was . . . never knowing. The constant uncertainty and fear. All my life I have kept as far from him as possible. If he came in a room, I would drift out the other door. I was waiting only until I could leave, to live with you if I could, but if necessary to find any kind of job that would support me. I know I could teach music. I never thought I would have to spend the rest of my life living with that kind of fear, constantly wondering if I had done something wrong, never knowing when the lightnings would strike . . . and living without love." She started to tremble uncontrollably.

Jessica held her until the shaking stopped, then said carefully, "I understand why the idea is abhorrent to you. But are you sure it is anger you feel in Radford? It might be just that he is intense. I knew a man rather like that once—he lived life as if two hundred years would not be enough to do all he wished."

She thought a moment, then added, "Everyone is angry sometimes. A quickly passing irritation is very different from being a child at the mercy of an adult. When you are sure he loves you, a burst of temper won't bother you anything like so much as your memories do now."

"Do you really think that is true, Jess?"

"I know it is true, just as I know that our fears are almost always worse than reality."

"I . . . I think you must be right. When I was little, it was the fear, the unknowing, that was hardest to bear."

"And if the reality is as bad as your imaginings, you

can come to me. You will not have to spend your life living with a man you hate, Caroline. I promise you that."

Caroline looked directly at her aunt for the first time. "You would take me in? Even as a disgrace, a failed married woman?"

"Yes, anywhere, anytime. But in return, you must promise me you will try as hard as you can with Lord Radford. Look at him as he is, not overlaid with your father's shadow. You may truly come to love him; the closeness and sharing of married life are stronger bonds than you can imagine. Will you try to love him? For me, if not for yourself?"

"Oh, Jess, of course I will! What would I ever do without you?" Caroline laughed shakily, than raised herself up on the bed. "I must look like an absolute fright!"

"That you do."

Caroline looked slightly affronted, then gave a watery giggle. "If I am worrying about how I look, I guess the patient is on the mend. Thank you, Jess. I don't know how I can possible repay you."

"Well, you can start by convincing Linda her kitten has no talent for the pianoforte. Sometimes it is more than even a loving mother can take."

"Consider it done. Indeed, I will even teach Wellesley to play creditably on the instrument if that is what you wish."

"I will settle for silence, love. And your best efforts with the Diabolical Baron."

"Well, perhaps he is not so very diabolical after all. Should we start to call him the Dashing Baron?"

"Much better!" Jessica said. "Now it is time we started working on making you fit to be seen tomorrow."

"Yes, Mrs. Major Sterling, ma'am." Caroline's patented demure look was not up to her usual standard, but Jessica decided it was a good step in the right direction. One could only hope the baron would cooperate by not being diabolical. He might be stern and insensitive to the fears of a shy young lady, but there was no reason to suppose he was a monster. She must meet him soon and draw her own conclusions about his suitability as a husband.

Jason was immaculately attired as he entered the Hanscombe town house, Hessians gleaming like obsidian and the discreet glint of a ruby in his neckcloth. After all, a man didn't make an offer every day, and he intended to do justice to the occasion. His only other offer had been made under a beech tree with both parties smelling of horse, and that had been a singularly profitless venture. Though his confidence had grown enormously in the last dozen years, he was not absolutely sure Caroline would accept him; she was the most unaccountable girl. He knew little more about her now than when his courtship had begun weeks earlier. The workings of her mind were a complete mystery. She showed very little interest in either his polished address or his equally polished person. It would be a serious blow to his pride if she refused him, quite apart from the fact that he would lose his wager. Still, uncertainty lent spice to the venture.

He got a prim, knowing smile as he handed the butler his hat and asked for Miss Hanscombe. Everyone in the household must know why he was here. As he entered the sitting room to wait, his mind returned to his interview with Sir Alfred the day before. His lip curled slightly at the memory; really a most unattractive man, effusive in his delight at Lord Radford's so-flattering offer for his daughter. For all his effusions, he'd bar-

gained like a Billingsgate fish peddler over the settlements. For the amount of money he was asking, he
should have thrown in Lady Hanscombe and all the
younger daughters. But an agreement was reached.
Jason could afford to be generous, and by this time too
much time and pride were invested in the business to
cry off.

His musings were interrupted by Caroline's arrival,
just in time to catch the unpleasant expression left on his
face by thoughts of Sir Alfred. He straightened his features immediately, but she had obviously seen the look
and perhaps thought it intended for her.

She was pale but greeted him with composure.
"Good morning, Lord Radford. Please be seated. I trust
you are well today."

"Very well, thank you," he said with some brusque-
ness as he sat down. Now the moment was at hand, he
felt unexpectedly nervous. "There is something I particularly wish to discuss with you."

"Indeed? Pray continue." Her neutral voice gave no
hint of her thoughts, though she must know why he
was here.

"You cannot have failed to notice my great regard for
you. Your charm, your ladylike demeanor, have convinced me you are the woman I have sought for many
years." Jason paused, finding it difficult to face those
unfathomably deep blue eyes. "I would be greatly honored if you would consent to become my wife."

"Is this what you truly wish?" she asked in a low
voice.

"Of course," he said, puzzled by her lack of response.
Perhaps she was hoping for a more passionate declaration. He opened his mouth to make the necessary statement but found that the words wouldn't come. To save

his life, he could not have spoken lies of love. While he sat in silence, Caroline gave a slight sigh and answered him.

"In that case, I will of course be pleased and honored to accept your most flattering offer, Lord Radford."

"Perhaps you could see your way to calling me Jason, now we are betrothed?"

From the look on her face, it seemed clear she had never thought he might have a personal name. Swallowing hard, she replied, "I shall try . . . Jason. Please forgive me if I take time to acquire the habit."

"Of course. I wish you to take a good deal more than that. For a betrothal gift, I would like to send you to Madame Arlette's for a whole new wardrobe to celebrate your new life."

This called forth a violent blush. So he had noticed her dreadful clothes! He must have thought that was how she preferred to dress. Not only had her protective coloring failed, he must think she had wretched taste. Well, it was time to start working for his good opinion.

"That sounds a delightful prospect, Lor . . . Jason. It will be a great pleasure, and is most generous of you."

"In addition," Jason continued, "I wish to take you to my home, Wildehaven, at the end of next week. It will give us a chance to become better acquainted before the wedding. You must of course bring your family. I'm sure you would wish for your mother's support, and perhaps your sister Gina as well."

Caroline hesitated for a moment. "My sister is just engaged to Gideon Fallsworthy, and she and my stepmother will be going to visit his family in Lincolnshire. Would . . . would it be possible to invite my aunt, Mrs. Sterling? She is a widow and free to come and go as she chooses. She would probably wish to bring her young daughter, but Linda is a pretty-behaved child and would be no trouble."

Jason shrugged indifferently. One chaperon was much like another. In this case, the aunt would doubtless be preferable to the dragon mother. Or rather, dragon stepmother. "Of course they will both be welcome. I want you to be as comfortable as possible. I was thinking of an August wedding date."

Caroline looked a bit dismayed. "So soon?"

"'If it were done, 'twere well it were done quickly,'" Jason said, then mentally condemned his choice of quotation.

Surprisingly, Caroline ventured a slight smile. "Surely *Macbeth* is not entirely appropriate on this occasion? Although I recall he and his wife were well-matched, so perhaps it is not so far afield. Still, I would be greatly miscast as Lady Macbeth."

Jason chuckled at the improbable thought of Caroline wielding even an imaginary dagger. "I expressed myself poorly. Say rather that I see no virtue in a lengthy engagement, and am anxious to see you installed as Lady Radford." And of course, the wager specified they wed within six months.

He added, "I know my Aunt Honoria will be anxious to do something in your honor, since I have no closer female relatives. She is Lady Edgeware, you know."

Caroline looked alarmed. "I did not know. I was introduced to her at a card party once. She is very . . . memorable."

"She's a proper Tartar," Jason cheerfully agreed. "However, she will be so pleased at my choosing a bride that she will be bound to like you."

Caroline looked thoughtful. If Lord Radford's relations had been urging matrimony, it might help explain why he had suddenly decided to marry at his age. He didn't appear to be a man easily browbeaten, so she supposed marriage suited his own purposes.

Jason stood to take his leave. "I trust you will accept my escort to the Stanhopes' ball tonight? I will call for you at nine o'clock." He moved toward her, towering above her small figure even when she was standing. He hesitated a moment, then bent to give her a quick kiss to seal the engagement. Had it not been for her slight but unmistakable withdrawal, the sensation would have been much like kissing a piece of Roman statuary. With so little response, the embrace was perfunctory in the extreme. Bowing farewell to his intended, his lordship beat a hasty retreat.

Jason felt an unexpected sense of depression as he left Adam Street. When he had entered into this damnable wager, he had assumed he would find some cheerfully avaricious wench who would be delighted to sell her body and breeding for his wealth and title. He might even have found a damsel who would fancy herself in love with him, although he hadn't wished for that; a lovelorn maiden would have been a great nuisance, sighing and demanding his attention. He hadn't bargained for a girl who was being coerced as he expected Caroline was. Not even an optimistic lover would have taken her attitude as anything higher than resignation. Still, there was no help for it now. Doubtless she would be more relaxed when she knew him better. And when he was in the mood for passion, that could be purchased easily enough.

Chapter 6

Jessica swept across her parlor to give Caroline a hug as the girl entered. "I presume you are officially engaged now. Was it as bad as you expected?"

Caroline hugged her aunt back, then took her bonnet off. "No, you were right—anticipation was worse than reality. Lord Radford was most considerate, though very far from loverlike. From something he said, I believe he just thought it was time to get married, and for some reason decided on me. Still, if he doesn't want much of me, no doubt we shall rub along tolerably."

She colored suddenly. If nothing else, his lordship was certain to want an heir. And the thought of how that would be done . . . She said hurriedly, "He wants me to go to Madame Arlette's for a new wardrobe. Apparently he was not impressed with my governess clothes. Will you help me at the *modiste*'s? Then I shall be rigged out in proper style."

"How delightful. I have never set foot in that august salon. It will be the greatest fun to spend large quantities of Lord Radford's money to put you in the first stare of fashion. I still think you must misjudge his feelings. After all, he chose you above every other eligible lady in London."

"He probably drew my name out of a hat," Caroline said darkly. She paused, then said diffidently, "There is something else. He wishes me to come to his estate, Wildehaven, at the end of next week. Mama and Gina will be going to Lincolnshire to meet the Fallsworthys. Do you think . . . could you possibly come as my chaperon? Lord Radford has agreed, and says Linda can come too. I'm sure the riding will be good, and you would have a pleasant time." She finished in a rush, with a hopeful look her aunt couldn't have resisted if she tried.

"Indeed, I would like nothing better than to meet the Diabolical Baron on his own ground," she said with a smile. "But I think I will take Linda to her grandparents'. It will be good for us to be apart for a time. I depend too much on her company. She is already halfway to being a young lady, and I had best start learning to live without her. She will have her cousins and her pony and shan't miss me at all. Do you think Radford could be persuaded to take us to Gloucestershire by way of my in-laws'? It is not too far out of the way."

"Splendid!" cried her niece. "It will be so much easier if you are there. I'm sure he won't mind the detour—he has been most obliging. He wishes to leave next Friday, so the sooner we get to Madame Arlette's, the better." She wrinkled her nose a bit. "He has asked me to call him by his Christian name, but I don't think I am ready for that yet. It would be like calling God by a nickname. I shall start by thinking of him as 'Radford' without the 'Lord.' I daresay when I am more comfortable with him, in five or ten years, I shall achieve greater informality."

"Truly, Caro, it won't take so very long. It was a fine

and considerate idea of his to let you get better acquainted before the wedding. You have always preferred the country anyway, and will doubtless take to being the lady of the manor very quickly."

"We shall see," Caroline said skeptically. "In the meantime, would you be free to go to the *modiste's* right now? Buying a mountain of expensive clothes should be diverting."

"Just let me get my bonnet."

The trip was quickly accomplished in the old-fashioned Hanscombe carriage Caroline had arrived in. Now that she was destined to be a peeress, her stepmother was taking great care of her consequence; no more walking around like a servant girl.

Madame Arlette's proved to be all one might expect of the most fashionable *modiste* in London: thick carpet, expensive furniture and draperies, a delicate scent of some exotic perfume. Plus Madame herself when her chief saleswoman informed her that Lord Radford's future bride had arrived. A stately woman of great dignity, one would never have guessed she started life as the illegitimate daughter of a Parisian prostitute. To the English, all émigrés were much the same; if she chose to present herself as an aristocrat fallen on hard times, who would care to dispute her?

Sweeping grandly up to Jessica, she said, "It is the greatest of pleasures for me to meet the future Lady Radford *enfin*. You will make a couple *très magnifique!*"

Jessica inclined her head coolly. "Permit me to introduce myself. I am Mrs. Sterling, and this is my niece, Caroline Hanscombe, who is to wed Lord Radford."

In the face of the proprietor's embarrassment, Caroline could only dimple and say, "Indeed, Madame Arlette, I am used to being overlooked when my aunt is around. I am trusting your skills to make me less invisible. Lord Radford wishes me to have a completely new wardrobe, and I am sure you will do a wonderful job of it. Where would you suggest we begin?"

Relieved to have her gaffe dismissed so gently, Madame Arlette studied her client carefully and pronounced, "For you the clear spring colors, delicate but vibrant, no? And a great simplicity of line. Leonora, bring some of the bolts of Italian silks from the back room. Yes, the ones I was saving for a very special customer. You will be of an unmatched *superbité* when we are done, *hein*?"

She looked again at Jessica. "If I may say so, Madame Sterling, your own toilette is most exquisite. Only a woman of Madame's magnificent coloring could wear that shade of dark teal blue. And the cut— subtle yet *très chic*. Might I inquire who is your *modiste*?"

"But of course," Jessica said affably. "Madame Sterling does her own clothes."

"A-a-h-h-h!" Madame Arlette said, giving Jessica the look of one artist to another. "It is most fortunate for my humble establishment you are not in the business yourself. You would take the honors from us all."

By no means averse to flattery, Jessica laughed and they settled down in earnest to the business of turning Caroline into a lady of fashion. Round gowns, morning gowns, riding habits, pelisses, walking dresses, ball gowns, bonnets, exquisite unmentionables, a domino for possible masked balls—nothing was left to chance.

After three hours of being draped with fabrics and discussed as if she weren't present, a dazed Caroline realized that being fashionable was much more work than she had anticipated. While she was being dressed—not unlike a leg of mutton, as she pointed out with resignation—she amused herself by drifting into a creative haze. The obvious subject was a musical fantasy on the subject of fashion: strong on the violin, to convey the gauzy fabrics; some delicate flutes show- ing the fluttering hands; an erratic oboe passage to add to a general effect most whimsical. A pity she lacked access to the musicians needed to turn the composition into living sound; she had the overall piece clear in her mind by the time her two experts declared the results worthy of Lord Radford. Now it only remained for his lordship to agree.

Ten days later, all was in readiness for the trip to Wildehaven. Madame Arlette's underpaid minions had labored mightily to create the staggering quantity of clothes deemed essential to Lady Radford. An ex- pert hairdresser had been called in to pull, trim, and tug Caroline's hair into a multitude of new styles, and her newly acquired personal maid was drilled in their execution until the master was satisfied with her com- petence. The new styles were pulled back more from Caroline's face, emphasizing the pure line of her pro- file, the exquisite complexion and delicate features, and the dramatically blue eyes. She felt uncomfortably exposed without her hair to hide behind, but she ac- cepted the change meekly, in keeping with her promise to Jessica to try her best with her future hus- band.

When he arrived to pick her up in Adam Street, Jason thought her appearance lacked only vivacity to qualify her as a remarkably attractive woman. Unfor- tunately, even the best shops in Bond Street could not

supply that, but he was well satisfied with her im-
provement. She was ready promptly, another point in
her favor. Not only could patience not be listed as one
of Jason's good points; it was so low on the list of his
virtues as to be nonexistent.

He bowed as she entered the salon and said, "You
look most charming today, Caroline. Madame Arlette
has surpassed herself." This last was no surprise; he
had learned of Madame's expertise while outfitting
various mistresses over the years, and knew her skills
could be relied upon. "We have perfect traveling
weather. The rains of the last two days will have laid
the dust, and now we have sunshine to light our way.
In truth, I am anxious to return to Wildehaven.
Courtship has kept me from home longer than I like."

Caroline's smile was less enthusiastic as she contemplated the ordeal ahead of her. "I look forward to traveling with your famous team of grays. If they are the
equal of the chestnuts that pulls your phaeton, they
must be praiseworthy indeed."

"That they are, and steady as they are handsome."
And mine to keep now, he added silently. "While my
men are loading the luggage, I would like to pay my
respects to your parents. I trust they will be able to
visit Gloucestershire soon."

While Jason was exercising his manners on Lady
Hanscombe, Caroline received a quick farewell hug
from Gina, who assumed that all newly engaged
maidens were as happy as herself. She and her mother
were leaving for Lincolnshire the next morning, and
Gina looked forward to meeting Gideon's parents
with a mixture of anticipation and anxiety.

It was not yet ten o'clock when they reached the
Sterling house, where they had arranged to pick up

Jessica and her daughter. The little square where they lived was not fashionable, but it was a pleasant pocket of peace that hardly seemed to be in London. When they had been let into the house, Caroline excused herself from Jason and went upstairs to see if her assistance was needed.

"You look particularly splendid today, Jess," she said, admiring the gold traveling costume that rivaled her aunt's red hair for sheen and brilliance. "Letting the Diabolical, sorry, Dashing Baron know that you are a force to be reckoned with?"

"Exactly so," her aunt laughed. "You know me too well. But in life's uneven battles, we poor females must use all the weapons at our disposal. We can't have the Dashing Baron think your chaperon is a cipher who can be ignored with impunity."

"A good excuse to justify a new dress, though I can't recall that you usually bother with excuses. And as for being ignored! If you walked down St. James in that dress, all the clubs would empty of gentlemen and they would follow you down the street as if you were the Pied Piper himself. Or rather herself. Is Linda ready?"

"I believe so. Apart from the fact that I said she couldn't take Wellesley, she has been ready to leave anytime this last week. If you'll go to her room and take her down to the salon, I'll be along in a moment." Caroline grinned inwardly as she went to Linda's room. Trust Jessica to make a grand entrance; she would have done splendidly at Drury Lane.

Pacing around a parlor too small for his restless energy, Jason was pleased when Caroline and her cousin entered so quickly. "Jason, I would like to present my cousin Miss Linda Sterling. Linda, Lord Radford."

The child bobbed a very proper curtsy. With the ruthless directness of the young, she said, "I am pleased to make your acquaintance, Lord Radford. I trust you intend to take proper care of my cousin?"

Caroline's stern "Linda!" was drowned out by Jason's chuckle. "You are clearly a soldier's daughter, with a talent for attack. I assure you I have every intention of treating your cousin as she deserves, and I will expect you to call me on my failings."

Linda nodded, satisfied with his answer. Jason continued, "Your name is unusual; how came you by it?"

Linda gave a pleased smile. "Linda means 'pretty' in Spanish. My mama says when I was born my father said I was the prettiest little thing he had ever seen, and insisted no other name would do." She paused; then her natural honesty compelled her to add, "Mama says I actually looked like a proper bit of underdone beef."

Jason chuckled again. "A surprising degree of candor for a new mother. No doubt your father was seeing into the future and realizing what a heartbreaker you would grow to be. It sounds like your mother coming now. I am anxious to meet her."

Moving into the entrance hall, Jason looked up the curving stairs to the source of the footsteps. The heart he thought had died in him more than a dozen years before twisted into painful and unwelcome life at the sight of the golden figure descending. Hair like flame, a figure that would keep a Cyprian wrapped in jewels for life, and he knew she would ride like Diana. Glowing with a radiant warmth that surpassed the dazzling loveliness of seventeen; beautiful even beyond dream and memory. Jessica.

* * *

Jessica was chuckling to herself as she came down the staircase, anticipating the trip and the challenges ahead. Though she maintained her own household for the freedom it gave her, London sometimes made her feel claustrophobic. Several weeks on a grand country estate with good horses and wide-open spaces to ride them in was a prospect that could not fail to please. And there should be a lively social life as well, since Lord Radford would wish to introduce his bride to local society.

As Jessica came from the brightly lit upper hall, her eyes took a few moments adjusting to the darker vestibule. From the stairs, she saw a tall, dark figure that could only be his lordship, and fixed her best social smile on her face. Her first impression was of leashed power and a formidable elegance. Midway down, her step faltered and she stopped, holding the rail to support herself as the blood drained from her face.

God in heaven, she thought wildly. How can Caroline's Diabolical Baron possibly be Jason Kincaid? As she stood stock-still, her eyes adjusted enough to see the dark frowning brows. Gone was the reckless, open boy, replaced by a man used to power and impatient of obstacles. It was still the handsomest face she had ever seen, but its hard lines made him seem older than his years, accounting for Caro's misjudgment of his age. The well-cut mouth was set in a tight line, and black eyes bored into hers, icy with anger. Clearly he recognized her, and had forgiven nothing.

As Caroline and Linda came into the hall, Jessica was pleased to hear her own voice saying coolly, "Such a surprise, Caroline. I had no idea your Lord Radford was an old acquaintance of mine from before my first

Season. When I knew him he was plain Jason Kincaid."

Continuing to the bottom of the stairs, she extended her hand to him and went on, "Indeed, your lordship, I must congratulate you on your high estate. Were you a cousin who came unexpectedly to the title?"

He bowed punctiliously over her hand and stepped back, answering, "My father was Lord Radford, but since my older brother enjoyed the rudest of good health, I had no expectation of inheriting. When Geoffrey refused to believe hard drinking and hard riding don't mix, I came into the title five years ago." He paused, then added coldly, "Of course it is not to be expected you would know how I was placed, since our acquaintance was of the slightest."

Jessica flinched at his casual dismissal of what had been the most intense experience of her life. Her emotions tilted wildly from believing he remembered her to being convinced he had forgotten—no doubt he hardly recalled her amongst all the famous society beauties he had known through the years. Consistency was not prominent in her thinking at the moment.

Since she was about to become his aunt by marriage, the dead past must stay that way—dead and buried beyond redemption.

Caroline looked uncertainly back and forth between the two tall striking figures. She heard the polite words, but deep in her viscera she could feel murky undercurrents swirling. Jason looked like Zeus about to hurl a thunderbolt, and even her aunt's unshakable composure seemed forced. Given his apparent preference for docile ladies, he must have hated Jessica's headstrong independence when he knew her in the past. Since she was now less wild but even more independent, he wasn't likely to appreciate her any better.

Given a choice, Caroline would have preferred to slip out of the room and disappear; anywhere would be preferable to seeing her betrothed looking like he wanted to murder her dearest friend and relative. But she was responsible for this meeting, so she bravely moved into the breech. "How interesting. You did not know my mother was a Westerly, Jason?"

His face was stiff but he answered civilly enough. "I must apologize for inadequate research into your antecedents. Having met you, I felt no need to know more. Shall we leave, my dear?" He offered Caroline his arm. She blinked a bit at the endearment and the speech; it was the most loverlike thing he had ever said to her.

As she took the proffered arm, she smiled brightly and said, "Of course. We have quite a journey to make and I am anxious to be off. Jess, are you and Linda ready?"

Jessica answered, "Since the luggage is going on the second carriage, there is no reason to delay. I'm sure Lord Radford's driver can be trusted to take care of the loading. Linda, do you have your shawl? It will be cooler outside of London."

Linda nodded. Oblivious of atmosphere, she was intent on her own affairs. Considering the states of mind of the three adults, it was hardly surprising no one noticed the straw basket under her cashmere shawl.

As they climbed into the carriage, Jason was cursing himself for having chosen to ride within rather than alongside. It had seemed a reasonable step in his plan to further his acquaintance with Caroline, but now the prospect of traveling in such close quarters with his future aunt appalled him. Since his shattered nerves still hadn't recovered from shock, he was abrupt to a point just short of rudeness to Caroline's conversational sallies. Jessica said nothing at all; only Linda showed any pleasure, peering out the window excitedly and pointing out worthy sights and familiar landmarks on the road.

Less than an hour sufficed to get them out of the city's confusion and into the green countryside. Caroline had succumbed to the atmosphere of vibrating tension and sat silent, feeling her temples throb. If this is how the next weeks are going to be, she thought miserably, I'll be ready for Bedlam. Why can't the wretched man make some effort to be civil? For lack of anything better to do, she took refuge in mentally transforming the situation into a concerto for chamber orchestra. Her knowledge of orchestration was imperfect, but she was sure of one thing: the composition would emphasize drums.

Lost as she was in her work, at first she missed the small, high-pitched cries. The unexpected noise was almost inaudible over the noises of the creaking carriage, horses' hooves, and jingling harness, but her sensitive musician's ear caught it. She looked sharply at Linda, who sat across from her, next to Jason. The next time the cry came, she noticed Linda quickly made some remark about the passing scene.

She had a lively suspicion of what might be the problem, but hesitated to mention it in the strained atmosphere. Her indecision was solved by a new cry that could not be overlooked by anyone present.

· Jessica looked sternly at her daughter and said, "What was that sound?"

"A . . . a hiccup, Mama," Linda said falteringly.

"I have never yet heard a hiccup that sounded like that. Have you disobeyed me and brought your kitten?"

Linda hung her head. "Yes, Mama." There was no point in lying; the evidence would have overwhelmed her in any case.

Apparently realizing he had attracted the attention he sought, Wellesley was starting to yowl in earnest. Jason looked on with a nasty glint in his eyes that clearly showed what he thought of women who couldn't control their children.

"All right, miss. Where have you hidden him?" Jessica said with resignation.

Linda reached down and pulled a covered straw basket out from under her trailing shawl. Lifting the basket's lid, she said, "Here he is, Mama."

Lifting the lid proved a serious mistake. Frantic at his confinement, the kitten gave a bloodcurdling cry and exploded out of the basket. He cleared his jail in one bound, ricocheted off the blue velvet squabs, and swarmed to the top of the highest available object, shrieking as if a pack of pit dogs were after him.

Unfortunately, the object he chose to treat as a tree was Lord Radford. The three females stared in horror as the orange ball of fluff came to rest on his lordship's impeccably tailored shoulder, mewing piteously and leaving a faint trail of colorful fur in its wake. Jason's face was a study in conflicting emotions, none of them pleasant. The appalling moment stretched interminably, punctuated only by continuing cat cries.

Just when it seemed the tension would explode of its own accord, the silence was broken by a burst of laughter from Jessica. Shaking in mirth, she bent her head toward her lap, gasping, "Oh, Jason, if you could only see!"

Freed of her paralysis, Caroline found herself joining her aunt's unseemly laughter. "Indeed, my lord, it is so very droll. That such an insignificant beast should perform such an act of *lèse-majesté*!"

Torn between outrage and the gales of merriment surrounding him, Jason's sense of humor finally won out. Chuckling in spite of himself, he reached up and detached the clinging needle-fine claws. Scratching behind the cat's ears, he held it up to eye level and said, "And who might this insignificant creature be? It is more than a kitten but much less than a cat."

"Wellesley, my lord," Linda said while she tried to subdue her giggles.

"After the Iron Duke, you know," Caroline added helpfully. Unfortunately, this useful information sent her and her aunt off again, and some time passed before they were sober. Jason continued stroking the cat; he was no feline expert, but the principle appeared to be the same as for dogs. Wellesley recognized safety in a fellow male and settled down comfortably on the lordly lap.

When she was capable of rationality again, Jessica said, "I am very sorry, Lord Radford. It has always been a mistake to give my daughter orders that don't make sense to her."

"Doubtless you were exactly the same at her age." Jason's tone was dry but no longer hostile. All of the strain in the carriage had vanished during the feline frenzy.

"Unfortunately yes," she sighed. "Linda, I should have explained that it was not caprice that made me forbid you to bring Wellesley. Cats make your grandmother ill; she sneezes and has trouble breathing. We really can't bring a cat into the house, and I'm afraid a kitten like Wellesley will not do well among the barn cats."

Before Linda could volunteer to sleep in the barn with her pet, Jason said to her, "We can take the cat on to Wildehaven. Unfortunately you will still be deprived of his company, but I trust we can keep him safe."

"I suppose that would be best," Linda said sadly. "And I'm sure you will take better care of him than he would have had in London."

"Indeed, it is most generous of Lord Radford," Jessica said.

"Since we still have a lengthy journey ahead of us, may I ask about the, er, practical arrangements for his care?" Jason inquired, still speaking to Linda.

Linda turned over what he said and then blushed when she realized what was meant. "Indeed, sir, I brought some food for him but I didn't think of the other thing."

"Never mind," Jason said soothingly. "We can get a box with some earth in it when we stop for a nuncheon."

The remainder of the journey was considerably more pleasant than the first part; it was hard to tell whether Linda or Wellesley was having the better time. Having had scant experience with either cats or small girls, Jason watched them both with amusement. Wellesley proved to be a good traveler when he was allowed the freedom of the coach, distributing his favors impartially as he moved from lap to lap.

They made good time and arrived at the Sterling family home in Wiltshire at sunset. The small manor had been the secure center for generations of military men and their families, and the party was welcomed warmly. Caught up by a gaggle of cousins, Linda raced off to the stables to see how her pony had survived her absence. The adults were glad enough to retire to their rooms with their various uncomfortable thoughts until the pleasantly informal dinner was served.

Always happy to see their daughter-in-law, Colonel Sterling and his wife urged them to spend more than one night, but no one wished to linger—Jason because he felt obscurely that he would be able to control his feelings more easily when he was on his home ground, Jessica and Caroline because they might as well get on with the business ahead.

The next day's journey was shorter than the first, and soon they were among the steep-sided Cotswold hills. The road twisted and turned to create ever-changing views of breathtaking beauty. Although she had grown up not far to the south, Caroline had never been into Gloucestershire and she was disarmed by its loveliness. It would be a major compensation for a loveless match.

Not long after their midday break, Jason signaled the coachman to stop at the crest of a hill and invited the ladies out to admire the view. The hills and woodlands seemed to have been designed by a painter; here and there a square stone church tower marked a distant village, and a small river curved away from them to the west. Following the river's turns, Caroline drew in a breath at the sight of the house in the middle distance. Designed and proportioned in the Palladian mode, its cool classicism blended perfectly into its setting. "What is that great house, Lor . . . Jason?" she asked.

With a warmth in his voice she had never heard before, he said, "That is your new home, Wildehaven."

She looked a few moments longer. "I can see why you are so pleased to come home. It is superb."

Jessica had been unusually silent during the trip; she conceded the irony of having her first love as her new nephew, but she wasn't quite ready to find amusement in it. She had thought long and hard on how Jason would suit her niece, and could not decide whether the match would succeed or fail abysmally. She would swear the young Jason Kincaid had had not an ounce of real vice in him, but this new hard-eyed stranger was an enigma. It was easy to see how intimidating he would be to a shy young girl. If he had the patience to deal gently with Caroline, the marriage could be comfortable, but patience had never been a feature in his youth and he didn't appear to have improved in that respect. For Caroline's sake she would hint to him the best way of winning her niece's trust and love, though it was not a task she welcomed.

As she looked at Wildehaven's distant majesty, it was impossible to avoid thinking that she could have been mistress of it. But any present that didn't include Linda would not have been worth the having, so the pang was easily suppressed.

It was only another half-hour's ride to the gates of Wildehaven. A magnificent drive lined with lime trees curved around the side of a hill and led to the main entrance. Jason bowed ceremonially over Caroline's hand after he had helped her from the carriage. "Welcome to Wildehaven."

Caroline looked at the broad facade dubiously. Close up, it was rather overpowering. The central section was three stories high, and long wings angled out on both sides. It seemed to have been built for a race of giants, not for undersized females of no great style or countenance. Her confidence was not aided by the hastily assembled line of servants waiting to greet her in the enormous high-ceilinged entrance hall. The butler and housekeeper were even more intimidating than Jason himself; impossible to think of giving either of them orders. They were introduced as Burke and Mrs. Burke, presumably a married couple. The rest of the names and faces passed in a blur.

"Would you care to rest from the trip, Caroline?" Jason's voice was a welcome break into her tired confusion.

"I would like that very much," she said. "What time do we dine?"

"We keep country hours here, but that gives you two hours for a rest. Mrs. Burke will show you and your aunt to your rooms."

Before they could leave, a giant dog came galloping into the room, heading straight for his much-missed master. He came to a screeching halt, skidding ponderously on the polished marble floor, his head exactly positioned for Jason's caress. Secure in Jessica's arms, Wellesley hissed in panic, his back arching and his tail fluffing to double its normal diameter. Intrigued by the sound, the mastiff swung his giant head toward the cat and moved to investigate. Before Wellesley's hysteria became completely uncontrollable, Jason snapped, "Rufus, you are not to touch the cat, now or ever. Do you understand?"

The dog looked at his master in what appeared to be perfect comprehension, and a look of doggy delight caused his jaws to loll open as Jason continued scratching behind his ears. "As for you, Wellesley," Jason continued with a hard stare at the little cat, "cease this un-seemly emotion. Rufus will not harm you."

Amazingly, the kitten appeared to accept this. His tail resumed normal proportions and he settled once more in Jessica's grasp.

The drama having ended, the housekeeper inclined her head infinitesimally and swept off with Caroline and Jessica trailing behind her. Jessica's long strides kept up easily, but Caroline felt like a child scurrying to keep up with an adult. The journey to their rooms seemed to encompass miles of corridors and hand-some rooms; by the time they reached their destination she was thinking wistfully of the ball of string Theseus took into the Labyrinth.

"Your room, Miss Hanscombe. If you should wish anything, just pull the bell rope. I will send a girl along later to help you prepare for dinner."

"Thank you, Mrs. Burke," Caroline replied. "I am sure I will be most comfortable here."

Her assigned chamber was beautifully proportioned and fitted with elegant Chippendale-style furniture. The predominant colors were rose and a delicate green, and the massive canopied bed would suit any fairy-tale princess. She moved to the window and found herself looking behind the house into the Wilde-haven gardens. Formal squares of grass and flowers led the eye to a small lake where a graceful bridge arched to a small island.

She was still gazing out the window when a knock on the door was quickly followed by her aunt.

"Goodness, Caro, it's magnificent! I feel as if I've wandered into one of my childhood fantasies. They've put me right next door." Jessica grinned. "I suppose that is the best place for a chaperon to do her guarding.

I'm lucky they didn't give me a pallet across your door to lie on."

Caroline turned from her window position. "It certainly is superb. I can't help feeling that Wildehaven is the wrong name. There is nothing at all wild about it. Everything appears to be under complete control. It gives me an insight into why Jason might have offered for me. He should find me easy to control."

Jessica chuckled and cast herself back over the bed, stretching her arms and legs catwise in sensual appreciation. "It was a surprise to have Rufus and Wellesley obey him so readily, though it benefited Wellesley's health. As for your being easy to control—what a whisker! I know you never indulge in open rebellion, but you have a talent for eluding unwelcome strictures. I've see you disappear like a wisp of smoke any number of times when you didn't like what was going on.

"In the meantime, I have a great desire to soak up every particle of luxury Wildehaven has to offer. It is hard to imagine an environment further removed from the dirt floor of a Spanish peasant's hut. It makes me so glad for those years of following the drum. I could not appreciate this half so much without my memories for contrast."

Caroline smiled warmly and crossed to sit on the bed next to her aunt. "Indeed, Jess, you were born to rule over a domain like this. Not like me—I should be much happier in one of those stone cottages we passed on the way."

"As long as it had a music room as large as the rest of the house."

"Exactly so." They both laughed at the thought.

"By the way, when did you meet Jason?" Caroline

was curious, and this was the first time they had been private since leaving London.

"Oh, it was just a hunting acquaintance. Father and I were visiting with one of his friends in the shires. He never had any money longer than it took him to lose it at cards, but he didn't lack for well-off friends who would keep him in comfort. I was seventeen and getting ready for my first Season, so I was old enough to be an asset to him. Doubtless he hoped some rich lord would fall in love with me."

A touch of bitterness was in her voice; she paused, then continued, "Jason Kincaid was there for the hunting also, staying with a university friend. They were just down from Cambridge, I believe. Our paths crossed at the hunts and the balls. After I left for London I never saw him again. It was quite a surprise to see him after all these years. I had no idea your Diabolical Baron was someone I knew when he was a fledgling."

"What was he like then?"

"A bruising rider, and always ripe for a jest. Much more playful than he seems now. I suppose his responsibilities have made him rather grim, but I'm sure a lighter side of him is still there, waiting for you to discover." Jessica looked earnestly at her niece, who seemed unwilling to pursue the topic.

Caroline stood and said, "You know, I've always wondered how someone like you who is always bringing in stray animals and patching broken wings can possibly hunt. Isn't there a contradiction there?"

"Yes, but what are any of us but a mass of contradictions? When I was a child, I would unstop the fox earths to foil the hunters because I couldn't bear to think of creatures dying unnecessarily, even if they were vermin. But riding in the hunt itself is so intoxicating . . . the excitement, the feel of the wind, the power of the horse you control. . . . It is the closest mere mortals come to flying. There is nothing like it. Ideally, the fox gives us a wonderful chase and escapes in the end."

Caroline nodded thoughtfully. "That explains a great deal. Now I understand better why people are so passionate about hunting. It was a favorite topic of the more boring young men I met at the *ton* parties. They were always going on about what great runs they'd had." She yawned and said, "And now to sleep. I'm going to need all my strength for the inevitable house tour."

Jessica slid off the bed. "With any luck you'll be spared that until tomorrow morning. In the meantime, I'd better check that Wellesley isn't on top of my canopy bed. If he had been a female, we could have called him Pandora, for all the things he gets into."

Then she retired to her own blue-tinted room to fortify herself for what promised to be the worst house party of her life.

Chapter 7

After Mrs. Burke had taken the ladies off, Jason lost no time in going to his room and changing into riding clothes. Ordinarily he would have visited his office to see if any urgent matters awaited attention, but today he hastened to the stables and saddled his favorite stallion, Caesar, without waiting for a groom. As soon as Jason and Caesar had cleared the stable-yard he gave the restless horse its head and they went blazing over the hills in a burst of explosive mutual energy.

They had reached the boundary of Wildehaven and were circling the perimeter before Caesar began to flag and Jason let the stallion slow to a more moderate pace. Jason had always been an intensely physical man, and the confinement and tension of the last two days had been a sore trial. With some of his energy released, he was now free to think on the unwelcome new complication in his life. He had gotten over his feelings for Jessica years ago, of course. It had merely been a youthful infatuation with a girl prettier than most.

An unwelcome voice in his head said: *Not pretty; beautiful.* He adjusted his thoughts. All right, she had been beautiful. *Had been?* Well, she was still beautiful.

But she was more than that. Jason shook his head irritably, trying to dismiss his unruly second-guesser. Before he had finished the gesture, he was rocked by a
flood of memories.

It was the first time he had been allowed to ride with
the Quorn, perhaps the most prestigious hunt in England. He was respectful of his elders, as befitted a
young man of twenty-one summers, but he knew his
riding was the equal of any man's there. A few women
were present, but the crowd of hunters that morning
was large and the pre-dawn mists heavy. He had been
impatient; the worst part of any hunt was waiting for
the hounds to find a quarry. When a scent was raised,
they were off on a wild chase across rough country he
had never seen before. The hunters were bunched at
first but thinned out as riders and horses refused
jumps, took tumbles, or became too winded to continue.

Jason was in the forefront close behind the hunts-
man when he realized a woman was in the small
group. He couldn't see her clearly in the half-light,
though he had been impressed by her riding.

There was a minor debacle when the fox was cor-
nered; the clumsy female somehow got her horse tangled with the hounds and the quarry had escaped. It
was a horrendous breach of hunting etiquette and the
Master had been furious until he had a closer look at
the transgressor. Jason was by this time near enough to
see her, and he would have gasped if he had had the
breath for it. The female was very young, very contrite,
and incredibly, breathtakingly lovely. She wore an
emerald-green velvet riding habit that matched her
eyes, and long strands of bright auburn hair blew
across her clear rose-petal skin. She batted her eye-

lashes as she apologized to the Master. So sorry! Overcome with excitement! The horse too strong for her; she would be ever so careful in the future! It would never happen again!

The Master, a retired general known for his steely eye and peremptory manners, harrumphed and muttered and even, Jason would have sworn, blushed. She was a foolish gel and had best be more careful in the future, but demmed if he'd ever seen a female who could ride like her. Best stay by him till they struck another scent and he'd explain the rules of the hunt to her. Did she know the fox that escaped was old Rufus, the wiliest beast in the shires? He'd been trying to catch the critter for years. Oh, she hadn't known, so *sorry*, General. Well, the fox had led them on merry chases before, and perhaps he would again. She wasn't to worry her pretty little head about it.

Jason had watched the little drama with deep appreciation. She might have fooled the Master, but no one who watched closely could think she wasn't in control of her horse. The gelding should have bolted or thrown her in that mad tangle of hounds, but she had shown effortless mastery. He saw the mischievous gleam under the fluttering lashes and would wager the minx had deliberately caused the incident so the fox could escape.

The Master and the girl rode off together, but Jason tested his theory at a hunt ball later that week. He had discovered her name was Jessica Westerly. Her father was the Honorable Gilbert Westerly, youngest son of a viscount, known as a gamester with never a feather to fly with. He spent his time moving from one great house to another, playing cards and paying the shot with lavish quantities of easy charm. The chit would be making her come-out in the spring; apparently he had brought her along so she could test her social wings in a more informal setting.

Based on what Jason could see, the wings had passed the test with superlative ease. There wasn't a man in the room unaware of Miss Westerly. They competed for her dances, for the right to fetch her orgeat, for a single glance of those dazzling green eyes. While two gentlemen were politely disputing the right to her next dance, Jason had swept her away.

She was dressed with great propriety in a white muslin gown edged with green embroidery to match her eyes. He accused her of letting the fox escape because it was a relative of hers; clearly they shared the same coloring. She answered with rich laughter acknowledging his hit, and he was lost.

The next two weeks had been sheer magic. Their constant companionship inspired excited gossip amongst the old quizzes, but Jessica gave no sign of noticing. During the hunts they hurled themselves across the shires with the mad confidence of those too young to believe in their own mortality. Jason had never known a rider to equal her. They danced together at evening parties, shared meals and mischief, talked of whatever entered their heads. While no words of love were exchanged, Jason was sure his every thought and feeling found an echo in her. The only small cloud came when he showed too much interest in a famous society hostess known for her taste in young men. Jessica treated him with ruthless civility for nearly three hours. Delighted by this sign of jealousy, he teased her out of the mood by evening's end.

On the night of the last formal hunt ball at the local great house, they had slipped outside under the full wintry moon. The night was bitterly cold, the garden a silvery enchantment belonging to them alone. For timeless moments they shared an embrace that left them both shaken. Jason had had his fair share of experience with women, but he had never before felt such passion and awed tenderness. Jessica's response was inexperienced but as enthusiastic as his own. Taking her back to the ball was the hardest thing he had ever done, and would have been impossible had his protectiveness not exceeded even his desire.

The next day he called early at the house where she stayed and asked her to go riding. No one could keep up when they chose to exert their horsemanship. They easily lost the groom detailed to Miss Westerly's protection, finally stopping and dismounting under a broad-armed chestnut tree. He kept his hands off her with great difficulty while he stammered his proposal in a stiff, brusque voice, saying how much he admired her beauty, how proud he would be to have her as his wife.

He would never forget the expression on her face changing from eager trust to shock, pain, and then blazing anger. She had cursed him in language she shouldn't have known, mounted her horse, and was gone while he was still reeling. He had thought he knew her to the depths of his soul, and found he did not know her at all. Perhaps the anger was because she thought of him as a friend, and was outraged when he acted the lover? She had not kissed him as if he were only a friend. Had she been insulted by the proposal of a young man with so little to offer her? But he had never discussed his circumstances. Or perhaps the night before was the casual experiment of a girl practicing her wiles on someone who didn't matter. That was the worst thought of all.

Hurt beyond words, two hours later Jason had packed and left his friend's house and was on his way to the small estate near Newmarket he had inherited from his mother. It was three months before he ventured out where friends or family could see him, and even then George Fitzwilliam complained he was like a bear with a sore ear. He spoke to no one of what had happened, and he swore never to be so vulnerable again. When he heard a few months later that the Divine Miss Westerly had confounded society by marrying a soldier of no great wealth or consequence, he merely raised a bored eyebrow and changed the subject.

Over the next years Jason turned his small estate into one of the finest horse-breeding farms in Britain. His hunters and racehorses were renowned for speed and endurance, his matched carriage teams without peer. When he went to town for the Season, men sought him out for equine advice, youths admired his sporting prowess, and women cast their lures to him. He was known as a devil with the ladies, always ready for an affair with a married woman but never giving away the smallest part of his heart. When his brother's unexpected death made him Lord Radford, he became even more sought after, and more cynical. The matchmaking mamas had been worse than the hot-eyed matrons.

His dynastic feelings were strong enough that he decided to marry, but he expected no particular pleasure. It had been a pleasant surprise when Caroline seemed to want nothing from him, in spite of her avaricious father. He had become confident of winning her affection as her shyness abated, so the union would be comfortable for them both.

Now his well-laid plan was blown to flinders. Who would have dreamed the long-lost Jessica could be Caroline's aunt? Or that her presence could still upset him so? Just shock, of course, but it was going to be deuced awkward having her around the house. Running into her in the halls, sharing coffee in the breakfast parlor—his stomach twisted sharply at the thought.

A soft canine whimper brought him back to the present. He found he had drawn the stallion to a halt and was staring west toward the Welsh hills. Rufus had found him and was now trying to attract his attention. He smiled without humor as he realized for the first time that he'd named his dog after the plaguey fox that had first drawn his attention to Jessica. What other tendrils had she left in his life?

He set the horse to a trot and signaled Rufus to follow him. The first thing was to get more people into the house. He had deliberately avoided a house party, to be more private with Caroline, but that was less important than his peace of mind. He must invite George, whose social skills had smoothed many a rocky path. Perhaps his friend would fall in love with Jessica and get her off Jason's hands.

Oddly, the thought failed to please.

And Aunt Honoria should come with her entourage. She wanted to meet the future Lady Radford, and it would be a courtesy to invite her. He was sure Lady Edgeware could keep even the most obstreperous redhead in check. The thought of the two women colliding brought a genuine chuckle; talk of an irresistible force meeting an immovable object!

Why couldn't the damned woman have had the
sense to marry a man who wouldn't get himself killed?

By the time he returned to the house his plans were
laid. While waiting for his new guests to arrive, he
would find some pressing business to take him away
for a few days. It was very rude to leave Caroline, but
she would have her aunt to bear her company. She
would hardly miss him.

He must remember to think of her as an aunt.

His unruly mind took over again. *She called you Jason
in the carriage.* But that was of no significance; she had
merely forgotten herself in amusement as he was sav-
aged by her beastly cat. It meant nothing. After all, she
had been married and traveled widely and must
hardly remember a foolish boy's ridiculous calf love. *Is
that what you want—for her to have forgotten?*

Even to himself, he couldn't answer that.

Just remember that she is Mrs. Sterling, his aunt.
Like Lady Edgeware. The voice in his head made a
rude and untranslatable noise. Well, not quite like
Aunt Honoria. And what was he doing carrying on a
conversation with himself? There was just barely time
to dress before dinner.

Satisfied that events would soon be under control
again, he strode up the steps of Wildehaven.

Caroline had tried to rest before dinner, but sleep
eluded her. After half an hour she rose and found her
lute and absently strummed as she considered how to
behave in the coming days. After all, she was setting a
course for the rest of her life, and should begin wisely.
Lord Radford—Jason—presumably wanted a gracious
chatelaine to run his household comfortably and un-
obtrusively. Actually, Mrs. Burke probably did that,

but Lady Radford should at least know what was going on. She must try to look older, and be careful not to be too absentminded.

As Jason himself . . . he still alarmed her, but perhaps he couldn't help having those eyebrows or that forceful voice. Certainly he had never been unkind. She suspected that missish behavior would give him a disgust of her, so she must appear more confident. Try not to quiver like a rabbit when he looks at you, she scolded. And do not always assume the worst of him—perhaps he has a shy, sensitive soul hidden deep inside. She smiled involuntarily at the thought; while everyone had unsuspected depths, it was impossible to imagine that Lord Radford's included shyness.

If she were to fulfill her promise to work at the marriage, she must keep Jason and Jessica from being at daggers drawn. She could feel the tension vibrating whenever they were together. They were both too independent, too used to going their own way; in short, they were too much alike to approve of each other. But she must make sure they stayed on terms; she would be unable to bear it if Jason forbade her Jessica's company. If he did, that alone would very nearly constitute grounds to leave him. Far better the situation never arise.

She had earlier considered breaking the engagement after Gina had married Gideon, but then Radford asked for an early wedding. She might be married before her sister. Besides, her sense of fairness rebelled at such shabby treatment of a man who had done nothing but honor her with a marriage proposal.

Jason's pride would be more injured by a jilt than his emotions, but that pride was so integral a part of him that the damage would be cruelly deep. He would naturally demand the return of the marriage settlement if she cried off; since her father had doubtless spent it, Radford could have him thrown in debtors' prison. At the moment she wouldn't mind seeing her father in jail, but the disgrace would devastate the whole family.

Caroline sighed. She had been through all this before, and had promised herself not to think of ways out of the match—it wasn't possible and would undermine her resolve to make the best of the situation.

At this point a timid knock interrupted her unwelcome thoughts. The knock was followed by a young maid no more than fifteen years old. "Mrs. Burke sent me up to help you dress, miss. Is it convenient now?"

Caroline smiled at the child. If she intended to work on being a gracious lady, someone even shyer than herself offered a good place to start. "Of course. You know that I am Caroline Hanscombe, but I fear I don't remember your name."

"Betsy, miss," she said, bobbing a curtsy.

"Well, Betsy, shall we see what we can find of my wardrobe? The baggage carriage was delayed with a broken axle, but there are several gowns in the one trunk that came on our carriage."

Betsy went to the trunk and opened it, making a small exclamation over the contents. "Oh, Miss Hanscombe, such lovely things!" she said, stroking the fine silks and muslins as she took them out.

"Have you never worked as a lady's maid before, Betsy?"

"No, miss. The only ladies that came here, Mrs. Burke said it weren't proper for a young lass like me to wait on them."

Caroline suppressed a smile at this artless information. It was fortunate she was neither in love with Jason nor of a jealous disposition. If she were, there would be plenty of material to send her temperature soaring. She had suspected at Madame Arlette's that Lord Radford had been a frequent visitor. And when the *modiste* had instantly decided Jessica was his intended, it was made clear his lordship had a preference for beautiful dashers. She wondered once more how he came to choose such an undramatic bride as herself.

"I think I shall wear the apricot gown tonight, Betsy. Could you have it pressed?"

"Of course, miss. And if you like, miss, there are some lovely miniature roses in the garden just this shade. Shall I bring some for your hair?"

"An excellent idea. I see you have a talent for this work. We shall have to find more opportunities for you." Caroline smiled warmly at the little maid, who blushed with pleasure.

"Oh, thank you, miss! I'll just take this off for pressing. Shall I send a footman with hot water for a bath?"

"Another excellent idea. I should like it above all things."

The girl quickly slipped out the door. Caroline was pleased to have made a friend in the house. The rather haughty dresser Lady Hanscombe had engaged for her had been called to a sick relative just before they left London; if Betsy were a capable abigail, she could keep the position.

An hour later she was ready for her first dinner at Wildehaven. The apricot dress was particularly becoming, and Betsy had a knack for hairdressing. Most of Caroline's glossy dark blond hair was pulled into a twist at the back of her head, with a few curls left at the sides and front. The exquisite little apricot rosebuds Betsy brought were carefully woven under the edge of the twist and complemented her dress perfectly. A single strand of pearls was her only jewelry.

Betsy was justly proud of her handiwork. "Oh, miss, you do look ever so nice. Everyone is ever so pleased the master is going to marry you."

Caroline asked curiously, "Are they pleased he is marrying *me*, or just that he is marrying?"

"Well, that he is marrying at all. But as soon as they know you, they will be glad it is you. You look just like a fairy-tale princess," the little maid said. *And nice as she can be, I'll tell the others.*

At this juncture a knock on the door was followed by Jessica. Betsy's mouth sagged in awe. If Caroline looked like a princess, clearly the maid had no image strong enough for Jessica's auburn magnificence. She dressed in her favorite emerald green, bringing her eyes to an improbable brilliance. The gown was simple enough for a country dinner, but its masterful cut and deep décolletage admirably displayed her superb figure. Her green jade necklace was not particularly valuable but it was beautifully crafted and perfectly matched her eyes.

"Jessica, sometimes I think you exist to cut me to size when I am in danger of getting a conceit of myself," Caroline said with a laugh. "Betsy, this is my aunt, Mrs. Sterling."

Jessica smiled at the maid. "If you are the one who did Caroline's hair, may I hope you will help me in the future?"

"Oh, *yes*, ma'am!" the child said fervently. She could hardly believe how her luck had changed. Earlier today she had been polishing silver with vague dreams of someday becoming a lady's maid; now these two beautiful women were complimenting her skills and asking for her services. As Caroline and Jessica left the room, she was sighing blissfully.

The butler, Burke, met them at the foot of the main stairs with the announcement, "It is a custom of the house to gather in the small salon before dining. If you will follow me?"

Since the small salon could have held two or three dozen people without crowding, Caroline could only be grateful the large one was not used. Burke gave them each a glass of ladylike ratafia and withdrew. While Jessica examined a collection of china miniatures, Caroline wandered to a window and admired the velvety lawns lying warm in the early-evening sun. She tried imagining children belonging to her and Jason playing there, but without success—it looked as if no one had ever taken that lawn in vain. The head gardener would probably have an apoplexy if someone walked on it. It was even harder to imagine the children. Lady Hanscombe had given her a blunt and unappetizing lecture on A Woman's Duty to Her Husband. While Caroline had had a general idea about the process, she had almost perished of embarrassment while her stepmother talked.

When the deep voice rumbled from behind her, "Please forgive my lateness," she started so violently that some of the ratafia spilled. She turned to her betrothed with a blush as deep as if he had been reading her thoughts. So much for being a gracious lady, she thought wryly. It was very hard to look him in the eye with A Woman's Duty still on her mind.

"I have been admiring the grounds, my lord," she stammered.

The dark sardonic face obviously recognized prevarication, but Jason answered readily enough, "The park is said to be one of the finest in England. If you are not too tired after dinner, perhaps we can take a stroll in the formal gardens."

"That would be very pleasant," she answered, making a mental note to be tired later. She didn't feel ready to be alone in the shrubbery with her fiancé yet. Perhaps next week . . .

Jason glanced at Jessica; an appearance that would have stunned most men called forth only a tightening of the lips from him. She nodded her head in cool acknowledgment of his presence and they adjourned to the dining room.

The meal that followed was beautifully prepared and served, but very quiet. With only three people, even the small family dining room seemed large, and no one was inclined to talk. Midway through the second remove, Jason announced, "I am afraid I must leave you for a few days. My bailiff has informed me of a problem at my Suffolk property that requires my personal attention. I will stay with you tomorrow but I must leave the next morning for perhaps a week."

He paused, unpleasantly aware that Caroline's face showed more relief than dismay. "You must make yourselves completely at home. The staff are at your command. Mrs. Sterling, perhaps you would like to take advantage of the stables. I recall you were a horsewoman."

The understatement drew a curious glance from Jessica, but she answered calmly, "It will be my pleasure. Doubtless your lordship has a good eye for a horse."

Jason looked her in the eye for the first time, wondering if she was baiting him. After all, it was universally acknowledged that no one had better judgment about horseflesh than Lord Radford. If she wasn't aware of his present reputation, surely her memory would remind her. The innocent look that met his eyes spoke of nothing but social blandness.

"I have also invited a few people to bear us company. You know George Fitzwilliam, Caroline. And my Aunt Honoria wishes to meet you."

This occasioned a small sound from Jessica. "She is known to you?" he said with a supercilious arch to his brows.

"Very much so," Jessica said dryly. "If you mean Lady Edgeware, I met her during my come-out. I believe she disapproved of me more than any other woman in London."

Now it was Jason's turn to look bland. "Doubtless she will be happy to see what a good douce matron you've become."

He was pleased to see Jessica grit her teeth at that. The girl he remembered would have preferred almost any fate to that of staidness, but the woman she had become refused to be drawn.

"I found that respectability is not inherently distasteful, Lord Radford. In fact, used in moderation it adds a certain savor to life. The contrast, you know."

Caroline watched the conversation uncertainly, feeling that some sparring was taking place beyond her understanding. "Will the guests arrive in your absence, my lord?"

"I think not. Even if they do, you will have no problems; the Burkes can take care of all the details. Please forgive me. I know it is very bad to leave you so soon."

The dinner party broke up shortly thereafter as Caroline pleaded fatigue and Jessica withdrew with her.

Jason lingered over his port, wondering what the devil he had done to himself.

The promised house tour began the next morning promptly after breakfast. Jessica considered crying off but decided she had best learn her way around the great house before she got lost. While Mrs. Burke accompanied the party, it was Jason who provided the commentary, forgetting himself in the history and anecdotes of Wildehaven.

"Originally there was one very large royal hunting preserve in this area. Henry II broke it into two manors and gave them to favorites of his. Wildehaven and our neighbor, Wargrave Park, are the results. Both properties have grown and shrunk with the family fortunes over the years, but the manor houses are only about a mile apart because of their common history." He paused, pleased by the genuine interest in Caroline's eyes.

"Surely it is unusual for two great houses to be so close?" she asked.

"It is," he confirmed. "Neither house lies in the center of the park. In the past, the two families were close allies in many ways, but that has changed in this generation. The late Earl of Wargrave was very unsocial, and conservative as well. He made it obvious he didn't approve of many of my innovations. He even considered this house too modern to be in good taste. Personally I believe he was envious; Wargrave Park is an old rabbit warren. It is empty now but for a skeleton staff."

"How old is this house?" said Jessica, curiosity bringing her out of her self-imposed silence.

"It was built just a hundred years ago on the site of an older house that burned. My great-great-grandfather was widely assumed to have set fire to the place because he was tired of its draftiness. Nicholas Hawksmoor designed this building, and it is considered his masterpiece."

Wildehaven was indeed magnificent. The lofty ceilings were superbly carved in the Italianate style, and each room boasted at least one lovely marble fireplace. The proportions were flawless and it had been furnished with love as well as taste.

Caroline found the portrait gallery of particular interest. As Jason gave a brief summary of his ancestors, she kept comparing him with the pictures. He caught one of her sidelong glances and smiled in genuine amusement. "You are quite right; the family look is very pronounced."

"I had thought your eyebrows unique, my lord, but I see I was wrong," she murmured. If there was one thing that distinguished the family, it was frowning brows. Rupert Kincaid, the sixth baron, appeared furious about the War of Roses. Rupert II, his great-grandson, seemed equally displeased with the cost of entertaining Queen Elizabeth on one of her progresses. Another baron, apparently at the time of the Civil War, left a scowl for his descendants. Either the family was permanently angry or Jessica was right: Jason wasn't really condemning her personally.

"Yes, I believe the brows go back to this reprobate here, Sir Ralph Kincaid. He was granted the original manor, apparently for his services in promoting Henry II's various affairs. Ralph the Panderer he is called by the family. He is said to have introduced Henry to the Fair Rosamund."

Caroline and Jessica viewed the small dark portrait with interest. "It certainly makes history come alive,"

Jessica said admiringly. "Was Ralph really such a scoundrel?"

"With that face, what else could he be?"

Caroline compared Ralph's visage to Jason's. "But he looks just like you."

"I rest my case."

That produced peals of laughter from both women. Caroline was beginning to appreciate the sense of humor lurking beneath the sardonic Radford eye. The aspects of him coming to light in his home made the future seem more plausible.

Her speculations on his character vanished at the sight of the large room behind the portrait gallery. "Good heavens!" she said. "I thought this sort of thing belonged only in Scottish castles." It was a genuine weapons room, with swords set in arcs on the walls, crossed pikes, morning stars and halberds, cases of firearms from the age of muzzle-loaders on, and suits of armor standing about.

Jason glanced casually around the assorted instruments of mayhem. "The previous Wildehaven *was* a castle. These weapons survived the fire, and my honored ancestor decided to house them in splendor. It is used now as a gun room, and sometimes for fencing practice."

The house contained one other surprise, but it was one of omission. They had reached the end of the house tour, and Caroline knew her comments were expected. "My lord . . . Jason, Wildehaven is the most splendid house I have ever seen. It has clearly been cherished and loved. But . . ." She hesitated, then went resolutely forward, "there is something missing."

"Oh?" Amazing how quickly the brows could turn threatening.

"There is no music room. Nowhere have I seen a pianoforte, nor any other instrument."

The brows remained drawn together, but now they appeared thoughtful rather than dangerous. "You are quite right. It is a sad lack but we have never been a very musical family. My mother's pianoforte was given to the vicar's daughters after she died. No one really missed it, so it was never replaced. I will be happy to buy you whatever instrument you wish. Just write down the name of the manufacturer and the kind you prefer. I am sorry my house has failed you."

"Oh, no, I meant no criticism," Caroline said hastily. She was a little startled by Jason's quick cooperation. She was not in the habit of asking for things because her wishes had seldom been considered of account.

Jason had not finished thinking. "It will take several weeks to get a suitable instrument here. If you like, I can arrange for you to practice at Wargrave Park. The late countess was very musical and had a fine pianoforte. We can go over now and I'll introduce you to Somers, the butler. He'll be happy to accommodate you."

Caroline turned a dazzling smile on Jason. "That will be wonderful! You are so kind."

Her intended looked startled. It was the first time she had directed any warmth or enthusiasm at him. He decided he liked it.

Chapter 8

Richard Davenport's first view of his ancestral home produced neither respect nor a sense of homecoming; his predominant emotion was amusement.

Josiah Chelmsford had stopped the chaise at the gates of Wargrave Park and invited the captain to step out and look at his inheritance. Richard was glad to comply. The long journey in cramped quarters had been hard on his injured leg, and it felt good to stretch out. They had stopped the night before near Witney rather than do the trip in one day, and as they neared their destination he felt some qualms about what he would find. He had not expected the eccentric building clearly visible in the early afternoon light.

As one side of his mouth quirked up humorously, he said, "It appears to have been designed by a committee over a period of five hundred years."

"You are almost exactly right," Chelmsford replied, pleased by his client's perception. "The oldest part of the house is thirteenth-century. There had never been a Davenport willing to tear the place down, so your ancestors just kept adding on."

The result was certainly unique. The central part of the sprawling building was Elizabethan, with handsome mullioned windows and twisted brick chimneys.

What appeared to be a medieval great hall stretched back to the left, while the right wing was of fairly recent construction. Someone had been unable to resist the lure of towers; from this distance it was impossible to tell if they were genuinely old or more recently applied follies. What appeared to be a small Greek temple lurked in the woods to the right.

Wargrave Park's saving grace was that it was entirely built of local materials. The gray-golden warmth of Cotswold stone created unity out of architectural disparity. The house appeared to have grown out of the underlying hillside; while it did not inspire awe, it had an undeniable charm.

Returning to the chaise, they soon drew up before the main doors. As Richard studied the asymmetrical facade, he wondered again why his father had turned away from his past so completely. Although duels were illegal under English law, the consequences were usually forgotten quickly—a few months abroad might have sufficed. What had driven Julius to leave forever when he was younger than Richard was now, no more than twenty-one or twenty-two? He had asked Josiah that yesterday, and received a shrug for an answer.

"I really don't know the whole story. There was a fearful scandal. Most of the details were hushed up, and the rumors that came my way are too lurid to recount. Your father killed his man in a fair fight, from what I understand, but Barford had influential relatives who got a murder charge against him. Julius came to see me the night of the duel, saying your mother was in the carriage and they were leaving England forever. He gave me authority to liquidate what assets he had and directed me to send the money to a banker in Paris."

The lawyer paused, then continued, "Your grandfather was an overbearing man and Julius resented his attempted dominance. Perhaps he could only be free away from England. But I find it interesting that he raised you to feel you were English even though you have spent so much of your life abroad."

Richard nodded. "It was deliberate on their part. We never lived in one place long enough for me to identify with the country completely, and when I was old enough for serious education, we went to Belfast so I could go to a British school. Then I was packed off to Oxford. But neither of my parents would set foot in England, even when it would have been more convenient in travel terms. I guess I'll never know the whole story of why they left."

"From what you say, they were very happy in the life they chose. Few people are so lucky."

Looking at Wargrave Park, Richard tried to imagine his father a boy, but without success. Like most children, he had seen his parents as an immutable law of nature, ever wise and adult. With maturity he realized their little family was unusual both for its contentment and for its rootlessness. They had belonged to each other, and to no one else. What would it feel like to be the owner of this place, with hundreds of people dependent on him? In the Army the objective was simple: defeat the enemy when necessary and stay alive and as comfortable as possible the rest of the time. Here the issues would be less clear-cut, the demands much more complex.

The lawyer said, "Come in now and meet the staff."

The next half-hour was spent meeting Somers, the impassively dignified butler, and Hain, the old earl's agent. Chelmsford introduced him as Captain Richard Dalton, saying that he would be taking an inventory of the property and was to be treated with every courtesy and given whatever information he required. Both of the old men stared at him solemnly and allowed they were pleased to make his acquaintance. After a few minutes of general conversation, Josiah said, "I have some business matters to take up with Somers and Hain, but you can start exploring on your own. I'll catch up with you when I've finished."

Richard nodded agreeably and left. After the door closed behind him the lawyer gazed sternly at Somers and Hain. Both had spent their lives with the Davenport estates and were exactly the kind of family retainers Richard had wondered about. "If you have any speculations about Captain Dalton, it would be well to keep them to yourselves. Do I make myself clear?"

Somers raised one eyebrow with the supercilious look of a man who would never gossip with the lower staff. Less discreet, Joseph Hain said, "We won't say anything. But unless my eyes are deceiving me, there may be hope for Wargrave yet."

"There may be—as long as he isn't scared away. In the meantime, I am sure you will do your best to make Captain *Dalton* comfortable."

His listeners nodded; a conspiracy of silence was under way.

Richard enjoyed his explorations; the house followed no particular plan but was full of interesting nooks and crannies. There was indeed a medieval great hall, complete with an ox-roaster fireplace and a minstrel gallery added at a later time. It looked like a fine place for dancing and entertainment, if less conventional than a modern ballroom. The furniture in most of the house was shrouded in holland covers but the Elizabethan

section boasted magnificently carved wooden wain-
scoting and a hanging staircase. The small staff had
done a reasonable job of keeping order, though there
was a general air of musty disuse.

In the modern wing he began hearing an ethereal
wisp of music. At first it seemed imaginary, but it
strengthened and led him to a thick oak door in the rear
corner of the building. Opening the door, he paused in
pure wonder.

Richard's first thought was that she was an angel.
However, no wings were in evidence, and he didn't
suppose angels needed sheet music. The girl was
seated on a bench before a window, backlit by a flood
of sunshine that burnished her hair to gold. A few
silken curls hung around the exquisitely delicate face
as her head bent over a small Celtic harp.

The tune was familiar to him, but he had never heard
it done with such feeling or virtuosity. Seeing her rapt
in a world of radiant sound, he thought of a pagan
priestess playing to her gods on a moonlit mountain.
The bell-like notes throbbed and pulsed, the echoes res-
onating from the ancient roots of Britain.

He had forgotten the sound of joy. When had he last
seen or felt such a passionate intensity of being? These
last months had held little but pain and stoic determination. Hearing that triumphant musical celebration,
he could almost feel the blood begin to sing in his
veins. The world took on added dimension and color—
weightless motes of dust suspended in the sun, polished wood glowing with inner light, and the vision
before him impressed irrevocably on his brain. He
wanted to laugh out loud as he remembered what it
was to *live*.

The music ended in a shower of golden notes, leaving a richly silent peace. As he was irresistibly drawn across the room toward the girl, she looked up at him with a complete lack of self-consciousness.

"It was you, wasn't it?" she said in a voice as pure and musical as that of the harp.

"I'm sorry, what was me? Or would it be 'what was I?'"

She gave an enchanting chuckle. "That didn't make sense, did it? I thought I was imagining the sound of a pipe harmonizing with the harp. It blended and counter-pointed with the main theme so perfectly, I didn't believe it was real. Were you whistling?"

He returned her smile. "I'm afraid I probably was. Whistling is my besetting sin—I often don't know I am doing it. My friends have threatened to throw shoes at me as if I were a back-alley cat."

"But you whistle so very well," she said seriously. "Surely you must have known this piece of music."

He nodded. "Yes, it is by Turlough O'Carolan."

"Oh, you've heard of him! I never have. Who was he?"

"A superb composer who lived in Ireland about a hundred years ago. His work was in the folk tradition but has Italian elements as well. It is unfortunate he is not better known outside his own country. But how did you learn to play a Celtic harp so well in England?"

She looked pleased at the praise. "The box that contained the scores also had notes on the kinds of ornamentation an Irish harper would improvise. I've been working on this all day. Was it correct?"

"I have never heard it played better." He gazed intently at her for a moment, then looked around. "What is this place?"

"I think of it as heaven," she confided, "but perhaps

it would be more correct to call it the ultimate music room."

Richard suppressed an inward laugh as he turned to investigate. Where else would an angel belong but in heaven?

The wall opposite the broad windows held a specially built cabinet with an incredible array of stringed and wind instruments. To his left were shelves of vertical boxes shaped like large books. He pulled one out at random and read the label on the spine: *Johann Christian Bach, Music for Strings and Chamber Orchestra*. A list of individual pieces followed, and inside were the sheets of music described. As he looked further, he saw that it was a completely cataloged music library, classified by title, instrument, composer, and date.

The young woman had followed him. "Is it not incredible?" she asked eagerly. "I have never seen such a wealth of music. I'm told the last countess was a fine musician—she collected all these instruments and compositions. It must have been her life's work. The instruments are all of superb quality, and the composers are wonderful. Some are men I never heard of, but all I have tried are more than worthy."

Richard looked around the room. It had the high molded ceiling and proportions of a fine library, and there was ample space for several standing instruments. A raised platform at the far end seemed designed for chamber concerts. "I see two dulcimers, a harpsichord, virginals, a clavichord, and a pianoforte. The only thing missing is a pipe organ."

The girl laughed. "It is a sad lack, but I'm told the countess had a very fine organ built in the parish church. Perhaps the earl objected to having plaster shaken loose from the ceilings."

"How very unhandsome of him."

"Perhaps the poor man had no ear for the finer things of life," she said charitably.

Richard was gazing at the pianoforte with a longing expression on his face. "Excuse me, but I haven't been near a pianoforte in over a year." He limped over and seated himself on the long bench, running some experimental scales. "It has a lovely tone. A pity I am so out of practice."

He started to play a Mozart sonata, forgetting he was not alone. For someone who hadn't played for many months, it was a remarkably fine performance. A few notes might go astray, but great feeling and skill were apparent. Caroline listened in appreciation for a few minutes, then walked to the instrument and seated herself next to him on the bench. With her right hand she started improvising a descant that blended with the main sonata. Richard accepted her presence without missing a note, and they continued through the piece in perfect harmony.

After completing the concerto, he turned and looked down at her. "Thank you. I don't know when I have enjoyed anything more."

There was a brief silence; then she said rather breathlessly, "Do you know any of the other Mozart sonatas?" He turned wordlessly and began to play again.

Caroline joined in readily but she felt curiously off-balance. When he looked at her with those warm, golden-flecked hazel eyes she abruptly realized they were nearly touching. She could feel a calm strength radiating from his body; it was disquieting, but not in the way Jason was. She felt no anger in him, but rather a deep and abiding kindness. She shivered slightly, then let herself be absorbed by the music.

He took liberties with the tempo but she seemed able to read his mind and followed his playing effortlessly. They passed the next half-hour in complete harmony, taking turns choosing the music and letting the other recognize and join in.

That was how Josiah Chelmsford found them. He listened at the door for a few minutes, enjoying the rare quality of the performance. He had had no idea Richard was so talented, but it shouldn't have surprised him—both sides of the boy's family had been musically inclined. The lawyer was loath to end the performance but finally intervened after a Mozart sonata.

"That was a treat for these old ears. Will you introduce me to your charming companion, Captain Dalton?"

The two young people looked at each other in surprise, then both started laughing. "I'm sorry, sir, I have no idea. We haven't gotten to names yet. If you will permit me to introduce myself, I am Richard Dalton, here at Mr. Chelmsford's behest to take inventory of the property. Do you live here? I was told only a small staff was present." Dressed as she was, the girl couldn't possibly be a servant.

She looked up at him, shyer with another person present. "My name is Caroline Hanscombe. I am staying nearby and . . . it was arranged that I could practice here."

Chelmsford looked at her keenly. "Caroline Hanscombe—then you would be Lord Radford's fiancée. I saw the notice in the newspaper. Delighted to make your acquaintance. Radford is held in very high esteem.

Richard watched closely as she cast her eyes downward. She was visibly withdrawing. "Yes, he has been everything that is kind. I am most fortunate."

The lawyer observed with interest as Richard resumed his usual calm, controlled expression. The girl was a taking little thing. Pity she was engaged; he had never seen the boy look so carefree. Still, it was best he understood the situation; Radford wasn't the man to let another poach on his preserves.

Having tracked Richard to the music room, Josiah decided to use the fine summer day to show him some of the property. As they walked to the stables, the general air of shabby neglect that was faintly obvious in the house became much more pronounced. It was clear that the estate had suffered from mismanagement or a shortage of funds or both. The captain noted it without comment, but Chelmsford found himself saying apologetically, "I've done all I could to bring it about this last year, but the income isn't sufficient to do all that is required in such a short time."

By this time they had reached the main stable block. While many of the stalls were empty, eight or ten good horses remained. No grooms were in evidence so Richard took a saddle from the tack room.

"This should be interesting," he said. "I haven't been on a horse in a year."

The lawyer's eyes shot to the injured leg, ashamed for having forgotten. Much as Richard might be determined to ignore his handicap, he would still run into problems controlling a horse. "Do you think you can manage?" Chelmsford said, reluctant to demur openly.

"There's only one way to find out."

Chelmsford was alarmed to find the captain heading for the largest and liveliest of the horses, a beast with a

wicked gleam in its eye and the unpromising name
"Rakehell" on a plaque above its door.

"If it has been so long, perhaps a quieter animal?"
the lawyer said with a hint of desperation.

"We wouldn't want to make it too easy, now, would
we?"

Chelmsford was stilled by the mischievous spark in
the captain's eye. Resigning himself to the inevitable,
he saddled a peaceful-looking mare called Daisy. If the
French hadn't killed the boy in seven years, a horse
probably wouldn't do it.

After mounting, the lawyer turned to see Richard
nose to nose in earnest conversation with Rakehell.

"What are you doing?" he asked.

"Asking him to take pity on a broken-down soldier."

"In Spanish?"

"Horses seem to like it." With this unanswerable
statement, the captain swung up to the saddle. Rakehell fidgeted a bit but refrained from the wild acrobat-
ics his appearance and name had suggested. As the
lawyer stared, Richard said cheerfully, "Now, what was
it you wanted to show me?"

Shaking his head, Josiah reminded himself once
again not to underestimate Richard Davenport.

*   *   *

Three hours later they drew up on a hill overlooking
the pretty village of Wargrave. It was about a mile
away from the house, and its gray stone cottages were
scattered casually along the banks of a small river.

Richard had been surprised at how large the estate
was; seeing was quite different from hearing about it in
London. There were a dozen tenant properties as well
as the home farm, with sheep and cattle, plus a variety

of crops. The estate itself was a complete community with dairy, laundries, succession houses, forge, brewhouse, dovecote, fishpond, and everything else needed for self-sufficiency. Now many buildings were closed or little-used. In its heyday Wargrave Park had bustled like a beehive; now it more nearly resembled a ghost town.

Looking down at the village, Richard asked, "Is everyone down there a Wargrave tenant?"

"Yes, in the sense that the estate owns the cottages. Most of the villagers earn their bread with different skills. There's a blacksmith, of course, and a shoemaker, a baker, a shop with a smattering of useful items. Much like any other village."

"How do the people feel about the Davenports?"

Chelmsford considered his reply for a moment before answering. "They don't confide in me, but my impression is that they are wary and watchful. Fifty years ago most of the villagers farmed the common land. Then the old earl had a private Enclosure Act passed and fenced off much of the estate. In most cases the villagers' shares of the common rights were too small to support themselves. Many had to sell their land to the earl and leave."

"Where did they go?"

The lawyer shrugged. "Some to the mills in Lancashire, some to the cities, some to the colonies. I doubt if there is a person in the village who hasn't a cousin in Canada or the United States. One of Julius' quarrels with his father was over the enclosures. He thought it disgraceful that people were forced off land their families had farmed for centuries. He did what he could. I know of half a dozen cases where he gave families enough money to emigrate, and I suspect there were more."

Richard gazed down at the village, imagining the rage and helplessness of those forced out of their ancient homes. "It certainly sounds like my father. From what I read in the newspapers, struggles over Enclosure Acts are still going on."

The lawyer said shrewdly, "If you are interested in social reform, you will have far more power as an earl than as a former Army officer." As he saw Richard's face close, he decided a change of subject was in order and continued smoothly, "I think most of the villagers are hoping that Reginald Davenport will quickly sell out to Lord Radford. There have been some dislocations at Wildehaven, but he has done a good job of minimizing the human damage. He is considered an enlightened landlord. And of course he's not a foreigner."

"What constitutes a 'foreigner'?"

"Anyone born more than fifteen miles away," was the prompt answer,

The captain laughed. "In that case, I would hardly qualify as from this planet."

"Perhaps. But Julius is still remembered fondly here. There would be no lack of cooperation."

"If we may turn this discussion to the present, what time will dinner be served? Riding has given me a country appetite."

"Whenever we're ready."

The captain turned his horse and they headed back to the stables. Richard's effortless control dismissed any concern Chelmsford had felt about his riding ability. As long as the boy could talk to the horse first, he'd be all right.

Chapter 9

The next morning, Caroline gave a delicate catlike yawn behind her palm before sipping the cup of coffee. Her aunt grinned at her with the ruthless cheer of the natural early riser. "I thought I heard you moving about late last night. Were you composing something?"

Her niece swallowed her coffee and said, "Yes, I got involved in a new piece for the harp. The instrument at Wargrave Park inspired me. Before I realized, it was almost two o'clock."

"You were born to be a night owl, Caro. Here you sit, barely alive for your breakfast at nine o'clock. *I* have already been for a ride, taken a bath, and written a letter. Why, the day is half over!" Jessica said teasingly.

Caroline eyed her with disfavor. "It occurs to me that if we shared a house, the only thing that would prevent me from committing morning violence is that my body would not obey commands to move quickly."

Jessica gave her rich throaty chuckle. "If you had Wellesley pouncing on your feet first light you would wake up early too. I actually did consider a little violence on him this morning, but he was too fast for me."

Caroline moved to the sideboard, shuddered at the braised kidneys, then decided she could face an egg with her toast. "Perhaps you could leave him free to prowl at night. I should think everyone in the household knows of him by now, so he should come to no harm."

"I might try that. I love morning rides, but after a late night they needn't be as early as that worthless cat demands. Are you going over to Wargrave Park again today?"

Caroline was beginning to look like she would survive the day. At her aunt's words, she brightened and said enthusiastically, "Oh, yes! It is the most wonderful place. In the three days since Lord Radford left, I've hardly touched the surface of the music library, and the instruments are just wonderful."

She stopped, then said guiltily, "Unless you would rather do something together today. I'm ashamed to admit it, but until this moment I hadn't given a thought to how you are spending your time. I hope you haven't been too bored."

"Not in the least," Jessica replied cheerfully. "It has been wonderfully relaxing. I've caught up on my correspondence and finished a dress I had cut in London. And of course I've done a lot of riding. Lord Radford's horses are superb. Since he gave me the freedom of the stables, I've been exploring every inch of the estate." She smiled impishly. "I bought a shirt and breeches from one of the stable lads and have been riding astride again—at least in the early morning."

Caroline shook her head with amused resignation. "Incorrigible as always. Which of us is the chaperon?"

"I am working on becoming an eccentric old lady. I assume a man invented the sidesaddle as a way of handicapping female riders, and riding astride is my way of protesting."

"I have never heard that a sidesaddle slowed you down. Still, you might as well enjoy your freedom here. I think that is why I prefer the country. London was too full of rules and critics." As an afterthought, Caroline added, "I shouldn't think you would have to work too hard on becoming eccentric. It is the 'old' part that people won't believe."

"All things come to her who waits," her aunt said serenely. "Especially old age. I may stop by Wargrave myself to see the magical music room. Perhaps we can play some duets."

"That would be nice. I'll tell the butler, Somers, that you may be along." She busied herself pouring a new cup of coffee, then said offhandedly, "Yesterday the lawyer who is handling the estate came for a visit. He had someone with him who will be staying for a while. An inventory-taker, I believe."

Her mind strayed for a moment. Captain Dalton had such a wonderful voice, rich and deep as hot chocolate on a cold night. Caroline was always more attracted by voices than faces; perhaps that was why she didn't find Jason as devastatingly attractive as other women did. Not that his voice was really unpleasant, but it had an abruptness that was most unrestful. . . . She was recalled from her reverie by Jessica's voice.

"Oh? Perhaps the estate will be settled soon. Having an earl in residence should improve the neighborhood social life. I hope the heir and his family are pleasant people. You will likely see a good deal of them."

"I suppose." Caroline's response was lukewarm. Then she said hopefully, "Perhaps the new earl will be single and will fall passionately in love with you. We can be neighbors."

"Talk about rushing your fences! Earls never stay single for long unless they have no desire to marry. And I am sure they are entirely too used to having their own way to suit me. It would never do," her aunt said.

"Ah well, if you don't wish to be a countess . . ." Caroline said mournfully.

"If you can find me a doddering earl guaranteed to expire within two hours of the ceremony, I promise you I will consider it. In the meantime, shall we have dinner at seven o'clock?"

"That will be fine. I shall ask the Wargrave butler to remind me to leave at six."

"And tell him to remind you again at a quarter past the hour," Jessica prompted. "I'm sure that one reminder will be insufficient."

"Very true," Caroline said. "I should hate to be responsible for driving Lord Radford's chef away by my lateness and failure to appreciate his art. It would be a bad omen for my future here."

"Definitely. Keeping a cook happy is essential to a household's comfort," her aunt said as she rose from the table. "Enjoy your day. Perhaps I will see you later at Wargrave."

Caroline was thoroughly awake and filled with unanalyzed anticipation as she walked to Wargrave Park. The path passed through light woodlands with occasional clearings and it was popular with all kinds of wild birds and small animals. She had seen moles, rabbits, deer, shy red squirrels, and even a badger on a rare daytime mission. She was mentally working out a composition to describe the woodland walk: flutes for the birds, violins for the breeze rustling the leaves and long grasses.

The sound of real birdcalls ahead distracted her from her composing. Something about it sounded unusual, so she proceeded slowly. The path crooked, then passed into a clearing. She stopped on the edge, arrested by amazement. Captain Dalton was seated on a fallen tree trunk with a number of birds around him, some even eating from his hand. He was whistling birdcalls that sounded absolutely authentic. Apparently the birds agreed, because more were coming as she watched. She recognized greenfinches, robins, linnets, and a tiny blue tit hanging acrobatically below his hand. He held some kind of seeds, with more scattered on the ground. It was an amazing sight, and she held her breath for fear of disturbing it.

She saw the captain's eyes move in her direction, but he continued his silvery trills and chirps. A fight broke out between an aggressive greenfinch and a newly arrived great tit, and suddenly the whole flock whirled away.

She stepped forward. "I hope I wasn't responsible for ending that. I thought only Saint Francis could call the birds from the trees."

Richard smiled companionably. "I hope you won't tell anyone. It would quite ruin my reputation to be linked with a saint."

Unbidden, she sat on the log before he could rise, noticing how totally relaxed he was, and how his hazel eyes seemed always on the verge of laughter. "What were you saying to the birds?"

"I'm really not sure," he admitted, "but doubtless it means something like 'Dinner is served.' Cupboard love, I fear."

"*I* think it was the most extraordinary thing I have ever seen. How did you learn to do it?"

"When I was a boy I always enjoyed watching birds. And since I also liked whistling, one thing led to another. We moved about when I was young, so I had a chance to learn different species. Did you know that birds have different accents in different parts of Europe? Not as pronounced as human differences, but definitely there."

"How remarkable! Do you suppose there was an avian Tower of Babel, cursing them to different languages?" Caroline suggested.

"Perhaps," he added. "But I'm afraid I can't ask them. All I can do is mimic." His eyes grew distant as he said thoughtfully, "I didn't know I could still do that. I hadn't tried since I went into the Army eight years ago."

Caroline was silent as she thought through the implications of that.

"Besides," he added, "in Spain calling birds might have ended with them in a pot when the supply trains were too far behind. It is very squeamish of me but I don't think I could eat a songbird I had just conversed with. Or any songbird, really."

She shuddered. "A dreadful thought, Captain Dalton! Still, if one were hungry enough . . ."

"I have never been that hungry," he said firmly. "And I would prefer you not to call me Captain Dalton. I know that military titles tend to follow one around forever, but I am in the Army no longer and have not the least desire to give anyone orders. Actually"—he turned his green-golden eyes on her—"I would prefer you call me Richard."

She forgot she had met him only the day before; he

seemed as familiar as the face in her own mirror. "Only if you will call me Caroline," she said shyly.

The moment stretched between them, too deep to last very long. Richard stood and offered his hand to help her up and took her music case from her. "Shall I escort you to Wargrave? Mr. Chelmsford is probably looking for me. He wants to explain the accounts this morning."

"Will you be able to spend any time in the music room?" she asked.

"I will find the time this afternoon," he promised.

They walked to the house in companionable silence, Caroline enjoying the way he matched his strides to hers. With Jason's long legs, she sometimes felt like a small child being taken for a walk by a parent. Richard's gentle courtesy was pleasing. Not that she couldn't rise from a log or carry her music case herself . . . but she rather enjoyed the attentions.

They separated in the main hall, Richard to find the lawyer and Caroline to go to the music room. It took her uncharacteristically long to decide what she wanted to do. Play the pianoforte? The harp? Perhaps search out some new composers in the sheet music?

In the end she decided to work on the harp composition that had kept her up late the night before. Soon she was lost in trying to perfect a new fingering pattern she could hear in her head but not quite create out loud. She was startled when the butler, Somers, gave a discreet cough to gain her attention.

"Excuse me, miss, a light luncheon is being served in the family dining room. The gentlemen wondered if you might wish to join them."

"Oh! I had not realized how much time had passed.

Yes, that would be very agreeable. I shall be along directly."

As the butler left, she looked around for her reticule, but realized she hadn't brought it. Well, her hair would just have to go uncombed. At least her mint-green dress was presentable.

In the eyes of the gentlemen, she was more than presentable. The meal was a merry one, with Caroline being drawn out of her shyness by Richard's interested questions. Soon she was describing the horrors of a London Season, finding amusement in events that seemed an unrelieved ordeal at the time. Exercising a gift for mimicry she hadn't known she possessed, she parodied some of the more foolish society types.

Her favorite story was of the harridan who thoroughly investigated all young ladies at their first Almack's assembly. "I swear, I thought she would ask me to open my mouth so she could check my teeth. She asked about my parents and grandparents and would go 'Harrumph!' at every answer. She is known to be looking for a wife for her depressing son. While no girl could possibly be good enough, I did have one feature that her son lacked."

"What is that?" Richard asked.

"A chin!"

When the laughter from that subsided, the captain said, "I am reminded of some of the young aristocrats who came into the Army expecting romance, adventure, and all the comforts of home. Perhaps some of the Guards regiments could supply that, but the Ninety-fifth Rifles are a rowdy lot, and proved a sad shock for them. When these fine young sprigs of the nobility found they were really expected to sleep in tents and rise at dawn . . . !" He shook his head sadly. "But that was not the worst."

"What was the worst?" inquired Chelmsford.

"When they discovered that Army life would *ruin their boots*!" They all started laughing again. Young dandies had been known to suffer nervous collapse if they got even a scratch on their gleaming Hessians; the effects of campaigning in the Peninsula must have been dire.

After the meal, it seemed entirely natural that Richard accompany Caroline back to the music room. As he pointed out, account books must needs be followed by an antidote lest they prove fatal.

"I have been given as much information as Mr. Chelmsford feels I need," he said. "Or perhaps he assumes, correctly, that I can absorb no more."

"What exactly will you be doing here?" Caroline asked.

"It is none too arduous," was the reply. "The estate is in trust until the end of the year. There were several small bequests to servants, with the remaining property to go to the heir. Because the late earl was rather secretive, it is not sure just what the heir will receive. Mr. Chelmsford is a careful man and wishes to determine how things stand. I will be checking the reality against some of the old accounts of what should be in the house and on the estate."

"Who is the heir?" Caroline asked. "My aunt was wondering this morning."

Richard turned to one of the cupboards holding the more obscure stringed instruments. With his face averted, he said, "That isn't really clear yet. The heir presumptive is Reginald Davenport, the nephew of the late earl. However, Mr. Chelmsford thinks there may be a nearer heir. In the meantime"—he looked up at her with a smile—"I am having a fine holiday in the Cotswolds."

"Will you be staying here long?" Caroline said hesitantly.

"I really don't know. I haven't thought much about the future."

As he rummaged in the cupboard, she looked at his broad shoulders regretfully. It didn't sound as if he were likely to stay. Richard made a pleased exclamation and pulled out a flat instrument with six strings and a sound box shaped like an hourglass.

"What is that?" she asked.

"A *guitarra*. It is usually called a guitar in English. I learned to play one in Spain." He lovingly touched the inlaid pattern around the sound hole, then strummed the strings. He winced slightly at the discordant noise and rapidly started tuning it.

"It seems to be related to the lute," she remarked.

"Yes, but less delicate and much simpler to play. The sound is strong, coarse, perhaps, but full of vitality. The Spaniards could play them to make the hair curl off your head. My own guitar got lost with the rest of my baggage after Waterloo." He struck a dramatic chord. "I understand the lute is harder to keep tuned."

"That is certainly true," Caroline said with heartfelt agreement. "My music teacher says that if a lutenist lived to be eighty years old, he would have spent sixty of those years tuning his instrument. I know mine requires considerable attention."

"You play the lute?"

"Yes, it is my favorite instrument after the pianoforte. It is so very private. I can play mine late at night without disturbing anyone. But I am more interested in your *guitarra*. Will you play some characteristic Spanish music for me?"

Richard was happy to oblige. He was very skilled, and the Spanish music he chose was new to Caroline. She was bewitched by the performance, feeling the intense gaiety and the underlying sadness. Some time had passed before he called a halt.

"If I don't stop soon, I will have blisters on my fingertips. All my string-holding calluses have vanished, and it will take time to recreate them."

"I'm sorry," she said. "I could have listened all day and never thought of your poor fingers. May I try the guitar? My lute calluses should protect me."

With her natural talent and Richard's instruction, she was soon playing very creditably. They were laughing together over a chord gone astray when the sound of light footsteps interrupted.

Caroline recognized the step and looked up; she had forgotten Jessica said she might come by. Her aunt swept into the room like a queen, glowing in a topaz-colored dress and a delicious Florentine bonnet with matching ribbons. Caroline felt a slight twist in her midriff. She found she didn't want to see Richard with the stunned expression men got when they first saw Jessica.

She slanted a sideways look at him, but his expression wasn't stunned. Rather, it showed pleased surprise as he stood up and quickly crossed across the room.

"Jessica Sterling! Is it really you?"

Jessica laughed in delight as she reached out both hands. "Richard Dalton! This is beyond anything great. What brings you to Gloucestershire?"

Her aunt was almost as tall as Richard, and they

were looking into each other's eyes as they clasped hands. Caroline could feel the affection between them; she gave a slight shiver as the room felt inexplicably colder.

Richard said, "I am working at Wargrave Park temporarily, taking inventory. Do you live in this neighborhood?"

She shook her head, "No, I am visiting at Wildehaven with my niece, whom you have so obviously met. You see me dwindled to a chaperon!"

He laughed. "I am sure you can hold court there as well as anywhere else." He released her hands and turned to include Caroline in the conversation. "You will have deduced we are old campaigning friends from the Peninsula. Mrs. Sterling was celebrated as the finest hostess and the best rider in Spain."

Caroline firmly suppressed her faint sense of loss and moved forward with her sweet smile. "How lovely to find an old friend unexpectedly. Surely it is four or five years since you have met. It was 1812 when you left Spain, wasn't it, Jess?"

A shadow passed over her aunt's face, dimming some of its brightness. "Yes, Linda and I left very soon after Salamanca."

Richard hesitated, then said gently, "I know this is four years too late, but you have my deepest sympathy for your loss. Major Sterling was as fine a gentleman as he was an officer. I knew no one who did not grieve for him. He died as bravely as he lived."

Jessica swallowed and said in a low voice, "Thank you. It is never too late to hear such kind words. I have always been glad that I went, against everyone's wishes, to follow the drum. Without those years on the

Peninsula, I would have had no real marriage and no memories."

"Was everyone against it, Jess? Even John?" Caroline asked.

Jessica laughed, the shadow gone. "*Especially* John! He would have wrapped me in cotton wool if he could. It is amazing that anyone could think such a strapping creature as I could be fragile, but it was quite charming. At least he knew better than to try to make me behave with ladylike languor."

At this point Somers entered carrying a tray. "I thought perhaps you would wish some refreshments." Since the afternoon was well advanced, his offering was gratefully received. Over tea and cakes Jessica and Richard exchanged histories and queries about mutual friends.

Caroline sipped her tea and watched thoughtfully. She had never truly envied Jessica's dramatic beauty, but as she observed her aunt's lovely face ripple with vivid expression, she found herself wishing she was as interesting a person. Nothing noteworthy had ever happened to her. When Jess was twenty-one she was married, a mother, and had already traveled out of England.

Happened to her . . . Perhaps her problem was that she waited for events to come to her. Jess had always seized life with both hands. If she had lived richly, she had also paid the price; she had been the target of criticism and unkind snubs; narrow-minded women had been lavish with "I told you so" and "Serves her right" after she had returned to England a widow of small fortune. Though she had lived quietly these last four years, it had been by choice. Her sparkle and enthusi-

asm were undimmed, and she could talk to a man like
Captain Dalton about things that interested him.

Caroline had always admired her aunt as a wonderful, inimitable being, so different as to be almost from
another species. She knew she could never be wonderful in the ways Jessica was, but she might try adapting
some of that gusto and determination to her own life.
If she started working now, perhaps in ten years she
could be wonderful in her own way.

Her musings were interrupted when Jessica drew
her into the conversation. "Has Richard demonstrated
his guitar playing for you? Sometimes at informal par-
ities he would play and I would dance. The Spanish
dances are wonderful—much more primitive and dramatic than ours."

Caroline nodded. "Yes, he played some of the music
earlier. I would love to see how one dances to it.
Would you be able to give a demonstration?"

Her aunt cocked her head and considered. "I remember them well enough, but one really needs the
right costume. Our fashionable Empire gowns are very
comfortable but haven't enough *whoosh*! Still, it would
be great fun to dance them again."

She stood, kicking off her shoes and loosening her
hair, the auburn coils falling past her shoulders. With a
theatrical gesture she raised her arms above her head,
arched her back, and tilted her chin.

While Caroline watched in fascination, Richard was
reaching for the *guitarra*. With his first crashing chord,
Jessica came to whirling life. She looked a different
person, not really English and certainly not a lady. The
pantherlike power and grace of her movements
brought the passionate music to dazzling life as her
veils of hair swirled about, revealing and concealing. It

was a breathtaking performance; if Caroline felt a pang at how well her aunt worked with her accompanist, she suppressed it.

Walking back to Wildehaven later, Jessica was still exhilarated. She seldom referred to her time in Spain, but today she was in a mood to talk. "I'm sorry to chatter on like this, Caro." She broke off apologetically. "But it was so good to see an old friend again. For the last four years I have locked that whole part of my life away. Now I am ready to remember again."

She stooped to pick a white field rose, inhaling the delicate scent before she walked on. "I am so glad it was Richard Dalton. He is the loveliest man. In many ways he is like my John was—kind, steady, and wonderfully comfortable. And yet he had the most impressive military reputation."

Having seen the kindness, Caroline was curious about Richard's martial accomplishments. "What did they say of him?"

"Well, he had been mentioned in dispatches for outstanding valor twice when I knew him, and that was four years ago. He must have been no more than four-or five-and-twenty at the time. But I particularly remember the stories I heard from one of the other officers in his regiment."

Her eyes distant, she went on, "He had a reputation for imperturbability, always being in complete command of himself and his men. But his colonel told me of two exceptions to that."

"Yes?" her niece prompted when her aunt showed signs of disappearing into her memories.

"The first time, he was just a boy, only a few months in the field. He came across two of his men about to ravish a French girl. She was a camp follower, left behind in childbed when the troops she was traveling with had to retreat suddenly. They say young Dalton gave them a tongue-lashing that nearly removed their leathery hides. Told them they were a disgrace to humanity, asked them how they would feel if it was their sister or sweetheart or daughter in like case. I was told that when he finished, they were wishing he had flogged them instead."

"What was the other occasion?" Caroline asked curiously.

"That was only a few months before John . . . before I left Spain. Captain Dalton was leading a patrol over disputed ground when they were trapped in a ravine by French sharpshooters. Four of his men fell wounded in the open, bleeding to death in front of their comrades.

"Apparently Richard went into a cold fury and crawled across the field of fire, working his way around and above the sharpshooters. One of them put a bullet through his upper arm and he was bleeding badly, but even so he was able to pick them off and free his patrol. I'm told that it was an incredible feat of marksmanship, and he certainly saved the lives of the wounded soldiers. They say his men worshiped him."

"I can see why," Caroline murmured. It was a very different view of the man she had met, yet it sounded oddly right. He would be loyal to those in his charge, and would inspire a similar loyalty in those around him.

As they were entering Wildehaven, she realized she had left her music case at Wargrave Park. Engrossed in her thoughts, she shrugged it off; she would get it back tomorrow.

*   *   *

Josiah Chelmsford said his farewells the next morning at breakfast. Richard would miss him but looked forward to being on his own without the lawyer's unspoken hopes in the background.

The talk was casual until the two men were on their final cup of tea. Chelmsford considered subtly sounding out Richard's feelings about his inheritance, but decided the direct approach would work better; the captain was quite capable of ignoring subtlety if he didn't want to answer.

"Have you made your mind up, my boy?"

"No," Richard said baldly.

Since direct attack didn't seem to work either, the lawyer decided to retreat once more. "I've instructed Somers and Hain, the agent, to help you in any way they can. If you have any questions they can't answer, write to me in London. I can be here in two days if necessary."

Richard stood and offered his hand. "I want to thank you for all your help. Regardless of what I decide, I appreciate your efforts on my behalf."

The lawyer said gruffly, "You needn't thank me. I would have done as much for any child of Julius Davenport. Just see you don't vanish without a word."

Richard smiled and shook his head. "You won't be thanked and I won't be an earl. We make a pretty pair. I am a long way from knowing my own mind, but I promise you I won't disappear without telling you."

After seeing Chelmsford on his way, Richard contemplated the office with a shudder, then went to the music room to work on his calluses instead. After playing the *guitarra* for half an hour, he decided to explore the music room further while giving his fingertips a rest. It was then he noticed the flat leather music case. He thought it might be Caroline's, but opened it to see if there was any identification. The sheet music he drew out was handwritten on printed score lines, with brief notes written in a light but firm hand. At the top it said, "Sonata in E Major, by C. L. Hanscombe."

If it hadn't been for the name, he would have returned the music to the case, but he found himself studying it. After a few minutes he released his breath sharply, then went to the piano and began to play.

He lost track of time as he worked his way through the first three compositions. He was just finishing the third sonata when a sudden movement in the door caught his eye. He looked up to see Caroline poised like a terrified fawn ready for flight, her slight figure rigid and a stricken expression on her face. Realizing she was observed, she came reluctantly into the room.

"Good . . . good day," she said nervously. "I'm sorry to interrupt you. I will not stay. If . . . I could have my music case, I'll be off."

Under Richard's searching gaze she was trembling. "Please, can I have my music case?"

Richard got up and moved swiftly around the instrument. "I didn't mean to upset you. Is it because I was playing the sonata?"

She nodded without meeting his eyes.

"You wrote it, didn't you?"

She cried out in agitation, "You had no right to play it! Please, give it to me so I can leave!"

He reached a hand out and gently lifted her chin so she had to look at him. The deep blue eyes were drowning in tears. "I would never knowingly hurt you," he said gently. "Why are you so frightened of someone playing your work?"

"It was the way you *looked* at me, as if I were a freak.

Please, just give it to me and don't tell anyone and I won't ever bother you again. There is no harm in it!"

By this time the tears were pouring down her face and she was shaking all over. Richard led her to a sofa, sat her down next to him, and handed her his handkerchief. As she cried, he put an arm around her and she turned to bury both face and handkerchief against his shirt. After a few minutes her sobs abated and he asked, "Can you talk now?"

She sniffed through her reddened nose and nodded.

"My dear girl, I didn't mean to stare rudely, but I really didn't know what to say. If Mozart or Handel had walked into the room I would have felt much the same. What does one do when confronted by genius? Make a deep bow? Kneel? Lay my jacket down for you to walk on?"

Seeing that Richard didn't appear angry with her, Caroline tried to give a shaky smile. "If Mozart walked in, summoning a priest or a journalist might be more appropriate. After all, he's been dead for twenty-five years."

He smiled encouragingly. "That's much better. I didn't mean to invade your privacy, but I came across the scores and couldn't put them down. Your work is . . ." He paused, searching for a word. "Remarkable. It has something of Mozart's lyricism, of Beethoven's originality, but with a quality that is yours alone. You cover the full emotional spectrum, from joy to anguish to laughter. It is the equal of anything I have ever heard."

She looked at him with a mixture of shyness, embarrassment, and pleasure. "Do you truly think so?" He nodded. "And . . . you don't think it dreadful for a female to do such a thing?"

He said curiously, "Who has been frightening you? What could be wrong with an artist practicing her art?"

She looked down at the handkerchief she was twisting in her hands. "I'm sorry to be such a watering pot," she said haltingly. "My mother told me it was very unladylike and never to let people know or they would conceive a disgust for me. She said there has never been a female composer, that females were incapable of it.

"And . . . and my father found me composing once and . . . he became furious. He ripped up what I was working on and threw it at me. He said I was a cursed bluestocking and forbade me ever to do it again. But I didn't say I wouldn't," she said with an earnest glance. "I didn't make any promises." She stared at her hands again and grimaced. "I knew I would end up breaking them, so I didn't say anything. It never occurred to my father that he might be disobeyed. I have been very careful to keep my work hidden since then."

Richard clamped an iron control on the anger that welled up at her explanation. How could anyone behave so cruelly to such a lovely, talented girl? But he kept his quiet manner; she had been upset too much already. "Does anyone else know about your compositions?"

"Jessica does. She says there is no reason she can think of why a woman can't be a composer. And my music teacher, Signore Ferrante. He thought I should publish some of my work, but of course I couldn't."

"Why not? If you are shy or don't want to be judged as an oddity, you could use another name. And it seems a pity to deprive others of the beauty of your work."

She glanced at him sideways. "Do you truly think my work is good? Signore Ferrante always said it was, but he was too kind to say anything that would hurt me."

Richard said seriously, "The sonatas are splendid and could hold their own against the finest composers of Europe. I can't play the quartets by myself, but they appear to have the same freshness and power. I would like to copy some of your work for my own use."

He smiled at her starry-eyed look; he had seen the same expression on the face of a mother whose child had been sincerely praised. "There is a spot in the second movement of the D Minor Sonata I had trouble with—I'm not sure what cadence you intended. Could you be persuaded to demonstrate?"

His diversion worked perfectly. All the tears were gone and she looked happier and more confident than he had yet seen her. "I would love to."

As she played the composition in question, Richard's attention was divided between the glorious music and the sight of her performing. As he had suspected from their duets, she was an extraordinary pianist. For all her look of small-boned fragility, her long slim fingers had unusual strength and dexterity. And he rather thought no one else could bring quite the same feeling to a work as its composer.

When she had finished, she turned to him, seeking approval while quietly confident of receiving it. For all his intentions of moving carefully with her, he was impelled to take her right hand and kiss it. "Thank you," he said in his soft, deep voice. "Again you have shown me a beauty undreamed of."

Caroline reddened slightly but was in no hurry to retrieve the hand he held. She felt a sensation of warmth spreading through her, a warmth that seemed an integral part of this man with his quiet strength and deep-set eyes. A lifetime of anxiety over her unlady-like hobby had dissipated after a few minutes of his appreciation and acceptance.

While she had always been shy, she had never had much sense of the proprieties, and some moments passed before she realized how forward her behavior was. The thought did not disturb her overmuch, but she did let go of his hand, still feeling the imprint of his lips tingling on her fingers.

"I really should leave now," she said. "I just came to collect my music case. If you like, I will leave it here so you can copy some of the pieces."

Richard escorted her home as a matter of course. It was only when she was alone in her room before dinner that she permitted herself to think of that sweet moment after he had kissed her hand. Her fingers curled unconsciously as she remembered. If only Jason were more like Captain Dalton! He was so easy to be with, so understanding. She didn't feel awkward and tongue-tied with him; there seemed no end of interesting things to discuss. He had told her marvelous stories of some of the people and places he had seen—not just in Spain but Vienna, Ireland, Italy. Most of Europe, in fact, as well as a brief spell in North America before Waterloo. Perhaps that was why he was so relaxing to be with; he had seen so much, and seemed quite willing to accept people on their own terms. It was a refreshing change; sometimes it seemed to Caroline that everyone she knew had a different plan for how she should be. She never managed to satisfy her parents. And Jason seemed to see her primarily as raw material for molding into a comfortable wife.

For a few minutes she let herself dream of what it would be like to meet Richard Dalton if she weren't engaged, if her family had not been in such dire financial straits. Underneath her dreaming was a thread of rebellion; why was *she* the sacrificial lamb for the rest of the family? She had a mental image of herself bound and bleating on a stone altar before a frowning pagan god, and started giggling. She was sure that Lord Radford would not appreciate the metaphor—but he did make an excellent angry pagan god!

Chapter 10

Jason awoke at dawn and indulged himself with a satisfied leonine stretch. It was good to be home in his own bed after ten days' absence. He had intended to return sooner, but some genuine business had cropped up and delayed his return. He had collected George Fitzwilliam in London and they had arrived late the night before, after the rest of the household had retired. Knowing George's habits, he didn't expect to see him before ten o'clock even in the country.

He rose and looked out at the brightening sky. The dawn chorus of birds sang industriously and the Cotswold hills lay partially garbed in a pastel-tinted haze. It had been one of the fairest summers in his memory. The farmer in him wondered if there had been sufficient rain for the crops, but he firmly quashed the thought while he donned his riding clothes.

When he reached the stables his good mood was threatened by the absence of his favorite horse, Caesar. This early, even the stablehands were not stirring; certainly it wasn't a normal hour for exercising the stallion. Perhaps one of the younger lads was stealing a ride on the horse generally reserved for the master or the head groom. Making a mental note to check into the matter later, he saddled a large roan gelding he was schooling as a hunter.

The morning fulfilled its promise as he cantered east into the sunrise. He drew a deep breath of Wildehaven air, thinking how surprised his London acquaintances would be to know how much he enjoyed being home in the country. It was amusing to play the bored man of fashion in the city, but it was only a facade, suitable for short stretches of time. He felt a fierce sense of connection with his own land and could easily imagine defending it to the death in an earlier, more barbaric century.

He was reveling in his pride of place when he saw a horse cresting the hill above him. Caesar was readily identifiable by his size and gait, but he didn't recognize the rider silhouetted against the rising sun. The slim figure appeared to be one of the stableboys. He called out and urged the roan uphill. Caesar's rider reined back, apparently torn between fleeing and staying in the face of Radford's obvious desire to intercept.

The rider stayed. Had he sought to escape, it would have been difficult to catch him—Caesar was the fastest animal on the estate and didn't appear to be carrying much weight.

The windblown red hair gave her away. Slim and boyish, she was simply dressed in breeches and shirt with her hair tied back by a scarf. As she eyed him with the wariness of a lad caught in mischief, she looked even younger than the seventeen years she had when first they met.

Still feeling expansive, Jason hailed her cheerfully. "Good morning! I trust my favorite horse pleases you?"

Jessica looked defensive. "You did give me the freedom of the stables, my lord."

"A freedom you have taken advantage of," he said with a pointed glance at her costume.

"I am sorry, my lord. I would never knowingly offend someone in his own home," she said formally. The effect was undermined when she couldn't resist adding, "Your absence was lengthy enough that I was in danger of forgetting just whose home this is."

He grinned. "I take it you are chastising me for my failings as a host. Will you be pacified if I plead guilty on all counts? I had not intended to abandon you and Caroline for so long. Nor am I offended by your breeches. My grandmother often told me ladies had more freedom in her day and riding astride was commonplace. She found our modern manners tedious and hypocritical."

"Really?" Jessica said with interest. Then she remembered her formal role and said neutrally, "It is not my place to chastise you, my lord."

"While I appreciate your awareness of my exalted rank, it is not necessary to say 'my lord' with every breath you draw," he complained.

"No, your lordship," she said meekly, while her eyes started to dance.

"Very well, madam," he said with resignation. "I see that formality is to be the order of the day. If Mrs. Sterling has had her fill of riding, would she consent to accompany Lord Radford back to his humble abode?"

Jessica finally gave in to her laughter. "There is nothing the least bit humble about either Wildehaven or its owner! But I will be happy to accompany you in the hopes of an early breakfast."

The horses fell into a leisurely pace as they rode side

by side. Jason eyed her uneasily. He had thought absence would steady his nerves; there had been ample time to reflect on her cruel and unfathomable behavior so many years before. Admittedly it was a shock to see her so unexpectedly, but he had returned thinking himself immune to her undeniable charms. Now he found her presence was unraveling the previous ten days of work with shocking speed.

That lovely face looked so young and guileless that he was in danger of forgetting the intervening years—the same enchanted delight he had felt at the age of twenty-one was beginning to steal over him again. He knew she had grown and changed in many ways over these past years, but he sensed that her essential spirit was unchanged. As was his.

Fearful of forgetting his obligations, not least of them to this woman's niece, he said coolly, "You would be better advised to choose a different horse. Caesar is not what one would usually consider a lady's mount."

Jessica laughed, refusing to take offense. "I am not what is usually considered a lady."

Jason said sternly, "You should not talk so of yourself."

She shot a surprised glance at him. "Why ever not? I have been called a good deal worse by any number of people. 'Fast,' 'loose,' 'strumpet,' 'keeps her husband under the cat's paw,' 'hoyden,' 'hanging out for a rich husband—'"

"Stop it!" More calmly he said, "I am sorry if you have been the target of too many old cats. I expect they were jealous on behalf of their plain daughters."

Jessica shrugged. "I am used to it. I found that I could do nothing right, so I gave up trying. Fortunately, men have usually been more tolerant of my failings."

"I have no doubt of it," he growled.

She reined her horse in, causing him to pull up. She said, "You know, this is the most peculiar conversation. I think we are fighting, but I am not sure why." She looked at him earnestly. "We will be related soon. It would grieve me greatly to be at odds with Caroline's husband. Can we not cry friends?"

He looked at her with remote black eyes. "I never wanted to be your friend."

She shrank a little under his gaze but persevered. "Once we were a great deal more than friends. I was young and foolish beyond measure and destroyed all our might-have-beens. The past is beyond repair, but will you not accept that I wish you all possible joy in the future?"

He could not deny that earnest plea. He reached his right hand across to her and said, "Friends."

She took his hand gratefully. "As a friend, may I speak frankly?"

He smiled reluctantly. "Do you ever speak any other way?"

She blushed and shook her head. "Alas, no. I am afraid the good Lord was out of subtlety the day he assembled me. I expect that is why so many women find me alarming." She hesitated, then said, "I am not sure how to begin, but pray remember that I speak as a friend, and as an aunt."

His eyebrows drew together forbiddingly. "You wish to discuss my affianced wife with me?"

"Yes. It is . . . greatly to your credit that you have fallen in love with Caroline. She has such a sweet and loving nature, and a great talent as well. There is no malice or anger in her—she has always been an example to me of what I should strive toward."

"I will allow that she is a paragon if you will tell me where this is leading," he said dryly.

Jessica bravely soldiered on. "In some ways she is very young. While she has a great wisdom in some areas, her experience of men has been limited and . . . not such as to give her confidence. If you can be patient and move slowly with her, she will be the most loving wife a man could wish for."

"And if I forget myself and unleash my vile animal passions, I will terrify the wits out of her?"

By now Jessica was wishing she had never begun this wretched conversation, particularly as it was impossible to be with Jason without thinking of how much she had loved his "vile animal passions." "I would not use quite those words, but it is near enough to what I meant."

They were approaching the stables now and would have only a few more moments of private conversation. He said finally, "No doubt you mean well. It would take a more hardened rake than I to force her against her will—it is not my desire to have a wife that quakes in my presence. And your daughter has already warned me that I would have her to deal with should I mistreat your niece."

"Linda did what?"

He glanced at her. "In your London town house, before you came downstairs. I was told in no uncertain terms to behave or I would suffer her wrath. The women in your family appear to have a uniformly poor opinion of me."

Jessica closed her eyes and gave a mortified sigh. "Lord in heaven, we have been hard on you. Can we just forget this last five minutes of conversation and go back to being friends? Without me acting like an anxious nanny goat?"

"Perhaps that would be best." Jason didn't speak again until they were in the stables. He alighted from the roan, then went over to help Jessica dismount. "I really mean her no harm, you know," he said softly.

She looked up at his dark eyes, only a foot away. "I never thought that you did."

He stepped back, his gaze traveling from the jade-green eyes to the ripe curves of her body. He hadn't counted on the erotic impact of seeing her in the tight breeches, her beautiful face earnest and unself-conscious. He deliberately made his voice jocular as he said, "I have trouble believing I mistook you for a stableboy even from a quarter-mile away."

She answered in the same light tone. "Perhaps I'd best resurrect my riding habit so there will be no question in the future."

"That might be better in company, but suit yourself when you are out alone. I doubt if anyone would dare criticize you as long as you are on my land."

"Thank you, my lord." The improbably long lashes swept down over the sparkling eyes. It sounded like the lord of the manor was back in charge.

"You called me Jason once."

She raised her eyes to his. "That was at your invitation. I doubted whether the invitation still stood."

He resisted the temptation to brush a strand of wayward auburn hair from her cheek. "If we are to be friends, I would rather you named me as one. Or I warn you," he added wickedly, "I shall start calling you 'Aunt Jessica.'"

She choked back a giggle. "Very well . . . Jason. I

yield in the face of superior force. And on the condition you call me Jessica. After all, I've known you since my salad days."

"Which are decades in the past."

"Long, *long* ago," she said firmly. "You will become convinced of my dignified years when I start wearing my dowager caps."

"No, you wouldn't!" he said with a horror that was only partially feigned. After all, if she was middle-aged, what did that make him?

"You'll see," she warned. "Meanwhile, where is that breakfast you promised me?"

Contrary to expectations, George Fitzwilliam made an appearance in the breakfast parlor before they had finished a relaxed meal. He was rubbing his eyes and his elegant clothing was perhaps a trifle less impecca-ble than usual.

"I say, Jason, can't something be done about those wretched birds?"

His host looked up in surprise. "Good morning, George. What wretched birds?"

George waved his hand irritably. "I don't know 'em by their first names! Those dreadful creatures that were squawkin' in the tree outside my window. Demmed bad *ton* they have."

Jason said gravely, "My most sincere apologies. I shall notify my housekeeper to see if she can procure birds of better breeding who will keep more fashion-able hours. In the meantime, I fear you will have to consider the present lot as one of the hazards of coun-try living."

George nodded in satisfaction and turned to the sideboard to select a surprisingly hearty breakfast. Jessica was watching, much diverted. When he turned to the table and saw her for the first time, he was rendered almost speechless. She had changed to a cream-colored muslin gown before eating and looked a picture of modest womanhood. Watching George's mouth make small fishlike movements was almost too much for her gravity.

"Oh, I *say!*" he said reverently. "Who is . . . ?" He stopped abruptly and stared at his friend. Surely Jason wouldn't have brought one of his fancy pieces to stay under the same roof as his fiancée? She didn't look like a bit o' muslin, but the very best ones didn't. His confusion effectively destroyed any possibility of coherent speech.

Caroline entered the breakfast parlor in time to catch the tableau. Since poor George's transparent expressions seemed to be affording Jason and Jessica too much amusement to wish to enlighten him, she moved to the rescue.

"Good morning, Mr. Fitzwilliam. It is good to see you again. I believe you haven't met my aunt, Mrs. Sterling."

George gulped and said with disbelief, "You mean this is the dragon?"

At that, even Caroline had to laugh. "Indeed it is. But I promise you, she is a very nice dragon and scorches only those who deserve it. Jessica, this is George Fitzwilliam, who first introduced me to Lord Radford."

Mr. Fitzwilliam pulled himself together and executed a bow of exquisite grace in spite of the platter of ham, trout, and biscuits in his left hand. "Beg your pardon, Mrs. Sterling. Delighted to make your acquaintance. Not at all dragonish. Beauty and charm obviously common in Miss Hanscombe's family."

Jason rose and went to Caroline. "Good morning, my dear. You are in looks today."

"Thank you . . . Jason," she said in her low sweet voice. "I hope your business prospered. We missed you."

He looked down at her measuringly; he was pleased to see how steadily she met his eye. She seemed much more relaxed than when he had left, and there was a glow about her that was new. He would have been delighted at how well she was adjusting to the idea of becoming his wife—had it not been for the unreadable green eyes watching from across the room.

After Caroline and George had a chance to break their fasts, Jason said, "My aunt, Lady Edgeware, has written that she would like to host a ball here in your honor. She will be arriving in the next few days. If you are agreeable to the idea, perhaps you can work out the plans with her. It would give you a chance to become better acquainted."

Caroline nodded in agreement. He was happy to see she didn't shrink from the proposal as she might have a month earlier; Wildehaven definitely agreed with her.

She said, "My mother and sister Gina should be ending their visit in Lincolnshire soon. I trust I may invite them, along with my father? And I am sure Gideon Fallsworthy will be escorting them."

"Of course they are welcome to stay. My aunt will be inviting the local gentry. She grew up here and knows them well. I am sure they are all agog to meet you."

She hesitated, then said, "There is a man working at Wargrave Park, a former Army officer. He has little acquaintance in the neighborhood. May I invite him also?"

Jason waved his hand expansively. "Whomever you

like. The sooner you become comfortable as a hostess,
the better. This has been a bachelor establishment for
too long. I am looking forward to seeing my home
come to life again."

The former Army officer was busy increasing his acquaintance in the neighborhood, though not amongst
those who might be invited to Wildehaven. This morning's ride had taken him by the tenant farms. Since
farmers were of necessity early risers, he had taken the
opportunity to talk with several of them. One or two
had looked at him sharply; he was beginning to doubt
Chelmsford's bland assurances that no one would recognize him as a Davenport. As yet, no one had voiced
any suspicions. The tenants seemed a reliable lot,
though they all spoke of improvements needed to
maintain their productivity. Some had invested their
own money and time cobbling together repairs or improvements. He wished he knew more about agriculture; he felt sadly unqualified to run the estate.

His riding brought him near the village of Wargrave,
and on impulse he stopped by the parish church. Like
everything else in the village, it was built of warm gray
Cotswold stone. The square Norman tower appeared
to date from the thirteenth century, and parts of the
main sanctuary seemed even older.

He walked in slowly, savoring the sense of peace. He
had been raised in no fixed religion. His parents had
taken him to various churches wherever they lived, but
they had emphasized the beauty of architecture and
music as much as any creed. Since he gave equal
weight to the feelings he had when alone in the woods,
he thought he qualified as a pagan quite as much as a
Christian.

He was pleased to see the size and quality of the organ at the rear of the church; doubtless it was another example of the late countess's musical generosity. As he moved toward the chancel, a small figure unexpectedly straightened before him. She had been arranging flowers by the communion rail. As she turned, he halted, arrested by the proud hawk face. She must have been past seventy, but her back was gunrod erect and there was a fierce beauty about her. She had the look of an angel who had been cast from heaven, purified by fire, and reborn with her steely pride intact.

They looked at each other in silence for a few moments. "You would be the Army captain staying up at Wargrave Park," she said, her voice firm despite her years.

Richard smiled slightly. "I assume it would be useless to deny it."

A faint flicker of amusement answered him. "Entirely useless. If you have had any experience of villages, you will know why."

"My experience of English villages is not great, but I imagine any small isolated group of people is much the same. You would be amazed at the gossip of a company of soldiers."

Her look of amusement deepened. "I doubt it. Very little amazes me at my age." She looked at him carefully. "You look familiar, but then, almost everyone does. That and failing vision are other consequences of age. I am Lady Helen Chandler, the vicar's wife. Would you care to sit for a bit? Or is consecrated ground uncomfortable to a military man?"

He sat down on the front pew and she settled near him. "Not in the least. I have no more on my conscience than the average nonmilitary man. Possibly less; I haven't had too many opportunities for vice lately."

Her unexpected laugh had a rusty sound, as if seldom used. "You won't find many opportunities here. The fleshpots of London can offer a good deal more."

He looked at her keenly. "Is Wargrave so devoid of passion and scandal, then?"

She sobered. "No, we have our full share of human crimes and secrets here. But seldom will anyone talk of them." She added cynically, "That is the principal difference between a village and the fashionable world. Here we are more likely to be ashamed of our sins."

He wondered if she had lived here thirty years earlier, when Julius Davenport had left in a storm of scandal, but she didn't seem the sort to unearth old skeletons without a reason. "What other facts have the rumor mills provided about me?"

"Precious little, actually. It is known you were a captain of the Ninety-fifth Rifles, and assumed that you acquired that romantic limp at Waterloo. You are said to be gentlemanlike, and have been given the run of the great house. You observe much, say little, and have not been working overhard on your inventory. Your clothes are well-tailored but with the emphasis on comfort rather than fashion."

Richard burst into laughter. "I wish we had your intelligence-gathering talents in Spain! I hadn't realized my limp was romantic—I tend to think of it as a confounded nuisance."

"Very likely it is." She paused in thought for a moment, then added gruffly, "The village cobbler, Simmons, is no fashionable bootmaker like Hoby, but he's a dab hand at special boots for walking problems. His boy injured his leg in a bad fall, and Simmons has him fixed up so well there is hardly a trace of a limp." She didn't look at Richard, as if expecting him to be angry at her presumption in referring to his injury.

"I'm sure your husband's parishioners are glad to have you sort them out," he said, amused and a little discomfited at her remark.

She gave another rusty chuckle. "I'm sure some of them are praying for my rapid deliverance from this vale of tears to the care of Saint Peter. The vicar is in charge of their souls, but I take a much keener interest in their worldly doings."

He had no trouble believing either statement. He vaguely assumed that vicars' wives should be mild and discreet. Lady Helen did not seem heavily endowed with either of those rather boring virtues.

She added, "They are bound to be disappointed. I still have a great deal of atonement to do before I am ready to move on." He wondered at the sins she was making amends for; it was doubtful that she would waste her guilt on the trivial.

They were interrupted by the entrance of the vicar. Silver-haired and frail, he had the luminous face of a man who spent much of his life on a higher plane and remembered his mundane duties only in passing. His voice was soft, but had the carrying quality developed by decades worth of sermons. "Ah, there you are, my love. Are you finished with the flowers so we can have a cup of tea?" As his eyes adjusted to the dark church interior, he saw Richard and blinked doubtfully. "Do I know you, sir?"

Richard rose and offered his hand. "No, Reverend Chandler, but I am having the pleasure of meeting your wife."

The vicar beamed as he shook hands. "Isn't Lady

Helen splendid? The Lord sent her to take care of me in my old age. I can't think of what I may have done to deserve two wonderful wives in one lifetime, but I give thanks every day for my good fortune."

Since the good priest did not seem the sort to have had his two wives simultaneously, her ladyship must have come late to the vicarage. That fact and her aristocratic title would explain the lack of docility. The stern face softened as she looked at her husband; the sweetness of faith he radiated must be a balm to her acerbic nature.

"This is Captain Dalton, my dear. He is staying at the great house. Perhaps we can persuade him to join us for tea."

The vicar turned to him hopefully. "Would you like some tea, Captain? And perhaps a tour of the church first? We have some splendid old things here."

Richard smiled at him warmly. It would have been too cruel to deprive the old gentleman of the pleasure of showing off his beloved church. And the more he learned about Wargrave, the better he would be able to make the decision that must come soon.

The tour included memorials to sundry deceased Davenports. It felt strange to see the impassive stone face of Lord Hugh, dead in the Holy Land during the second Crusade; the brass plaque of Giles Davenport with his three wives and numerous children next to him; the stone inscription to Eleanor Davenport, beloved wife and mother. For all his desire to remain detached, he felt a pull to learn more about his ancestors. Like it or not, their blood flowed in his veins and gave him an anchor he had lacked since his parents' deaths. As the tour continued, he made interested comments to Reverend Chandler and filed his feelings away for later examination.

After an amiable tea he rode slowly back to Wargrave Park, absently whistling "To Be a Farmer's Boy" as he pondered what he had learned. The Chandlers' conversation had added to his understanding of the local situation, and even the perennial ache in his right leg was forgotten as he weighed the potential good he could do, as the local lord, against the heavy burdens.

He had been a good officer but never really developed a taste for military discipline. If he accepted the title, he would be losing his cherished new civilian freedom. The head of this miniature kingdom called Wargrave would be trapped by more restrictions than the youngest stableboy. There would be serious lessons to learn about agriculture, law, and finance; a seat in the House of Lords, with lawmaking responsibility for the whole country. Toadeaters and other such parasites would seek him out to further their own interests. Would he ever again be free to wander as he chose, without being constrained by well-meaning dependents? To argue philosophy or politics without deferential agreement? It had been easy to identify young noblemen in the Army; they were treated differently by those around him. He hated the idea of being perceived as an earl rather than a man.

Richard tried to be objective about the compensations. His life would not lack for purpose, even if freedom were in short supply. The estate might take years to return to full productivity, but even now there was more income than he'd ever dreamed of. He sighed; it was an unconvincing advantage, since money meant very little to him. A simple village cottage would be luxury to him after these last years; he felt no great need for anything more. But he was deeply drawn to those lovely green hills with their morning mists and hidden brooks. He didn't know if it was an ancestral call of the blood or his desire for their peace; either way, he could imagine a life among them.

And now there was a new factor, one that could make all the difference in the world to his future . . . .

He was still trying to balance comfort against captivity when he reached the stableyard, where a minor war seemed to be in progress. A sporting curricle and a trunk-filled carriage were pulled up in front of the rear entrance to the house and an imperious voice was yelling, "For God's sake, you imbeciles, that is *wine* you are unloading, not bricks! *Gently!*"

The crash of breaking bottles was followed by an explosion of curses that would have done credit to a master sergeant. Richard pulled in Rakehell and listened with deep appreciation. If his ears didn't betray him, Cousin Reginald had arrived.

As he rode around the wagon he found Reggie howling at two bemused-looking Wargrave servants, with a superior valet and a bored groom watching. Clearly they had come with his cousin and considered themselves above menial labor. Reggie's face was a good match for the claret wine spreading across the cobbled yard. "You cowhanded loobies! I'll have your jobs for this! I'll—"

His tirade broke off as he saw that his audience had increased. He looked at Richard suspiciously and said, "I've seen you before." His eyes narrowed; then he said between gritted teeth, "It was at the lawyer's office. You were wearing a captain's uniform. Ninety-fifth Riflemen. What are you doing here? Did he set you to spy on me?"

Richard answered mildly, "If Mr. Chelmsford knew you were coming here, it is more than he told me. Do you keep him informed of your movements?"

"Of course not!" Reggie snapped. "I didn't know I was coming myself until yesterday. Who are you, anyway?"

The captain bowed slightly from his horseback height. "Richard Dalton. When you saw me, the lawyer and I were discussing my coming here to inventory the estate in preparation for winding up the trust. While you and Mr. Chelmsford appeared"—he paused delicately—"incompatible, I'm sure that you must acknowledge his conscientious care of the property."

"He's said to be honest enough," Reggie said grudgingly. "Will you come down from that horse? I'm getting a sore neck from talking to you."

Richard obligingly dismounted and turned to lead the stallion to the stable. His cousin's voice stopped him. "You can subtract these two yokels from the inventory. They'll be leaving today."

Richard turned to face him, saying calmly, "That won't be necessary. Since you have no authority to dismiss them, they'll be staying. I've found them to be competent workers." He spared a glance for the miscreants. Not only were they looking entirely unashamed of their clumsiness, one of them actually winked at him as he said mournfully, "It whar a sad accident, Captain Dalton."

"What do you mean, I have no authority? I'm the next earl and I *own* this rock pile, and everyone in it!"

Richard raised an eyebrow. "I've never heard that freeborn Englishmen could be owned. And while you may be Lord Wargrave soon, for the time being Mr. Chelmsford is in charge. And here I am his deputy."

"Are you trying to tell me that I am not welcome in my own ancestral home?" Reggie's face was turning an interesting shade of puce that clashed seriously with his burgundy-colored coat.

"Not at all," Richard said gently. "I understand that you have not been allowed within its doors for some years, and I am sure that you are anxious to become reacquainted with the household. Doubtless it is an excellent place in which to avoid creditors."

Reggie gave a short bark of laughter at the words. "Perhaps you are not such a gapeseed as you appear. I'll admit the bailiffs had something to do with my desire to summer in Gloucestershire. Brighton would have been preferable, but the plaguey bill collectors always look there first. By the time they run me down, my luck will have changed."

"Perhaps. If you will excuse me, I need to rub my horse down."

"Gentlemen don't rub their horses down," Reggie said flatly.

"Gentlemen might not. But soldiers do. A bad habit I picked up on the Peninsula," Richard said as he headed toward the stable.

"Is that where you were crippled?" Reggie's raised voice reached him clearly. He turned to face his cousin and said in his quietest tone, "No, that was Waterloo."

Reginald paused suddenly. He was in a vile mood, his head aching from too much Blue Ruin the night before and his temper frayed from the longest spell of ill luck with the cards he'd ever had. He had been quite ready to pick a quarrel with this nonentity, years his junior and half a head shorter. But when Dalton turned and looked at him in that cool way, he felt a sudden disinclination to continue his baiting. "They say it was quite a battle," he said inanely.

"It was indeed." Richard waited a moment to see if his cousin had anything to add, then continued to the stables. He had a feeling that if Reginald Davenport inherited, half the servants on the estate would be off to find new jobs. The man certainly had a talent for unpleasantness.

Richard's opinion of his rakish cousin moderated a bit over the luncheon that was served. Lacking clear direction to the contrary, the servants had laid the table for two and called them at the same time. Reggie was in a better mood, possibly from the discovery that the Wargrave cellars harbored some excellent claret to replace the case that was broken. He made no attempt to provoke, and his cynical comments were slyly amusing.

Peaceable as always, the captain listened and answered noncommittally. Privately he thought Reginald would have been a better man if he had been born with less money or more responsibility. His natural gifts were frittered away in drink and gaming while he lived on his luck and his expectations. Mentally Richard thanked his father for raising him away from Wargrave's long shadow; it was better to know you were poor than to hope you might someday become rich by someone else's death.

The meal was just finishing when Caroline hurried into the dining room. "Somers said you were in here. I . . ." She stopped abruptly. "I'm sorry, I didn't know you had company."

She made an enchanting picture as she caught her breath, her cheeks flushed a pale rose that matched her

dress, a nimbus of glossy dark blond curls framing her
face. Both men stood at her entrance. "Well, well, *well*,"
drawled Reggie. "Life in the country has more attractions than I remembered. Permit me to introduce myself. I am Reginald Davenport, very much at your
service." He made an elegant leg that would have been
a credit to any courtier.

Richard completed the introduction. "This is Miss
Hanscombe. She is staying at Wildehaven."

Reggie's mouth tightened, his pale blue eyes becoming overlaid with something darker. His voice retained
its unctuous note as he said, "Then you would be Radford's fiancée. May I offer you my congratulations? He
must have been very difficult to catch."

Caroline gasped and turned red. Cold as steel,
Richard's voice cut across the silence. "I assume that
you wish to rephrase that comment, since there can be
no reason for you to wish to insult a lady you have only
just met." Reggie shot him a startled glance, suddenly
reminded that Army officers needed more than politeness to maintain order amongst rowdy soldiers.

"Of course no insult was intended," he said
smoothly. "I fear that Jason Kincaid and I have been acquainted any time these last thirty years, and have disliked each other a bit more each time we have met. My
envy of his finding such a lovely lady misled my
tongue."

He sketched another bow, then stared at Caroline in
frank admiration. The light muslin day dress clung to
her slim waist and soft curves; clearly she neither wore
nor needed corsets. She seemed unaware of her comeli-
ness, adding to her charm. And she was Jason's. How
delightful it would be to seduce such innocence while
serving an old enemy a backhanded turn. Pity he

wouldn't have the opportunity; young misses were usually so heavily guarded. Chaperons were the bane of his existence.

While Reggie was mentally licking his chops, Richard stepped forward and offered Caroline his arm. "Shall we adjourn to the music room?" She took his arm gratefully and they turned to leave.

"It was very nice to meet you, Mr. Davenport," she said uncertainly. "Perhaps I will see you again soon."

As they entered the music room she gave way to the shudder she had held in check. "What an unpleasant man! His eyes seem to leave slimy tracks like slugs. Perhaps it is just as well that . . . that I won't be able to come here as often now." She ended her words in a rush, looking at Richard with wide, unhappy eyes.

He disengaged his arm and said gently, "Lord Radford has returned?"

She nodded. "Yes, late last night. I expect I will be more busy now. Perhaps we can still play together some, but . . . there won't be as much time." *And it won't be the same.* She didn't say the last words out loud but she could hear them hanging in the air between them. She looked up at Richard's face, studying it carefully as if to memorize it. He looked less tired and drawn than when they met. It had been hardly more than a week, yet she felt she had known him forever. These last few days she had drifted in a happy haze, never thinking how quickly it must end. The intent hazel eyes were looking more green than gold today. She noticed with mild surprise how handsome he was; he had seemed so familiar from the very beginning that she hadn't studied his face closely. For the first time she saw a faint hairline scar along his left cheekbone. She put her hand up and touched it, lightly as a butterfly wing. "How did this happen?"

"A piece of shrapnel at Badajoz. A very minor thing."

She shuddered. "An inch higher and you would have lost an eye, yet this is 'a minor thing.' What is war like?"

He led her across to the benches where they often sat and played. He looked thoughtful as he took his guitar and absently tuned it, finally saying, "That is a hard question to answer. Why do you want to know?"

She said shyly, "I want to make music about it, and I can do that only if I understand. I have led such a quiet life. There is so little I truly know about that it limits what I can create."

She paused, then added in an almost inaudible voice, "I am just beginning to think of myself as a composer. I never dared do that before. But if I am a real musician, I must reach out to learn more about the world, if only through others."

Richard settled against the back of the bench, unconsciously straightening his bad leg out in front of him. "For someone of limited experience you have already created great depth in your music. But if you wish, I shall try to explain war," he said musingly. "It is a day-to-day business of boredom and discomfort, looking for whatever small way you can improve your lot. It is terror so intense it ceases to have meaning. It is going forward knowing that many of your company will surely die, and all that keeps you moving is a fear of disgracing yourself that is stronger than the fear of death."

As he talked, he plucked chords from the instrument in a counterpoint underlining his words. As she listened she could see the desolation of the field after the battle, feel the loneliness of the night watches, the diseases that killed more men than the bullets, the intense companionship, the awestruck wonder of survival, the inexpressible thunder of the guns. She never knew how long he spoke, but when he finally ended with a last haunting minor-key chord she found herself with tears in her eyes.

"'Thank you' seems inadequate, I feel you have taken me to another world." Beyond that, she felt he had shown her a glimpse of his soul, but she knew no words to say that. "Will you sing with me?" she said impulsively. "I have thought our voices would blend well."

She couldn't judge how they would sound to others, but she had never loved singing more. His beautiful dark velvet voice supported and harmonized with her clear tones. Once again they seemed to share the same musical taste and rhythms. They sang old songs from all over the British Isles, modern Italian duets, French ballads. As the afternoon drew to a close, Richard lightened the mood with a series of playful Spanish songs. After hearing one verse, she could harmonize without words. She would try to guess the song's meaning from the music; then he would translate it for her.

"The one we just sang was about . . . Sorry, I had better not translate that one!" he said with a laugh after the fifth or sixth Spanish tune.

"Is it improper?" she asked, making her eyes huge and innocent.

"Most improper," he said firmly. "Now that I think of it, I believe I have exhausted my supply of Spanish songs that can be sung in mixed company. Shall I play some of the Spanish dances for you?"

An hour later they walked slowly back to Wildehaven, reluctant to end the afternoon. Caroline had the heavy feeling that it was her last free, unconstrained time with Richard. Lord Radford's forceful energy seemed to be engulfing her; from now on most of her time would belong to him. She wondered if it would matter to the captain. He seemed to enjoy her company, but he had never said anything indicating a stronger feeling.

She determinedly pushed speculation from her mind; there would be time enough for brooding later. For the moment, she still felt free, and alive with passionate Spanish rhythms. As they entered a flower-floored glade where the slanting sunshine gave a strange, magical glow, Caroline paused and said, "I've always felt this would be a place where the Small Folk would dance. Whenever I come through, I feel like joining them."

"Why don't you?" Richard asked with a half-smile. "I'm sure they wouldn't object. Sometimes you seem to be half-fairy yourself; they should welcome you."

She looked up with an eager glance, then paused, unable to avoid a quick look at his damaged leg. Richard saw the direction of her eyes and said quietly, "I'm afraid my dancing days are done. You shall have to do it for both of us. Go ahead, Caro."

It was the first time he had used the diminutive of her name; it felt astonishingly intimate. She gave him a slow sweet smile, then moved into the center of the glade. Closing her eyes, she reached out with all her senses, absorbing the leafy scent, the small bird sounds, the slight breeze that caressed her cheek and rippled her thin muslin gown.

Her whole life had been lived to a background of music, like a great river flowing through her spirit, highs and lows blending into magical rhythms she could never quite express aloud. Often she would let them run free in her mind when she played or dreamed or composed. Now for the first time she let the torrent she felt in her soul run free in her body.

She began a slow swaying, then started to glide and turn in a dance as natural and graceful as eiderdown on the wind. Her eyes were open but unfocused as she listened to music only she could hear. All she had known of joy in her life was bound together with a profound new emotion coming from the center of her being. Her voice sang a wordless accompaniment to her dance, the crystalline tones filling the clearing like a sorcerer's incantation.

At the end she drifted across the grass and swept into a deep formal curtsy in front of Richard, one hand lifted toward him. She realized now what she had danced: it was the most ancient of mysteries and its name was Love.

As Richard moved toward her she studied the bright brown hair; the wide hazel eyes, a little remote now; his handsome face, inexpressibly dear. The broad-shouldered figure moved smoothly in spite of the limp that kept him forever earthbound, unable to dance his soul as she had just done. All thoughts of propriety had vanished as she danced in the clearing, and she wished with every fiber of her being for him to kiss her.

Instead he took her hand, his strong brown fingers enclosing hers. Even that simple contact affected her more than she would have dreamed possible, and she wondered if she were visibly trembling. Could he feel it too, the slow fire that spread from her fingers and through her body?

He said gently, "Come, Titania. I must return you to the lands of men."

She rose from her curtsy and shook some twigs from her hem, too moved by her newfound feelings to attempt speech. If she had known how, she would have told him of her love. Even if he didn't return her feelings, she knew he would be kind, be she ever so much a fool.

There has never been anything important in my life that I have been able to find the words for, she thought wretchedly. The logical part of her mind said it would be wrong to speak of love. She was bound past redemption to another man; and no lady would behave so forwardly. But I've never been a logical creature, she thought with wry humor. Any number of people have told me so.

With all of her emotional nature she wanted to tell him how she felt because she feared there would never be another chance. It seemed unbearably cruel that such an intensity of caring would never see the light of day.

She was still mute as they reached the clearing around Wildehaven. As was the custom of these last days, he waited at the edge while she crossed alone to the great house. She stood at the side door and looked back at the brown figure in the shadows of the wood until he turned and vanished, feeling the tightness in her chest of a grief too deep for words. If she couldn't speak in the aftermath of that ancient mystery dance, she would never find the courage in the future. Her face was set in the remote lines of a Greek statue as she returned to her chamber to dress for dinner.

* * *

Richard walked in the woods for hours before returning to Wargrave, his emotions in a tumult. From the moment he had first seen Caroline glowing with sunlight, to this afternoon's fey dance of unearthly beauty, she had touched realms of his heart entirely new to him. He had never wanted anything or anyone as he wanted Caroline, yet she was pledged to another man. It had been madness to spend these last days together, oblivious of her commitment and the world's possible censure.

He smiled without humor; if Radford found out and took exception to their intimacy, he would be within his rights to call Richard out. That was no great worry in itself, but the repercussions for Caroline could be devastating.

He had studied her carefully these last days and seen no sign that she was in love with Radford. If he were absolutely sure of that, he would be courting her openly. Not the act of a gentleman perhaps, but social conventions were a thin facade compared with the primal emotions Caroline aroused in him.

He felt he knew her, perhaps better than she knew herself—the sensitivity, the innocent clarity of spirit, the stunning musical talent. Being with her was pure joy—the sound of her light rippling laughter, the sweet dreaminess, the unexpected flashes of dry wit. He loved them with as much intensity as he desired to touch that delicate face, as fine-grained as a rose petal.

Yet it would be the act of a vandal to force unwanted attentions on her. She was happy in his company, but perhaps it was just the pleasure of their shared love of music. She was as unconscious of her loveliness as a flower; he doubted if she had any idea of the effect she had on him.

He found that he was whistling "Greensleeves." *Alas, my love, You do me wrong, To cast me off so discourteously* . . . Not entirely appropriate, perhaps; but the melancholy sweetness of the ancient tune haunted him the way her graceful movements did.

He was limping badly when he returned to Wargrave, his leg aching from the long walk and the chill evening air. He knew he must speak to her, and soon, before time ran out. He would never forgive himself if he lost her through inaction. And hadn't he fought other forlorn hopes in the Army?

Richard was unusually quiet that night, even for a man who had been known to say that few things improve on silence. Apart from asking the butler, Somers, for any mail from London, he seemed lost in thought. Reginald wondered idly if the captain were sulking over the scene at lunch, but decided not. The man certainly had nothing to say for himself.

Already growing bored with life in the country, Reggie tried various conversational gambits but his companion seemed singularly uninterested in *on dits*, boxing matches, wenching, gaming, and every other interesting topic that was introduced. Having spent much of the afternoon drinking, topped with a bottle and a half of hock with dinner, the Despair of the Davenports was in a surly mood by the time the captain pushed back from the table to leave.

"You're a dull dog, Dalton," he said pugnaciously. "Or perhaps a cow, chewing your cud."

Richard raised one eyebrow, his attention finally caught. "Surely 'bull' would be more accurate than 'cow'?"

" 'Gelding' would be better yet," Reggie said with an ugly glint.

Disconcertingly, his quarry laughed with genuine humor. "Come now, Davenport, you disappoint me. Schoolboys make insults about eunuchs. Surely a man of the world like you can do better than that."

Volatile as always, Reggie felt a certain reluctant respect for someone so impervious to attack. "What does it take to anger you, Dalton? I can't believe the Army didn't teach you something about fighting."

Richard smiled. "I'd best not tell you my weaknesses, for you would feel compelled to test them. And then I might have to kill you."

Angry again, his cousin spat out, "You and how many friends? There isn't a man in England I can't beat in any fair fight, pistols, swords, or fisticuffs. I've beaten Jackson himself at his salon."

"Ah, yes. That is one of the places where men of fashion play at fighting."

"Play?"

"I don't know what else to call it. You're right that I learned something in the Army. Avoid unnecessary battles. But when you fight, fight to win."

Dispensing with the formality of a glass, Reggie took a swallow direct from his latest bottle of wine. "I was going to invite you to a mill near Bristol tomorrow, but no doubt you would consider that too much like play."

"Alas, yes. I'm a workingman and can't take time for the treat." Richard made only a token attempt to look disappointed. Really, his cousin was the most unaccountable man, full of idle malice, yet so desperate for company he would extend an invitation to someone he was doing his level best to provoke. It would be no loss to have him away for a day or two.

Rising from the table, he said with unimpaired good humor, "Enjoy your mill, but don't put your blunt on the Cornishman. The word is he's off his form."

Reginald was left to stare at the closed door as the captain limped out. Where had the damned man learned who was boxing in Bristol? Shrugging, he reached for a new bottle of wine.

The evening seemed interminable. Jason looked at her with a slight frown and Jessica shot occasional puzzled glances. Caroline refused to let her aunt catch her eye, excusing herself as early as possible on the grounds of an all-too-real headache.

In the safety of her room she reached for her lute rather than her night robe. Singing softly, she plucked out many of the old ballads she had sung with Richard earlier in the day, so intent she never saw Jessica open the door.

I know where I'm going, And I know who's going with me, I know who I love, and he knows who I'll marry . . . She sang the words with the feelings she had been unable to express earlier. Her aunt listened for a few moments, then silently withdrew.

The clock was striking midnight when Caroline's songs were done, but she knew that sleep was still out of the question. Instead, she reached for her pen and her blank music paper. It was nearly dawn when she finally closed her burning eyes. One long night was over. There was still a whole lifetime to get through.

Chapter 11

The corridor past the guest rooms was still gray in the dawn half-light. Jason walked softly, telling himself it was perfectly logical to go to the stables by this route, and there was no reason to suppose that Jessica would be going out to ride this early. Even though their paths had crossed in the stables for the last three mornings and they had gone riding together, it wasn't as if they had arranged any of the meetings.

Nonetheless, he was listening closely enough to hear the muffled curse coming from behind her door. He paused, then tapped gently at the oak panels. Moments later, Jessica opened the door, dressed in her skintight breeches and a white shirt that strained across her breasts.

"Oh! I thought it would be one of the servants," she said as she looked up at the master of the house. He smiled at her smoothly, carefully keeping his gaze on her face rather than her all-too-revealing clothes.

"I heard what sounded uncommonly like a cavalry oath. May I offer any assistance?"

She smiled "You are exactly what I need. Come in." Apparently oblivious of the implications, she stood back and let him enter her bedchamber. Walking to the massive four-poster, she waved her hand at the canopy. "There is the problem."

Jason looked up and blinked, wondering if it was earlier than he thought. His initial impression was confirmed when the triangular orange patch opened a surprisingly large pink mouth full of needle-sharp teeth and said, "Mrro-o-o—o-wp!"

"He's gotten himself up there and can't seem to get down. I'm not tall enough to reach him and I'm reluctant to stand on your brocade chairs. If I leave him there, he'll either fall and break his neck or spend the day shredding the silk canopy."

"Allow me," Jason moved to the edge of the bed and reached up. The little cat seemed disposed to be skittish, but stood still after hearing "Wel-l-l-le-s-l-e-y," uttered in a warning tone.

Jason lifted him down and stroked the soft head carefully. His reward was a high-pitched purr of delight. "He certainly gets into a quantity of trouble, doesn't he?"

"He does that, my lord," Jessica said with a smile. "He is excellent preparation for having a child. Never where you expect him, able to move incredibly fast, and can charm you out of your irritation when you'd like to wring his neck."

"You have the greenest eyes I've ever seen," Jason said involuntarily as he looked down into her shining morning face.

She dimpled at him. "Then you can't have looked closely at Wellesley."

He smiled in reply. It was so very hard to stay on his guard with Jessica. "You have the greenest eyes I've ever seen on a human, then." They really were most remarkable, not the light olive shade usually called green but a clear true emerald with a dark rim around the iris. Eyes to drown in. . . .

He snapped his concentration back with an effort. "Since you appear to be ready for riding, would you care to join me?"

"I'd be delighted." She slipped on a worn brown jacket against the morning chill, then hustled her host into the corridor. Widows were relatively scandalproof but it wouldn't be at all the thing for her niece's fiancé to be seen coming out of her bedroom. It was even less the thing to know she didn't want him to leave.

As they walked outside, she darted a quick glance at him out of the corner of her eye. Why did he have to be so very handsome? The irresistible smile lurking behind his dark eyes, the rangy athlete's body, designed to make a tall lady feel fragile and feminine . . . She turned her attention forward as they entered the stables.

"Come down here. I want to show you something." Jason led her to the left, away from the area where most of the riding horses were kept. At the end of the passage he stopped in front of a large box stall. "What do you think?"

Jessica drew her breath in with delight, then reached out to the dappled gray mare. She was an exquisite creature, with huge dark eyes and dancing hooves. She trotted over to Jessica and gently pressed her velvet muzzle into the shoulder of the brown jacket.

"She seems to like you," Jason commented.

"Say rather that she smells the carrot in my pocket. I was going to give it to the roan I've been riding, but this beauty has talked me round." Jessica produced the treat, then stroked the glossy neck as the mare daintily nibbled. "She is mostly Arabian, isn't she?"

Jason nodded approvingly. "Quite right. She was just delivered yesterday afternoon. I think she is the finest mare in England, and have been after Lord Hudson to sell for two years now. I may give her to Caroline as a wedding gift."

Noticing Jessica's doubtful look, he said dryly, "Surely your niece does ride?"

"Of course she does! She is a very pretty rider when . . ." Jessica's voice trailed off.

"You are going to have to complete that sentence, you know," Jason said. "Particularly if it helps me to understand my elusive bride any better."

Jessica smiled with a trace of embarrassment. "There is no great mystery. Caroline tends to be a bit of a woolgatherer, as you may have noticed."

"The matter had not escaped my attention."

"Well, we have always made sure she has placid horses. She has gotten thrown several times by paying insufficient attention. A spirited horse like this would have her in the hedgerows constantly. She is always quite cheerful and apologetic about her lapses, but there is a risk of serious injury."

Jason sighed. "Perhaps the pianoforte will be a better gift."

"Without question. Meanwhile, what is this little lady's name?"

"Cleopatra. A fit mate for my Caesar." Jason noticed Jessica's doubtful look, and asked, "Does that not meet with your approval?"

"We-l-l-l . . . remember that Caesar and Cleopatra did not make a match of it. Perhaps she should be named for Caesar's wife rather than his bit of muslin."

Ignoring the strangled snort from her escort, she ran her fingers through the dark gray mane. "And like Caesar's wife, this one is above reproach."

Jason laughed suddenly. "How did an introduction to a horse turn into a lecture on the classics? If you prefer, I will call her Calpurnia rather than Cleopatra. She needs some exercise today. Shall I saddle her for you?"

Eyes shining, Jessica nodded enthusiastically. "Yes, *please!*"

As they cantered across a meadow several minutes later, Jessica threw back her head and laughed in sheer exhilaration. She knew how unwise it was to savor the company of the man by her side, but in affairs of the heart she had never been wise in her life. If she chose to enjoy now and suffer later, it was no one else's concern. She put Calpurnia through her paces, delighted by the mare's smooth gaits and powerful response. "Shall I put her at a few fences, my lord? I want to see if she can jump as well as she rides."

Without waiting for an answer, she turned her mount and headed for the nearest hedge, bounding over it with two feet to spare. Jason followed, thinking that few sights could improve on watching a beautiful woman on a beautiful horse. It occurred to him that almost the whole of his relationship with Jessica had been conducted on horseback.

She had pulled up on the other side of the hedge, beaming happily. "I swear this little beauty could outrun and outjump that big heavy brute you're on. Not that Caesar isn't a good fellow in his way," she added soothingly.

"That's coming it a bit strong," he snorted. "There isn't a mare born who could outrun this stallion."

Jessica looked disdainful as she effortlessly controlled Calpurnia's curvetting. "Possibly Caesar could make a creditable showing if he wasn't carrying so much weight. But since he is, I'll stand by my statement."

Provoked by the slur on his favorite, Jason answered with a dangerous glint in his eyes, "Would you care to put that to a test?"

"Certainly. Pick your time and your course."

"I choose right now. As for the course . . . are you familiar with the giant oak in the western sheep pasture? It's about two miles from here over mixed country." Jason considered adding a wager to the race but decided against it. He still hadn't recovered from his last foolish bet. He added, "Any route will do as long as no crops are damaged."

"Done!" With a last flashing smile, Jessica whirled her horse around and was gone over the next hedge before Jason had Caesar properly in hand. He cursed admiringly as he put the stallion at the hedge she had just jumped. The wench certainly didn't let any grass grow under her feet! He knew he had an unfair advantage; she couldn't possibly know his land as well as he did. There were three potential routes but the flattest was blocked by a thick tangle of woods and the shortest was split by a narrow but very deep ravine.

Jessica was already out of sight as he topped the first hill, so he urged Caesar into a full gallop. Delighted by the order, the giant black horse flew over the countryside.

Two-thirds of the way to his goal, Jason still hadn't seen a sign of his opponent. She couldn't have had that much of a lead; was she on a different path? She must know enough to avoid the woods; they had skirted that area the morning before.

An icy finger touched the back of his neck and sent a chill down his spine; did she know about the ravine? Coming from this side, a stone wall had been built along the edge to keep livestock from falling. It would appear a simple jump to a rider coming on it unaware. Though an expert horse and rider could cross it, it would be sudden death to anyone unprepared. In Jason's lifetime, two hunters had died there; new riders were always warned and watched when they first hunted the area.

Abandoning the race, he cut Caesar right over a hill that would give him a clear view of the route that ran to the ravine. His heart froze when he saw the rider flying toward the deceptive stone fence, her small figure nearly flat along the mare's gray neck, her flaming red hair the only bright note in the scene.

"Jessica!" He shouted at the top of his lungs as he set Caesar down the dangerous hillside, willing her to hear him and pull up. Uttering a quick prayer that Caesar wouldn't put a foot in a badger hole, he concentrated on avoiding visible obstacles as he crashed down the hill at a suicidal pace, barely aware of stinging branches from the scrubby trees.

He was less than a hundred feet behind her when he burst onto the path, but she was only yards from the stone fence. He called out again and saw her glance back briefly before she launched Calpurnia upward over the barrier. Time slowed almost to stopping as they floated . . . over . . . hanging above the impossible ravine for a frozen eternity, then landing safely on the other side.

Jason's panic barely registered relief before being washed away in a flood of fury. Beyond reason, he set the tiring Caesar at the fence, lifting them over the ravine by sheer force of will. Jessica had pulled up the mare and was waiting with a puzzled look on her face as he thundered up to her, drawing the stallion up at the last possible moment, then reaching out to grab Calpurnia's bridle.

"Are you insane?" he raged. "That is the most dangerous spot on the estate. Two men have died there! Have you no sense at all?"

Surprised, Jessica gave him a hard stare from her suddenly cool green eyes. "But you see, we made the jump quite handily. Do you think I would risk your horse's life?"

"I'm not worried about the damned horse! You haven't been here long enough to know your way around. You could have been killed!"

Barely holding on to her own temper, she said through clenched teeth, "You forget, Lord Radford, I had nothing to do for the last fortnight but explore your land. I know perfectly what this ground is like. Was the great sportsman hoping for my ignorance to improve his chances of winning?"

"I don't worry about being defeated by paper-skulled females! But I am your host, so if you are going to kill yourself through your own stupidity, don't do it on my land!"

Bidding good-bye to the last shreds of self-control, Jessica exploded with all the frustration that had been building in her for the last two weeks.

"My safety is none of your concern! I knew exactly what I was doing. Neither the horse nor I was in any danger. What right have you to rail at me like a fishwife?"

Goaded beyond sense and discretion, Jason let go of her bridle and wrapped one arm around Jessica, half-pulling her across his saddle. "*This* right!" he said gratingly, before crushing his lips down on hers. His anger disappeared as rapidly as it had come and he released his own reins, wrapping both arms around her and burying one hand in her tangled auburn hair. She had jerked violently at his first touch, but now she clung to him, her warm mouth as urgent and demanding as his.

"Oh, Jessie, Jessie," he breathed into her ear. "I thought you were going to die right in front of my eyes and I couldn't bear it. I've been fourteen years in hell, and with you gone I would have spent the rest of my life there. Better to have thrown myself into the ravine after you."

Caesar shifted uneasily, nearly unbalancing them both. It occurred to Jason that his sporting acquaintance would never believe that he, the great horseman, was foolish enough to make love to a woman when they were both astride spirited horses.

He shifted Jessica's weight upright, then dismounted, securing the reins of both mounts to a convenient branch. As she slid wordlessly into his arms, he saw that his peerless, indomitable Jessica was crying. He studied the drowning emerald eyes, open and vulnerable as when she was seventeen, and began kissing each crystal tear. Her body shuddered against his as he ran his hand down her long back. She started to break away, so he forbade his hands to wander and held her against his chest until her movement stilled and she rested her head against his shoulder.

"Why did you leave me, love?" he said softly. "There wasn't a day in the five years after that I didn't ask myself what I had done wrong."

She raised her head to look at him, her control still

fragile. "It was because of my own youthful foolishness, Jason." She drew a breath shakily. "I have often
thought that youth is greatly overrated. The pain that
is given and received without intending, the lack of
understanding, the unintentional crimes against the
heart . . . A thousand times I wished I could go back,
but it was beyond mending."

Her breath caught as she looked back over the years;
then she continued, "At least I am being given the
chance to answer for my wretched behavior."

She pulled away from his embrace and sat with her
back against a nearby log, patting the place beside her.
Jason lowered himself where she indicated, taking the
opportunity to put his arm around her. As she leaned
her head back against him, he prompted, "What do
you mean about your foolishness? All I could imagine
at the time was that you were set on a title or a fortune,
but when you married neither, I had to accept that I
never had really known what you wanted."

She smiled ruefully at him. "I wanted what every romantic young girl wanted." She paused to organize
her thoughts, then said, "You knew my father, didn't
you?" He nodded and she asked, "What manner of
man was he?"

Jason cast his memory back, then answered, "A
charming wastrel. Delightful company, held his liquor
well and his cards badly, completely selfish."

Jessica looked pleased at his perception. "Exactly so!
You obviously took his measure. He could be quite af-
fectionate with his daughters when he remembered
our existence, and he would indulge us when it cost
him nothing, but he looked on us primarily as a source
of revenue. He had inherited an easy competence from
his father, Lord Westerly, but he had gambled it away

by the time I was five. My mother died soon after, worn out by the effort of keeping the household going. My older sister, Emily, was left to raise me and juggle the accounts. My father would be off with his grand friends. Now and again he would send some money when his luck was in. We managed."

She drew in a deep breath and continued, her eyes fixed on the grazing horses. "Emily was a lovely girl; Caroline much resembles her. She caught Sir Alfred Hanscombe's eye and he offered Papa a large settlement in return for his consent to a marriage. Emily loathed him and begged Papa to refuse, but he just laughed and said every girl needed a husband and Alfred was as good as any.

"I lived with them after the marriage—there was no place else for me. Sir Alfred's infatuation didn't last long, so I watched my sister dying before my eyes— withering away from neglect, casual cruelty, and beastly selfishness. After Caro was born, she just gave up. It wasn't the birth that killed her—it was the lack of love." There was a hard edge in her voice as her story went on.

"Caroline and I lived with one of my father's sisters until Sir Alfred married Louisa a year later. Louisa is not a very warm woman but she believes in her duty and she brought Caro back to her father's home. I would have kept her if I could, but I was only a child myself. For the next few years I was shuffled around among various relatives. Lady Hanscombe would have me sometimes—she considered it only fair that Caroline should know her aunt. Every year or so my father would pop in for a visit wherever I was staying." She laughed bitterly.

"He was quite pleased at my progress. He said I was

turning into a rare beauty and would fetch a fine price
in the Marriage Mart—that he wouldn't settle for less
than an earl, and he'd not be surprised if I ended up a
duchess. He said any man would be 'proud to possess
me.' That I would be an ornament to any position."

Jason drew his breath in sharply as he began to understand where her story was leading. She turned to
look at him now, her lovely face intense with memory.
"I swore I would never follow the path he was choosing for me. That I would marry only for love, and I
didn't give a tinker's dam for wealth or position."

She looked down at her hands, and her voice came
haltingly. "When I met you at that hunting party, my
father was grooming me for a Season under the aus-
pices of an aunt. I knew you were what I wanted—I
had never felt so alive, or so close to anyone. I was sure
you felt the same. When you offered for me that day, I
was so eager to hear that you loved me. I didn't know
about your family or fortune, nor did I care. I just
wanted to hear you say that you loved me and wanted
to be with me always." Her voice was almost a whisper. "I wouldn't even have cared about marriage, really, I just wanted your love."

Jason continued the story. "Instead I said you were
the most beautiful girl I had ever seen, that I would be
proud to have you as my wife. That you would be a
credit to my position, that I could provide you with all
of the comforts and some of the elegancies of life. And
I said no word of love."

He put his other arm around her and pulled her
against his broad chest, raising her chin with one hand
so her green gaze met his dark eyes. "Let me make up
for that now. Jessica, I love you. I have never loved
anyone else. As angry and bewildered and hurt as I

was, I never stopped loving you, and I never could. You are maddening and independent and can ride as well as I can, and I love you the more because of that."

He touched his lips to hers in a gentle, passionless kiss that was a pledge to all he said. Drawing back, he continued, "I too was raised in a home where love was a valueless currency. I was a younger son, of no great significance except as a . . . a spare heir should my brother be untimely plucked. In a world that values fortune and position, I had only a small share of both. I hardly dared believe that you loved me for myself, so I offered what I thought you would value. I never dreamed that what you wanted I had in endless supply. I was very young then."

He bent his head to give her another delicate kiss. "It would have been well-nigh impossible to say clearly what I felt, how much I desired and needed you."

She laughed a little, deep sadness in her voice. "I understood that later. I was so crushed with disappointment that my beastly temper took over and I said all those terrible things. After I left you, I rode for hours, trying to understand what had happened. When I finally came to believe that my heart could not have been wrong about how you felt, I rode to the house where you were staying. But it was too late."

He looked at her in surprise. "You went to Longford's house? I never knew that. I had left a bare two hours after you rejected my suit—I knew I couldn't endure being near you. I suppose you would not have known where to write to me."

She shook her head. "I knew so little about you—not even where you lived. I didn't dare make inquiries— the butler who told me you had left made it very clear what he thought about brazen hussies who called on gentlemen without so much as a groom for escort. I was sure my foolish anger had given you a lasting disgust of me, and I hated myself for throwing away what I wanted more than anything in life.

"There seemed no help for it, so I went off to London as my father wished. I knew I couldn't fall in love like that again, but the social rounds helped distract me. Papa received a great many offers for my hand, but he didn't mind refusing those he considered unworthy of me."

She smiled with a trace of mischief. "He never knew the heir to a dukedom was so ill-bred as to propose to me directly. Papa would have expired on the spot if he knew I had turned down such an offer. And I got offers of quite another sort from no fewer than two royal dukes."

"Dare I speculate which two?"

"A lady never boasts of her conquests," she said primly. More seriously she said, "During that spring I came to know John Sterling better. He was a captain then. He came from Wiltshire near the Hanscombes' and had known me from when I was a child. As the Season came to an end, he told me he had always loved me but had been waiting for me to grow up and see something of the world. Even when I said I loved someone else, he wanted to marry me."

She stopped again, then said haltingly, "I needed very much to be loved. My father objected, but I had a stronger will than he, and swore I would elope if he didn't give his permission. He knew I would, so he threw up his hands in despair and let me go. We were married quietly and left the country soon after."

She smiled nostalgically. "I learned so much about love from John. He was all that was generous, always giving, never asking for more than I was willing to give in return. And soon I loved him too, though not the same way I loved you. One never loves two men in the same way, I suppose."

She started to rise, saying, "And that is how I came to be here. I am grateful for the chance to explain myself, and to beg your pardon for the wrong I did you."

Jason grabbed her hand and pulled her down again. "Do you think you can just leave now, as if you had finished a morning call? Do you think I will let you walk out of my life again?"

She looked at him steadily. "I might be willing to be your mistress under other conditions, but not when Caro is your wife."

"To hell with Caroline! It's *you* that I want to marry. Can you deny you love me?" There was an unfamiliar note of pleading in his voice; he daren't even consider losing her again.

She reached out her hand and traced the lines of his beloved face—the thick frowning brows that intimidated Caroline, the dark weathered skin, the unexpectedly warm lips. She said gently, "You are promised to her."

"I know that only women are supposed to break engagements, and I've always thought it was just so much fustian. Do you think I care what the gossips think of me? Does it matter to you?" He turned his face to press a burning kiss into her palm.

She sighed and withdrew her hand. "I wouldn't care for myself, though perhaps I would for my daughter's sake."

"There would be some embarrassment for Caroline, but I doubt she would really mind," he agreed. "I think her father was selling her, much as your father sold her mother."

"There is some truth to that," she admitted. "Sir Alfred needed the settlement or she would never have consented."

"She was willing to wed the ogre for money?" he asked sarcastically.

"She cares less for money than anyone I ever met. But she loves her sister Gina, and she was told Gina would not be allowed to wed her Gideon unless she agreed to marry you."

"So she was the virgin sacrifice for her sister's happiness. You are certainly bent on destroying my self-esteem! Why can't I let Sir Alfred keep the damned settlement in return for the blow to his daughter's spirits?"

"You know that isn't possible."

"Why not? It's my money, and I can do with it as I like. Or would I then be unable to afford your bride price?"

She refused to take it as a jest. "If it were only money, and a minor scandal, I would marry you tomorrow. But it has gone beyond that. Have you looked at Caroline closely?"

He nodded reluctantly. "She is looking very well. The country agrees with her."

"It is more than that," Jessica said earnestly. "I have known her all her life, and I have never seen her glow as she has these last two weeks. She is a very private person and hasn't confided in me about her feelings. Indeed, I doubt if she herself knew. But did you observe her three nights ago?"

He frowned. "Yes, she looked distracted and moody.

She was hardly there at all. She has been quiet ever since."

"I know. I was worried and went to her room later that night to see if she wished to talk. I heard her singing when she was unaware of my presence. If ever I have heard love, it was in her voice."

Jessica stopped, then went on painfully, "I think she had only realized it herself. That is why she seems withdrawn. Being in love is shattering, particularly when it is for the first time. Seeing you here in your home, coming to know you better . . . of course she came to love you. Who would not?"

There were tears in her eyes as she finished. "Do you see now why it is impossible? I could never buy my happiness at the price of hers. And soon you will love her too. She is a far better woman that I will ever be. And she is ten years younger, just beginning to blossom into her full beauty. What you and I had and lost belongs to the past. She is your future."

He grabbed her shoulders and shook her in desperation, seeing her slipping away from him. "Do you think I care about your age or her saintly disposition? I have never been truly happy but in those hours I spent with you. Would you buy your peace of mind at the price of mine?"

He moved his fingers into the tangled silk of her hair, pulling her close in a violent embrace. With every fiber of passion in him he tried to bind her with hands and mouth and body, to persuade her in ways beyond words.

She yielded for long moments, then shoved him away with startling strength. He fell back against the log as she scrambled across the clearing, untethering her horse and mounting in a blur of movement. The reins in hand, she looked down at him in anguish. "I will love you always," she said in a small clear voice.

Then she was gone. He stood slowly and crossed to Caesar, leaning his forehead against the horse's sweaty neck. He was grateful for the paralysis that gripped him. It held in check the pain he knew would devastate him when it was released—when he let himself know that she had ridden out of his life for the last time.

Caroline sighed and pushed a tawny curl off her face as she looked at the music score on the desk before her. Usually she composed directly on the pianoforte, relying on her near-perfect musical memory to hold the sounds in her mind until she could record them. Three nights ago it had been different—she worked in a blaze of creative energy, the notes pouring from her pen onto the paper as the composition pounded in her blood, demanding to be set free. When the music finally released her to her bed, she did not truly understand what she had written.

She had not looked at the sonata till this morning, unable to confront the intense emotions that had generated it. Now, as it lay on the desk before her in the late-morning sun, she wondered how she could have been so blind. The composition was a declaration of her love for Richard—all her inchoate feelings transmuted into pure melody. She didn't need to play it aloud to know it was the best thing she had ever done. It should be; every note had been drawn out of her blood and being.

Letting the music speak her heart had given a curious sense of peace after the confusion of the last weeks. She could see now how innocent she had been, living in her own dreamy world. Unlike most young girls, she had seldom thought of love and marriage; that was why both had caught her unaware. Her violent initial reaction to Jason had been caused as much by shock at the idea of marriage as by his alarmingly forceful personality. She had never fancied herself in love, not even the schoolgirl infatuations her sisters had suffered. Now the reality of loving had changed her whole world. Her emotions were hitting highs and lows she had never dreamed of, while her body stirred with barely comprehended yearnings.

She had never loved before, and she knew with aching certainty she would never love again. It was equally certain there could be no possible future with Richard. The engagement to Jason had taken on an unstoppable life of its own; her family's needs were not changed by the fact that she had lost her heart to the wrong man. To a slightly damaged former soldier, in fact. Her lips curved involuntarily to a smile as she thought of him.

Even if she were free to love as she chose, she had no reason to believe he felt anything stronger than friendship for her. She suspected he and Jessica were half in love with each other; she had seen how happy they were to meet again. Jess had mourned her husband long enough and was ready to move into a new life, while Richard had once told her that every officer in Spain had been expiring of love for the magnificent Mrs. Sterling. She had been a symbol for them of the best of English womanhood, not just beautiful and brimming with vital charm, but patently loving and faithful to her husband. The major had been the most envied man on the Peninsula.

She hoped they would make a match of it; better to

have Richard in her life that way than not at all. And
they were the two people that she loved best in the
world; she thought she had enough generosity to wish
them happy. *Uncle Richard?* Her heart twisted a little at
the thought. If that happened, she hoped it wouldn't
be too soon—she wasn't quite ready for that yet.

After she married Jason, she would be busy pre-
tending to be a lady. And there would be children—
another subject that she had never much considered,
but found more appealing now. She no longer feared
or hated Jason—might she someday feel a kind of love
for him? Perhaps it would be best if she didn't; he
showed no desire for a doting wife. He wanted a presentable and undemanding partner; she wasn't sure if
he even knew what love was. She hadn't known herself.

Her musings were interrupted by a soft knock at the
door, and her maid, Betsy, came in. "Excuse me, Miss
Hanscombe. I know you said you didn't wish to be
disturbed, but the gentleman said it was important."

Caroline looked up in surprise. It couldn't be Jason;
the maid would never apologize for bringing a summons from the master of the house. "Who is calling,
Betsy?"

"It's the military gentleman staying at Wargrave,
miss. Captain Dalton."

Caroline felt her face draining of color. She had been
sitting here, pleased with her calm resignation, and
now it was shattered at the mere thought of seeing him
again. How could she look at him normally when her
whole world had irrevocably changed? Forcing herself
to reply steadily, she said, "Tell him I will be down in a
few minutes. Is he waiting in the small parlor?"

The maid nodded and left the room with the message. Caroline stood and gave a despairing glance in the mirror. It was another irony that she who had never cared for her appearance was now as anxious as any other love-struck maiden. Fortunately, all her new dresses were flattering; the soft peach-colored morning gown she wore looked well enough to disguise her slight pallor. Her hair had been dressed simply that morning, and it required only a touch with the comb. Unconsciously squaring her shoulders, she went down to the small parlor.

Richard was looking grave as she entered, but his face softened to a warm smile at her entrance. She offered him her hand, saying, "This is an unexpected pleasure. It is your first visit to Wildehaven, is it not?"

He nodded. "Yes. The house is splendid and the land is in good heart. Lord Radford has earned his reputation as a good landowner. But I didn't come here to talk about Wildehaven." He stopped, apparently unsure how to continue.

"Yes?" Caroline prompted, seating herself on one of the brocade-covered chairs while her visitor chose another.

"I've taken a great liberty, Caroline. It is not irrevocable, but you may well be angry with me."

She raised her eyebrows in surprise. "Indeed?"

He gave her a rueful smile. "It might be easiest if you read this." He pulled a letter from inside his coat and handed it to her.

She opened it curiously. The paper was headed with the style and address of London's largest music publisher. Her eyes widened as she read:

Dear Mr. Dalton,
    We are delighted to be chosen as publishers of

the compositions you submitted. They are works of stunning power and virtuosity, equal to the very best of the modern European composers. I am particularly pleased that the man you represent is English-born; our island has produced few musicians of the top rank. We will be happy to comply with your principal's desire for anonymity; simply let us know what name or initials he wishes to use.

I think I can say with confidence that we will be honored to publish any future compositions. I hope you will be able to come to London soon to discuss the financial arrangements.

Your most obedient servant,
Silas Winford

"What does this mean?" she breathed, hardly believing.

"I copied the works you had left at Wargrave and sent them to Winford, saying only that they were by a wellborn person who desired privacy. If you truly do not wish them to be published, I can retrieve them for you. Though Mr. Winford would be sadly disappointed."

He looked at her earnestly, saying, "I understand your shyness, Caro, but your work deserves to be heard. The beauty of it can bring such joy to others. It need never affect your privacy. I know you will not need the money, but I hoped it would please you to share your work with others."

She looked at him, too moved to find the right words. "I can't believe someone would wish to publish my music. My friends have admired it, but of course they would feel bound to. I just can't believe . . ." She stopped and bent her head, feeling tears beginning to run down her cheeks. Her thoughts were jumbled in broken fragments; her father's anger, Signore Ferrante's encouragement, the nights when she lay awake with melodies dancing in her head, fitting themselves together in different patterns. It seemed incredible that an unknown expert really valued her work so much.

Ever practical, Richard handed her a clean handkerchief. She thought she felt a feather-light touch on her head as his hand withdrew, but wasn't sure. She wiped her eyes and looked up apologetically. "I'm sorry to be such a watering pot. I can never think what to say when I feel something strongly."

"Does this please you?" he said, watching her keenly.

She nodded. "Yes. I don't want my name on the music. Having people talk about me, criticize me for composing—that would be dreadful. I don't like to be noticed; indeed, it makes me very uncomfortable. I shan't make a very good peeress, I fear. But it means a great deal to me that others should care for my work."

Richard broke into a relieved smile. "Then I am forgiven?"

"Of course." She gave him a shining look as she started to feel the first tendrils of excitement. "I am just beginning to believe it." She stood up suddenly, then whirled in a circle, throwing her arms wide in an unladylike gesture. "In fact, I feel *wonderful!*"

Richard stood also, saying, "I will be going to London tomorrow for two or three days to complete the transaction. Mr. Chelmsford can accompany me to ensure that your interests are protected. I will contact you when I return."

Caroline stopped, her exhilaration dimming. "Wait for a moment. There is something I wish to give you." She hurried from the parlor and upstairs to her bedchamber. When she returned, she carried the sonata she had just written. Looking up at him shyly, she said, "This is not for publishing. I wrote it for you only." She turned and fled the room, unwilling to stay and see his reaction.

When Richard returned to Wargrave, he went immediately to the pianoforte to play the composition. The message came through as clearly as if it had been written in English, the gentle opening melody developing richer themes of great complexity, from innocence to love, with darker stirrings of lambent passion. There were joy and pain together, discovery and wonder, and the sonata ended in haunting echoes of loss. He sat at the instrument long after the final notes had faded into memory. When he finally rose, he knew what needed to be done. It only remained to discover how.

Chapter 12

There were two arrivals at Wildehaven that afternoon, both demanding Jason's reluctant attention. The first was Caroline's pianoforte, accompanied by a high-strung Italian gentleman who refused to consign it into the hands of a mere butler. It was a magnificent instrument, made by the great Broadwood himself, and its escort insisted on seeing that it would be properly appreciated. Faintly amused even through his black depression, Jason had Caroline summoned to oversee the installation and tuning.

While the Italian gentleman chattered delightedly to this satisfactorily musical lady, Jason was observing her very carefully. He was forced to admit that Jessica might be correct in her assessment of her niece's emotions. This was not the same shy child he had met at Almack's a bare two months before. She had a grave dignity about her, a confident womanly beauty. And she no longer shrank from him.

He was turning to quietly withdraw from the salon when Caroline began to play. He had heard the piece before at some musicale, but this time its lyrical passion affected him as music had never done before. When she had finished, the Italian, for once bereft of words, kissed her hand in genuine awe. Jason quietly asked, "What was that, Caroline?"

The deep blue eyes had looked directly into his. "It is by Ludwig van Beethoven, and is from the Moonlight Sonata. Did you enjoy it?"

He nodded, unwilling to describe how deeply it had resonated within his newly lacerated heart. Moved in spite of himself, he had an insight into what music meant to Caroline. Ironic that such understanding came at the same moment he was wishing her at Jericho. The world was entirely too complicated, he thought glumly as he retreated once more to his study.

The second intrusion of his privacy was occasioned by the long-awaited arrival of his Aunt Honoria. Lady Edgeware, after a token diatribe against the roads and a few acid comments on changes made in Wildehaven since her last visit, retreated to her chamber to rest before dinner. Jason could only be grateful, though he expected she was sharpening her tongue so she could do justice to dismembering his houseguests. The evening was to prove him correct.

The vicious ache at Jessica's temples gave her ample reason to avoid dinner, but she chose to go down. She had decided to leave Wildehaven as soon as the Hanscombes arrived, but would be unable to avoid seeing Jason a few more times.

Dressing for dinner, she found herself regretting her love of clothes: her heavy heart could not begin to live up to the dashing image in the mirror. The dark teal-blue evening dress was the most subdued one she owned; unfortunately, it had an extremely low-cut *décolletage*, and the color enhanced the brilliance of her auburn tresses while turning her green eyes to turquoise. But no other gown would be better, so she resigned herself and went next door to collect her niece.

As they joined the two men in the small salon, she couldn't help noticing what a dour party they were. Jason was at his most sardonic, Caroline was withdrawn in distant silence, and Jessica thought she herself must look cold and forbidding.

Only George Fitzwilliam showed a semblance of normality, manfully searching for topics that would draw some response from his companions. His struggles ended when the dowager Lady Edgeware swept in, resplendent in a purple turban with three nodding ostrich plumes. She had obviously recovered from her journey and was eager for victims. Jason hadn't mentioned her arrival and now took an unholy pleasure in watching his guests girding themselves for battle.

George blanched as she looked at him dismissively and said, "I'll never understand what you see in this nodcock, nevvy. All the Fitzwilliams have attics to let."

"But such good *ton*, Aunt Honoria," Jason murmured.

Naturally interested in her future niece, she then fixed Caroline with a gimlet eye, examining her from head to foot before barking, "So this is the chit. You look a milk-and-water miss to me. Do you have enough bottom to deal with a Kincaid, girl?"

Caroline flinched but her eye didn't drop under the examination. "I shall certainly try my best, Lady Edgeware."

"Trying isn't good enough. If you haven't produced an heir within a twelvemonth, you'll have *me* to answer to."

Impressed that his betrothed had not collapsed

under a stare capable of rendering strong men craven, Jason intervened to drawl. "Surely I would also bear some responsibility for that."

"Nonsense. The Kincaids have always been a lusty lot, unless the blood has run thin in you." She glared at her nephew as if daring him to proclaim his virility, but wisely changed her target before he actually could.

Turning to Jessica, she narrowed her eyes in concentration before saying triumphantly, "The Incomparable Miss Westerly, spring of '03. Married a red-coated rattle and disappeared. What are you doing here?"

Fearing Jessica might react badly to such bald description of her much-mourned husband, Caroline hastily said, "Lady Edgeware, may I present my aunt, Mrs. Sterling?"

Her ladyship waved her hand impatiently at Caroline. "No need. I remember her clearly from her come-out. Are you still a hoyden, girl?"

Jessica lifted her chin and said coolly, "Yes. And I see you are still rude."

Lady Edgeware surprised the group with a cackle of laughter. "Of course I am. Not many other pleasures left at my age. Glad to see the spirit hasn't been crushed out of you. Your behavior was quite improper for a gel of seventeen years—much like mine at the same age. If you live as long as I, you'll end up much like me, terrorizing your descendants for sport."

A faint smile playing over her lips, Jessica replied, "Perhaps. But I hope I will be able to find other amusements."

While the rest of the party watched in fascination, Lady Edgeware led Jessica into a corner and started a cheerfully malicious monologue that lasted through the ensuing meal and obviated the need for anyone else to converse.

When the ladies withdrew after dinner, she spent some time grilling Caroline about her family and health, approving of her Westerly connections ("a much better stable than the Hanscombes") but clicking her tongue over the news that her mother had died after producing a mere daughter.

At that, Caroline had opened her eyes wide and pointed out that a similar performance on her part would clear the way for a second wife to attempt an heir. Lady Edgeware gave her a sharp glance, unsure whether the girl was serious or was poking fun at the inquisition. Met by Caroline's look of blameless innocence, she transferred her attention back to Jessica. By the time the tea tray arrived, her ball had been set for the night of the full moon on Friday week, and Jessica had been conscripted as chief assistant for planning and logistics.

The party broke up early that evening, Lady Edgeware having tired and none of the others showing much interest in general conversation. When they reached their bedchambers, Caroline invited her aunt in with the promise of good news. Jessica followed willingly, thinking it was time something good happened, though she wasn't sure she wanted to hear that her niece had formed a lasting passion for Lord Radford.

Instead, Caroline perched on the bed and shyly handed her the letter from the music publishers. Her aunt read it twice, then leaned over and gave her a hug. "Caro, this is wonderful! I assume that Richard Dalton sent your compositions to Winford?"

Caroline nodded. "Yes, I'm glad he didn't ask me

first. I would never have had the confidence to submit anything. But it makes me very happy to know a stranger truly likes my work."

Jessica joined her niece on the bed, her eyes dancing as she said, "Did you think Signore Ferrante and I would endanger our immortal souls by lying about how good your music is?"

"I didn't precisely think you were lying," Caroline laughed. "But I did assume some bias." She frowned slightly in concentration, then said, "I knew my compositions were good for an amateur. The surprise is that they can be considered good on the level of serious musicians."

"But you have always been serious about music, Caro," her aunt objected.

"To be serious does not automatically make one good," her niece said rather dryly. She lay back on the bed, her voice taking on a dreamy note. Jessica could not see her face as she continued, "So much has happened lately, Jess. I am a whole different person than I was three months ago."

Her aunt kept a light tone as she asked, "A better or worse person?"

"Better, I think," Caroline answered seriously. "More understanding, wiser I hope, and much, *much* older."

Jessica gave a throaty chuckle and said, "Oh, to be twenty-one again and to *know* I was grown up!"

Caroline giggled. "I do sound rather pompous, don't I? But surely, the fact that I didn't bolt out of the room under Lady Edgeware's interrogation is a sign of mature strength."

"By that standard, I must be a century-old Hercules."

Caroline sat up and looked appropriately apologetic. "You were so brave. You have my sincerest sympathy on having taken her dragonship's fancy."

"Oh, she's not so bad now that I know she doesn't despise me. Though it is a lowering thought to reflect that she may be right about my ending up like her."

"Never," Caroline said firmly. "You are forceful as needed, but you have a kind heart. I misdoubt Lady Edgeware does."

"You must accustom yourself to thinking of her as Aunt Honoria," Jessica said maliciously.

"Heaven forfend!" Caroline gave a ladylike shriek and rolled over on the bed, grabbing a pillow to bury her head under.

Jessica reached over to peel off the pillow. "One must take the bad with the good. As Lady Radford, you will be gaining much more than you lose."

Caroline looked suddenly sad, her playfulness gone as quickly as it had come. "I will strive to remember that."

Richard returned from London late Sunday night after a hard ride. His leg aching from the strain, he took a glass of brandy and retired to a long dreamless sleep. He felt unreasonably refreshed the next morning, and wondered if his well-being stemmed from a sense of coming home. He firmly repressed the thought; he wasn't quite ready to make that decision.

Besides finalizing the contract with Caroline's publisher, he had taken time in London to discuss his legal options with Chelmsford. He was leaning toward making a private settlement with the Wargrave estate that would give him one of the smaller unentailed properties with enough cash to make it viable, and leaving the title and the rest of the estate to Reginald Davenport. He doubted his cousin would object, since the alternative would leave Reggie without a feather to fly with.

Richard had been bemused to learn that his cousin's sole income was an allowance from the estate that had been paid even though he and the old earl had been at outs for years. That knowledge had contributed to Richard's feeling that he himself was not cut out to be an English aristocrat; they didn't seem to act like normal people.

After breakfasting, he rode over to the village church to set a plan in motion. His eyes took several moments to adjust to the dim light as he walked down the aisle in search of Reverend Chandler. It was the sound of stifled sobs that drew his attention to the figure kneeling in the small Lady chapel to his left. He hesitated, uncertain whether to pass in silence or offer what comfort he could. Reluctant to walk away, he stepped into the chapel.

Lady Helen Chandler raised her head from the railing and turned to him, tears running down the proud hawk face. Richard handed her his linen handkerchief, reflecting that he had seen more than his share of distraught ladies recently. She pressed it against her eyes for a few moments, then said in a steady voice, "My daughter would have been fifty years old today."

"Would have been, Lady Helen?" Richard questioned gently. If she wished to release some old sorrow, it would not be the first such tale he had heard.

The old woman nodded. "I am sure she is dead these last three years. But I had not seen her for thirty."

Richard felt a faint prickly uneasiness at the base of

his skull, but his voice was still calm as he asked, "Had she married and moved to a foreign country?"

She said in a distant voice, "In effect. But the tragedy is that she was forced from her home. I hold much of the blame for her leaving. For many years I had hoped I would see her again, to beg her forgiveness. I felt in my heart she was well, and I think happy. Then three years ago my sense of her ended, and I knew she would never come home again."

Richard said nothing, torn by the shadow of old tragedy that combined with his own growing speculation. But Lady Helen needed no encouragement: she had a compulsion to talk, the story pouring out of her in a spate of words.

"My daughter was nineteen, and a lovely young girl. A crony of my first husband's wished to marry her. We both approved, but Mary wanted nothing to do with him. She was in love with a young man she had grown up with. A rather wild young man, I thought."

Lady Helen grimaced. "It is one of the ironies of the story that I preferred Lord Barford for her because I myself had married a childhood sweetheart and could not say it was a success. Were it not for my son and daughter, I would have left Randall and be damned to the scandal."

She drew a deep breath and continued, "Mary wept and pleaded with me, but I was convinced she would be best off married to a solid, mature man who could take care of her. The boy she wanted, Julius, was scarcely a year older than she, a younger son with no prospects. So I in my pride, my wisdom, coerced my daughter into a betrothal with a man she loathed. As it turned out, her instincts were far sounder than my 'wisdom.' Had I known of Lord Barford what I learned later, I would not have let him in the same room with Mary, much less used my authority to force a marriage. But it is one of those conspiracies men have, keeping information from women. Barford was corrupt and vicious, attracted by Mary's sweetness because he desired to destroy it. He had been married long before. His wife hanged herself."

Richard was cold with a chill deeper than the sunless stones of the church. Here at last was the full story of why his parents had left England, and he hoped he was strong enough to bear it. "It sounds as if you acted from the best motives."

Lady Helen made a sharp, angry gesture with her hand. "Intentions are not good enough. I tried to guide my daughter's life, and it caused a tragedy. One I will never atone for."

"Would your husband have forced the marriage even without your cooperation?"

She lifted her head with the ghost of old pride. "No. I am the daughter of an earl. I had influence, some fortune of my own. He could not have prevailed against me and my family's consequence.

"My son, Robert, supported his sister. He was much of an age with Julius, and they were close friends. But I no more listened to him than to Mary. Instead . . ." she paused, then said doggedly, "I warned my husband that I feared she might elope. She was too docile. I couldn't believe she had given up so easily.

"We were staying in our London town house a fortnight before the wedding. My fine husband was drinking late one night with Barford. I am not sure of the details, but apparently he said Mary might run away before the ceremony. Barford suggested that he should make her his that very night. After all, they were betrothed, as good as married. It was no great crime to anticipate the ceremony, and it would prevent the girl from ruining herself by an elopement. Besides, what other man would want her after he had taken her?"

Lady Helen's voice changed, becoming taut with anger. "And so her father, who should have been her natural protector, stood by and watched his daughter raped in her own home. I was asleep in the opposite wing and heard nothing, but I heard later that the servants in the attic above were wakened by her screams. When he was done with her, somehow she found the strength to escape. She left the house before Barford and my husband realized her intent. She ran bleeding and barefoot through the streets in her shift. Thank God the house where Julius had lodgings was only a few blocks away, and nothing worse befell her on the way over."

Oblivious of her present surroundings, Lady Helen had turned her eyes to her inner vision as she continued in a hoarse whisper, "I learned the rest of this from my son, Robert, who was with Julius Davenport. Mary pounded on the door, crying hysterically. Julius ran down to let her in and she poured out the whole story on his front steps as he held her. Barford and my husband came up then and tried to take her away."

She gave a faint smile, a smile of vengeance satisfied. "They fought a duel right there in the streets, by torchlight. My son stood second to Julius, my husband to Barford. Barford chose swords. He was reputed to be one of the best duelists in England, but young Julius was better. Apparently he could have killed Barford quickly, but he didn't. Instead he played cat and mouse, slashing him, causing him to bleed from a dozen wounds. In a proper duel it would have been stopped, but my son wouldn't interfere and my husband didn't dare."

She stopped for long moments. Her voice was a whisper as she said, "Finally Julius had enough of butchery and stabbed Barford through the heart. He turned to my husband and said the only reason he wouldn't kill him too was to avoid distressing Mary further. Then they went inside. Robert had been holding Mary throughout the duel; he said she refused to leave."

Lady Helen shrugged. "The next morning Julius and Mary were gone from his house. Robert came and told me what had happened and said they were leaving England. My son and I left my husband's house that day, never to return. I received a short note from Julius several months later, saying they were married, Mary was well, and neither would ever set foot in England again.

"I bought a house near here, thinking if they ever came back, they would visit Wargrave. Even that was a faint hope. Julius' father, the Earl of Wargrave, had not gotten on with the boy for years, and now he publicly disowned him. The full story was hushed up, but enough was known to cause a ghastly scandal."

"How did you come to where you are now, Lady Helen?" Richard asked the question almost absently as he studied the face of his grandmother.

This time when she smiled there was peace in the expression. "God was good to me. Reverend Chandler helped me come to terms with my guilt. He and I were widowed about the same time. Eventually we married and have been happy these fifteen years. My son is Lord Randall now, with his main estate a dozen miles east. He married whom he chose and is content with his life. You can be sure I cast no rub in his way."

"So you learned by your mistakes. That is no small thing."

She sighed, sadness returning to her eyes. "Perhaps not." Her eyes sharpened on the captain. "Why am I telling you this? Reverend Chandler is the only one I have ever told before."

Richard crossed and knelt by the railing a scant foot away from her. "Your heart knows why. Look at me."

Her faded blue eyes widened as she examined him closely. "Who are you?" she breathed as wonder dawned on her face. "Is it possible . . . ?" She stopped, unable to continue.

Richard completed the thought for her. "I am the son of Julius Davenport and Mary Randall. And you are the grandmother I never knew I had."

"Had it not been for the vanity of not wearing my spectacles, I would have known you before," she said with ironic amusement. "You are very like your father, but I see my Mary in your face as well. Tell me about her."

So he described the life they had shared across Europe, the sailing death in Greece, ending with, "She was the happiest woman I ever knew, with love to spare for everyone who crossed her path. It is possible the unusual closeness she had with my father was born from the pain their marriage began in. They both had the gift of living in the present day. I can understand now why she had no wish to look back, but I would swear on the sanctuary Bible that she had no anger or resentment against you."

The old lady closed her eyes, a sparkle of moisture

on her cheeks. "Thank you," she said softly. "I want very much to believe that.

"And you, young man," she continued, her eyes now open and worldly, "are the new Earl of Wargrave."

"Not yet, and probably never. I am nearly decided to take a small estate near the south coast, and leave the rest to my cousin Reginald Davenport. He wants it, I don't. I can't say that consequence and money seem to have made any of my relations very happy."

"But . . ." she started to protest, then smiled dryly. "The lesson of minding my own business is one I must teach myself over and over. You will stay in England? I don't have so many grandchildren that I would wish to lose any."

He smiled and took her hand. "I promise you I shall stay in touch, no matter what transpires. In return, I ask you to keep my secret from everyone except your husband and son until matters have been resolved. In fact, I would ask a favor of you. I came here to ask permission to use the organ. Not for myself, but a . . . friend of mine might wish to soon."

"That is easily arranged," she said briskly as she rose from the chapel railing. "There is an extra key to the organ loft in my husband's office. I will get it for you now."

She stood on tiptoe, placing her hands on his shoulders and brushing his cheek with her lips. Her voice was soft again as she said, "Thank you for bringing my Mary back to me." She turned and was quickly gone.

After receiving the key, Richard headed back to Wargrave Park. Halfway through the home wood he stopped, found a tree trunk to sit on, and let his feelings about the recent interview loose; he hadn't dared in front of Lady Helen. The thought of his gentle, loving mother raped by a vile old man . . . He took a fallen branch and methodically broke it to pieces with explosive violence. The one consolation was knowing his father had been amply qualified to avenge the crime.

Julius had been a brilliant swordsman, and often taught the art to young sprigs of the nobility in cities where they had lived. Though Richard much resembled his father physically, his disposition was more like his calm, slow-to-anger mother's. But on a few memorable occasions he had lost his temper with a violence and thoroughness that would have done justice to his intense and volatile father. It was always instances of innocent people being threatened that roused his fury; perhaps on some unconscious level he had sensed what happened to his mother. In this, his rage was thirty years too late.

After a few minutes of giving vent to his anger, he threw the fragments of wood away and drew a deep calming breath. It would be some time before he came to terms with what he had just learned; turning branches into flinders did not begin to release the rage he felt. But his parents had learned to live with the past, and he could do no less.

At the moment, it was more pertinent to consider his new relatives: a grandmother of distinction, worthy of respect and eventually love; a step-grandfather of saintly disposition; an unknown uncle and cousins he would surely like. Robert had already won his allegiance by championing his mother.

The Davenport side of the register was less prepossessing, but even Reginald had his worthwhile moments. After three years of being absolutely alone in the world, it was strange to think a whole network of people and relationships were waiting for him. But cousins or even grandparents were not what concerned him now. What he really wanted was a wife.

Caroline pushed herself back from the writing desk, checked the clock, and stretched her cramped fingers. It was time to make her escape. For the last three days, Lady Edgeware had kept her busy writing invitations to the ball and making lists of things to do. If Lady Edgeware was a general in the social wars and Caroline was a line trooper, Jessica at least qualified as a major. Many of her ideas on refreshments and decorations had been reluctantly accepted as worthy. Caroline was as amused to listen to the genteel skirmishing as she was appalled to realize she would be expected to participate on a future occasion. At the moment they were discussing whether it would be paltry to have a mere twenty dishes in each course of the dinner that would be served before the ball.

On the previous day, Caroline had received a note from Richard, inviting her to the Wargrave parish church to play some organ music he had found in the music library. She had not felt like discussing the note even with Jessica, so now she said a few vague words about going for a walk as she wafted out of the room. Her gift for slipping away unnoticed stood her in good stead; they barely noticed she was gone.

She was so eager for the meeting that she was halfway to the church before noticing that the long spell of fair weather seemed about to end. The sky was filling with dark clouds while the air hung heavy and motionless. She shrugged; if she went back for a cloak, she would be late, as well as running the risk of being caught again in the party preparations. It wouldn't hurt her to get wet, and every moment spent with Richard was precious because it might be the last. He was coming to the ball in four days, but that hardly counted; as guest of honor, she could do little beyond greeting him. Propriety and marriage would be catching up with her very soon, and she would no longer be free.

He was sitting on a bench by the side door when she reached the church. When he rose and gave her his warm, intimate smile, she wished time could stop right there, holding her in this moment of happiness. It was easy to pretend he felt as pleased to see her as she was to see him.

"I'm glad you could get away," he said as he took her hand. "I wanted to give you the publisher's agreement and the bank draft for your compositions. Mr. Chelmsford and I have devised a way for you to handle all your business through him without exposing your identity. You may choose another business representative if you like, but you know Mr. Chelmsford and he is an honest man. Is he acceptable?"

She let go of his hand reluctantly. "That will be fine. I liked him very much. I never thought to make money from my work, so anything is a bonus." She paused, then continued shyly, "Is there really any organ music or was that a ruse to get me here?"

"Not at all. Look what I found." He handed her several sheets of music. She knit her brows and asked, "Johann Sebastian Bach. Is he related to Johann Christian Bach?"

Richard nodded. "His father. Apparently there have been many generations of Bach musicians in the Germanic states. Johann Sebastian is not so well kn this country as his son, but if this sounds as I imagine it, he is surely as fine a composer."

She studied the score with rising enthusiasm. "Toccata and Fugue in D Minor. Not an exciting title, but it looks wonderful. Let's try it!"

After unlocking the organ loft, Richard went behind the instrument to pump the bellows that produced the necessary volume of air. Caroline forgot his presence as she warmed up, gaining a feel for the splendid instrument the last Countess of Wargrave had donated.

After a few minutes, she attacked the music—and "attack" was surely the best word. It began with a magnificent explosion of sound that caused every stone in the old church to vibrate in harmony. She had always loved the organ and frequently played at services in the parish church in Wiltshire. It was immensely satisfying to let her performing instincts loose on a work of such incredible power. After the splendid climax of Mr. Bach's masterpiece, she moved into an equally dramatic rendition of Handel's "Messiah," and ended her concert with "A Mighty Fortress Is Our God." She was in a mood for the Church Militant, and the energy of the music left her in a state of exhilaration.

Leaving the loft to join Richard, she stopped halfway down the stairwell in shock. An audience had collected in front of her, and they looked as if they would have applauded if they were not in a church. Th̶ ̶̶derly vicar was nearest, with a distinguished-̶ ̶ ̶ older woman at his side. Several women ̶ ̶ ̶ servants were in the back of the church, ̶ ̶ ̶ dozen people who might have been ̶ ̶ ̶ ̶wn in by the music. She was blushing ̶ ̶ ̶ the options for flight when the vicar stepped up to her and said, "Thank you, child. I am not sure whether that was man talking to God, or God talking to man, but it was a blessing to hear. I hope you will come and play here often."

She murmured a few words of thanks, nodded at her audience, and took Richard's arm with relief as he came forward. "Do you wish to escape?" he asked understandingly.

"Please!" She didn't fully relax until they were a quarter-mile from the church. "I'm sorry to be so idiotish," she said with an apologetic shrug as they walked toward Wildehaven. "I hate being the center of attention, especially so unexpectedly."

Richard chuckled at her expression. "You don't find it gratifying to be regarded with awe?"

"No, I really don't," she said slowly. "If I have any special musical gifts—"

"Which you do, to a remarkable degree."

Ignoring his interruption, she continued, "Any special gift I have is something I was born with. I no more deserve credit for that than I do for having blue eyes. It makes me uncomfortable to be regarded as superior for what is an accident of nature."

He reached out to guide her around a branch that she nearly walked into as she expounded. "All the talent in the world would be meaningless if you hadn't worked hard. How many thousands of hours have you spent studying, practicing, and composing?"

"But that was not work," she protested. "I enjoy it."

"In other words," he said with a twinkle, "we deserve esteem only when we have suffered?"

"It does sound a bit silly when you say it like that." She laughed. "But I do feel the honor belongs higher being than I. Do you understand what

ing to say? I have never tried to put this into words; I
just know that I dislike being singled out."

He nodded. "I think I understand. And I also think
you are a remarkably unegotistical young woman,
Caroline Hanscombe."

"Now, don't be too impressed with *that!*" she said.
"It is something else I was born with."

Absorbed in their conversation, neither had noticed
how the sky was darkening. Now a thunderclap broke
almost directly over their heads, accompanied by a
torrent of drenching rain. Richard took a quick glance
around, then said, "There's a gamekeeper's hut just
over there. We can take shelter until this is over." Taking her hand, he led her down an embankment to the
left.

Laughing and trying to brush wet hair from her eyes
with her free hand, Caroline paid little attention to her
footing. When she tripped on an exposed root, she lost
her balance and stumbled out of control down the
bank. Richard turned quickly and scooped her out of
the air before she could fall, catching her against his
chest to steady them both.

Still laughing, she looked up into the face inches
above hers. Suddenly breathless, she locked her gaze
into his searching hazel eyes. With the air of someone
throwing caution to the winds, he bent and claimed
her lips with the urgency of a man who had too long
suppressed his desires.

only experience of kisses had been Jason's
ute on their engagement and the clumsy ex-
a neighbor boy when they were both thir-
as totally, unequivocally different. She
asp of pleasure, instinctively opening
th his and pressing the whole length

of her body against him. She could feel the pounding of his heart against her breast, and the contrast between his burning warmth and the chill of her saturated muslin dress was unforgettably erotic.

She slid her arms behind him, reveling in the feel of his broad shoulders, the hard muscles rippling as he enfolded her more tightly. One of his hands was doing indescribably wonderful things along her spine while the other cradled her head. Leaving her lips, his mouth moved across her cheek with leisurely skill, kissing away the raindrops. She exhaled sharply in delight when he reached her ear and delicately ran his tongue along the edge. Brought back to reality by the small sound, he loosened his hold, stepping back while keeping her within the circle of his arms.

"Please, don't stop," she entreated. Her senses were completely focused on this moment, the fury of the rain echoing the rising passions of her own body. The physical intensity was completely new to her, and it possessed her as utterly as the blazing needs of her music would sometimes possess her mind. Her identity as Caroline, her engagement and family obligations, were not so much forgotten as meaningless. The two of them seemed alone in the world, as primal as Adam and Eve.

"If I don't stop now," he said with a shaky laugh, "I don't think I will be able to. Then we will both be in the suds. If we don't drown first. Come along, lady mine."

He inclined his head and touched her lips in a kiss as full of promise as the previous ones had been full of passion. Pulling off his jacket, he held it above their heads as he quickly guided them the last fifty yards to the hut. The unlocked door opened to a room simply furnished with a wooden table and bench, plus a storage cabinet and a small fireplace. The rain battered the thin roof and coursed down the one dim window.

Steering her to the bench, he draped his coat around her, then scooped her onto his lap. His encircling arms protected her from the damp chill and created the greatest sense of warmth and security she had ever known. She laid her head on his shoulder, as mindlessly happy as a kitten cuddled against its dam.

Silence and harmony reigned until Richard tenderly brushed the wet curls from her face and said, "We must talk, Caro. The rain won't last too long, and there is much to be said."

She gave a purring sound and burrowed closer to his chest, reluctant to face the problems that lay just outside the shelter of his arms. He traced the line of her jaw with his forefinger and said softly, "Each man carries an image of his perfect love in his heart. When I first saw you, I knew you were my own impossible dream come true. I have loved you from that moment.

"At least," he said with an involuntary chuckle, "I fell in love with you as soon as I determined that you weren't an angel."

She straightened up in surprise. "You thought I was an angel?"

He smiled reminiscently. "It seemed possible. You were the most beautiful creature I had ever seen, golden-haired, surrounded by a halo of light, and playing a harp. Much too lovely and ethereal for the mundane world."

Stroking her cheek, he continued, "And unless I have totally misunderstood the sonata you wrote for me, you love me too."

She looked at him shyly, her blue eyes meeting his

hazel ones without flinching. "I do. It was impossible for me to say it aloud, so I spoke my heart in the way I know best. I . . . I love you more than any of my words can say."

He pulled her to him for another kiss that disrupted rational conversation for some minutes. It ended when he lifted her again and deposited her on the bench a foot away from him, saying, "We will never get anywhere at this rate! I asked you out today primarily because it seemed bad manners to propose to you under your fiancé's roof."

She looked up at him, the happiness seeping from her face as the impossible situation returned to her. He touched her lips with a gentle finger and said, "The only solution for us is that you break your engagement to Lord Radford. I watched you from the beginning, and I saw no sign that you loved him. If anything, you seemed wary. Has he been unkind to you?"

"Oh, no! No!" she said quickly. "It is true that I was frightened of him at first, but that was my own foolishness. He has never been anything but generous and honorable. But . . . but . . ." She stopped, unable to continue, her eyes drowning pools of anguish.

"What is wrong?" he asked quietly.

"I *can't* break my engagement. I must marry him!"

Richard's face was very still. "Why?"

"It . . . it is the money," she stammered.

"It is true that I haven't the fortune Lord Radford does, but I promise I can keep you in comfort. I think I will be acquiring a small estate on the south coast. It would be the quiet life of a country squire, but there should be money for an occasional trip to London and perhaps the Continent to see what other musicians are doing."

Her gaze held his as she said quietly, "I could ask no happier life than, what you would offer me. But it is not only my desires that count. My father is . . . in great financial difficulty. Lord Radford made a settlement that takes care of his problems and ensures the future of my younger brothers and sisters. And . . . my father would have forbidden my sister Gina's marriage to the man she loves if I didn't accept Lord Radford's offer."

He reached over and squeezed her hand sympathetically. "My poor little love! I suspect your own needs have always given way to others. Is Lord Radford in love with you?"

A furrow appeared between her brows as she frowned slightly. "I don't know. I suppose he must be, for there would be no other reason for him to have offered. But I do not understand him at all. I have never felt love from him."

Richard was silent. He had known of rich men who were collectors, acquiring rare and precious objects for the simple joy of possession. Such a man might easily want Caroline, for her delicate beauty and talent. It could be considered a kind of love, but not one to warm the heart or soul. He had seen Caroline blossoming in these last weeks. If Radford were the sort to consider his wife a bloodless treasure, she would dwindle to a pale and unhappy shadow.

"Do you want me to speak to him?"

She considered, then shook her head slowly. "It is very tempting, but . . . it is too soon, I . . . I need time. My spirit is at war. I want to be with you more than I've ever wanted anything, but there are so many others involved. How can I turn my back on them? And I gave my promise to Jason as well."

He made no attempt to touch her. "It is your honor, and you must decide. But when you are weighing everyone's welfare, pray do not forget mine."

She gave him a forlorn look. "And if I decide I must go through with the marriage?"

The hazel eyes were steady. "I will leave here. I could not bear to see you belonging to another man."

Her heart felt as if it were being torn into bleeding shreds. She stood abruptly. "It is time to go. Will you be coming to the ball on Friday?"

He stood also, looking down at her gravely. "Yes. I will be here until you accept me or send me away."

She nodded, then walked out the door. The cloudburst had ended and pallid sunshine shafted down through the trees as showers of droplets shook from the leaves. She pulled Richard's coat around her, shivering with a chill that had nothing to do with temperature. The rest of her life was in her hands, and she feared that her strength was not equal to the challenge.

Chapter 13

The Hanscombes' descent on Wildehaven late Wednesday afternoon signaled the start of two days of upheaval. Lady Hanscombe and Lady Edgeware circled each other like wary cats on neutral territory. Gina threw herself into her sister's arms, bubbling with happy chatter, while her fiancé, Gideon, followed her around like a love-struck moonling. Sir Alfred eyed the rich acres and fabulous stables with barely concealed cupidity, elated at the prospect of such a rich son-in-law.

Jason steeled himself against the invasion with tight-lipped politeness. While Caroline's relations might be vulgar, he could be grateful that she wasn't. Not for the first time, he gave thanks that his mad wager hadn't produced a really disastrous bride. He could not even blame her for standing between him and Jessica; had it not been for the betrothal, he would never have found his love again. The pain of losing her a second time lay just under the surface of his iron control, but a thread of peace was woven through. There was comfort in finally understanding why she left, and knowing she loved him as intensely as he loved her. It was a feeble thing to support him for a lifetime.

As Jason pointed out to George Fitzwilliam over a

late brandy on Thursday night, he had won the basic principle of their bet: his fortune and title had easily gained him a randomly chosen bride. George cheerfully conceded the point; he cared little for abstract ideas. His chief problem at the moment was deciding whether he should be more enamored of Caroline or Jessica. On the whole, Caroline's imminent marriage made her a safer choice; with Jessica, there existed at least a possibility that his passion might not remain unrequited. He sighed romantically and said, "You're a lucky dog, Jason. Perhaps the hand of the Divine was at work when you made your wager."

Jason raised an eyebrow ironically and replied, "What is that cryptic remark supposed to signify?"

"Why, that you and your exquisite bride were Destined for Each Other. Since your paths might never have crossed under ordinary circumstances, the bet was part of a Higher Plan." His soulful look was composed of equal parts sentiment and brandy.

Jason snorted disdainfully, half-amused, half-pained. If a Higher Power had involved itself, it showed a damned unpleasant sense of humor to bring Jessica so close while keeping her out of his grasp. "You have been reading too much Byron."

His friend looked hurt. "One could hardly find a better leg shackle than Caroline! Her beauty, her grace, her sweetness of disposition . . . why, she is a diamond of the first water!"

Jason suddenly felt very tired. The face he saw in his dreams was not that of a paragon—merely the most vital, lovable woman he had ever known. "Perhaps you should marry her yourself."

The offer was not quite a jest. If it was money Sir Alfred wanted, George Fitzwilliam had more than enough. But the problem was not the money. It was Caroline's ill-timed passion for himself that was causing her aunt's regrettable attack of nobility.

Even half-disguised, George was not about to fall into that trap. He looked sorrowful and said, "Not fit to touch the hem of her dress. Content to worship her from afar."

Fortunately, Lady Edgeware entered the study before the conversation could deteriorate any further into mawkishness. George almost choked on his brandy as he struggled to his feet, since even drink could not destroy his manners.

She waved a hand in his direction. "You needn't rise on my account. Unless of course you are about to retire?" The last sentence was accompanied with a meaningful glare that had the hapless George mumbling his goodnights and fleeing the room in less than sixty seconds.

Jason watched his friend's rout with a dry half-smile. "I can only hope you are not persecuting my servants as much as my friends. Would you like something to drink?"

Her ladyship lowered herself into the still-warm chair so recently vacated. "I'll have some of the brandy you hide away from your guests."

Her nephew silently poured the dark amber fluid into a glass and passed it to her. She took a deep swallow and sighed in satisfaction while Jason watched her through narrowed eyes. Since there was a decanter of the same brandy in her room whenever she visited, it seemed unlikely she had come merely to drink. She obviously wanted to discuss something but showed uncharacteristic hesitation to do so. Suddenly bored, he prompted her, "Did you wish to say something to me? A comment on my land management perhaps? Or a criticism of my politics?"

Her chin came up sharply and she glared at him. "It's your marriage I want to talk about! Are you really going to marry that child?"

He raised a dangerous eyebrow. "You disagree with my choice? I have done exactly what you wished—found a healthy young woman of respectable birth to carry on the Kincaid line."

She scowled. "It's not her birth that is deficient. It's her spirit."

He found himself defending her. "She has strengths and resources that I doubt you have seen yet."

"She's too soft for you, boy—you'll be bored in a week. Someone like that aunt of hers would be much more in your style."

Jason felt as if a fist had slammed into his stomach. Had Honoria noticed something in their behavior? Still, it was an excuse to talk about Jessica. "She's a glorious creature but what makes you think she is my 'style'? She said once that you disapproved of her more than any other woman in London."

"She was a headstrong wench but she's grown into a woman of character. She'll stand up to you, make you think." His aunt took another draft of brandy, then added in a neutral tone, "Besides, I've seen how you look at her when you think you are unobserved."

"Are you proposing I jilt my betrothed to marry her chaperon? A fine scandal that would make!"

His aunt looked suddenly sad. "It would be quickly forgotten. A marriage of convenience is well enough if you have no special preference. But when Kincaids fall in love, we never get over it. I never did."

Jason felt acutely uncomfortable at his formidable

aunt's display of vulnerability. "I didn't know you considered love a worthwhile component of marriage."

She shrugged. "I never had a chance to find out for myself. When I met someone who made the blood shout in my veins, we were both married past redemption and found little joy in it. But it's not too late for you. Unless the fool woman won't have you."

"You exceed the limits allowed even to opinionated elderly relations," he said forbiddingly. He rose, downing the rest of his brandy in one gulp. "Can I see you to your room?"

"You may not," she said acidly. "I may be elderly and opinionated, but I am quite capable of finding my way around the house I grew up in."

He nodded indifferently. "In that case, I will see you on the morrow. Unless you are too foxed to show yourself then."

She banged her glass down on the polished mahogany table and glared after him as he left the study.

He left feeling mildly pleased at having scored at least one point on her, but a wave of depression prevailed by the time he went to bed. Even the brandy he had consumed could not still his restless twisting and turning. His mind tormented him with imaginings of how she would look in his bed, the glorious auburn sweep of hair patterned across his pillows, her arms open to receive him . . .

Knowing that she was under his own roof was wellnigh unendurable. He was still tossing at two in the morning when he was disturbed by a small sound at the door.

For a moment he permitted himself the fantasy that she had come to him, but the crazy hope died as the sound resolved itself into a scratching, accompanied by a distinct "Mre-oo-o-wp!"

He heaved out of the tangled covers and opened the door before Wellesley could do permanent injury to the carved panels. His unwelcome guest was half-grown now, no longer a kitten. The light of the nearly full moon was so bright in the hallway that he could see green glints in the hopeful eyes. He exhaled wearily and considered his options. He could leave the beast to cry and scratch at the door for the rest of the night. He could summon his mastiff Rufus and offer the cat for a snack. He could drop it from the window and find out if felines were as resilient as generally supposed.

"All right, then," he said. "Come on in. But mind you don't snore."

While having the cat in his bed in no way compared with having its mistress, there was comfort in lying there and hearing friendly purrs from a spot near his head. He rubbed his face once against the soft fur, then lay back and relaxed. In a few minutes they were both asleep.

Caroline Hanscombe was a badly frustrated young woman. For two days she had been attempting private speech with her father, with a singular lack of success. He kept slipping off to evaluate the Radford property, visit an old crony in the neighborhood, or absorb his host's port in breathtaking quantities, while Caroline spent much of Thursday and early Friday greeting guests arriving for the ball. Though Lady Edgeware was the official hostess, Caroline was the main object of attention and had to make herself continually avail-

able. It confirmed her in her belief that becoming a social lioness was not to her taste.

She determined to fight free of her unwanted engagement if at all possible, and had decided on her
strategy. First and most important, she must talk with
her father to find just how desperate his financial
straits were. She would offer him both her inheritance
from her mother and the money from the music publisher. The latter was not a great deal, but she was
preparing to send off a collection of quartets and trio
sonatas she thought would be acceptable and there
should be some profit from them.

Even if the money were enough to take care of the
worst problems, she knew her father would be reluctant to release her from her daughterly obligations—
she had seen his covetous examination of Wildehaven.
Therefore, the next vital step would be talking to Gina
about her engagement to Gideon. Would her father be
able to forbid the marriage even if he tried? Caroline
was hazy about the legalities but knew that settlement
papers had been signed. Perhaps that would protect
Gina.

And finally, she would have to speak to Jason. Socially it was acceptable for a female to end an engagement, though a man would be greatly censured for the
same act. Still, she owed him respect and gratitude
even if she didn't love him. How would she react if he
dropped his polished detachment and confessed that
he loved her? If he did indeed care, it would be shat-
teringly difficult to break the engagement. Only the
thought of Richard—the slow smile, the harmony of
their minds and interests, the sense of rightness—gave
her courage to go forward. If they were to be together,
it would have to be through her actions.

Midafternoon Friday had brought her no closer to her peripatetic parent, so she determined to accost him that night at the ball. After all, he would have to be in attendance for hours; at some point she would carry him off to a side room if she had to use brute force. Meanwhile, she had been packed off to her room to rest before the evening's festivities, so she invited her sister Gina in for a comfortable coze. It was their first chance for private speech and there was much to discuss.

Gina was as bouncy as ever but she had a new maturity and confidence; being in love suited her. Gideon's parents had welcomed her warmly and an August wedding date had been set. "And *then* we will take a wedding trip to Italy! Gideon has always wanted to go there, and since the war is over it is safe to travel. He says he would rather have me as a companion than *anyone!*"

"It sounds wonderfully romantic," Caroline smiled. "Do you think you will find antiquities interesting?"

"If Gideon was there to explain them to me, I would find"—she cast about for a suitable object—"*icebergs* interesting!"

Caroline hesitated, then decided it was time to introduce her questions. "Gina, if Papa were to get . . . difficult, would he be able to forbid your wedding?"

Her sister looked indignant at the thought. "He wouldn't dare!"

Caroline tried again. "But you know the odd fancies he gets. Suppose he took it into his head to say you couldn't marry Gideon. Could he do that when the settlements have been signed?"

"What a shatterbrained notion, Caro! If Papa tried any such foolishness, he'd go home by Weeping Cross. Neither Gideon nor his parents would permit him to back out of the contracts, and *I* certainly could not be persuaded to cry off. Besides"—her voice softened—"it is too late. Gideon and I are already one."

Caroline started at this artless piece of information. "Do you mean," she asked cautiously, "that Gideon has . . . ?" She stopped, unable to think of a sufficiently delicate way of asking for confirmation of her suspicions.

Gina nodded vigorously, half-shy and half-proud. "Yes, it is what you think. Although it would be more accurate to say that I caused it. My poor lamb was so determined to be a gentleman. I was shameless in my persuasions. It made no sense to wait," she said earnestly. "We wanted each other so much. You must know what I mean. Think of how you feel about Radford."

Caught off guard, Caroline blushed a violent crimson but she was saved from answering by Jessica's entrance into the bedchamber. Her aunt had heard the last part of Gina's speech, and she watched Caroline's reaction carefully. "Spare your sister's blushes, Gina," she said in an artificially bright tone. "She is not such a brazen piece as you or I."

Gina looked at Jessica and chuckled, one woman-of-the-world to another. "Not on the surface. But I daresay that behind her ladylike manner her thoughts have been the same as mine. Whose wouldn't be, with a man like Radford!"

If Jessica's smile became a trifle stiff, neither of the younger women noticed. Gina was rapt in lecherous fantasy and Caroline distressed by the implicit falseness of the situation. For a moment she was tempted to tell these two closest friends about Richard, but caution held her tongue. It would be unfair to burden them with her problems prematurely. There would be time enough to ask for comfort when the fat was in the fire.

"Actually, Caroline, I had another reason for coming in," Jessica said. "I have been missing Linda, and thought I would return to Wiltshire after the ball. Since Gina and your parents will be staying on, you will not lack for chaperonage."

Caroline looked at her aunt with a slight frown. Something felt off-key about the statement, but she couldn't quite put her finger on it. "Of course, if that is what you wish. I shall miss you, but I cannot keep you by me forever. Will you visit again soon?"

When hares fly! was Jessica's thought, but she said merely, "I will be at the wedding, of course. After that, we shall see. I am sure you and your husband will want to be alone at first."

She saw Caroline regarding her with unfathomable blue eyes. They had talked little but commonplaces since coming to Wildehaven. Falling in love was making each of them private—especially since it was with the same man. She swore once more that Caroline would never be hurt by a love affair that should have been over more than a dozen years before. In six months Jason would be totally absorbed with his lovely young bride, perhaps looking forward to the birth of a child. It would be harder for her, alone and aching. She only knew that she must remove herself and give them time to become truly wedded.

She continued, "I am going to lie down now, and I suggest you young ladies do the same. It is going to be a long night."

Her words were far more prophetic than she realized.

* * *

Not having been invited to the dinner at Wildehaven, Richard partook of a light meal before going to
the ball. There had been no contact with Caroline since
the day they were caught in the rainstorm, and he was
anxious to see her. Intuitively he felt matters were
nearing the crisis point, and he hoped he would be
near if she needed him. He was sure she loved him,
but the forces of family and society were ranged
against them. Many would be critical of his desire to
take her from a splendid match; his justification lay in
his belief that she would dislike being a fashionable
lady, and in his own driving need for her.

His thoughts troubled, he was unenthusiastic when
Reggie joined him for dinner; their paths seldom
crossed, even though they shared the same roof. His
cousin had been drinking and was in a surly mood.

"You were right about the Cornishman being off his
form in Bristol," he said abruptly, helping himself to
roast woodcock.

Richard pulled his mind back to the present and
said politely, "I'm glad I could be of service."

Reggie scowled. "Unfortunately, I didn't trust your
information and dropped some blunt on the match."

"A gambler and his money are soon parted," the
captain murmured.

His cousin glared at him. "I am sure you are too
much a dull dog to risk anything."

"Very true," Richard agreed as he pushed his plate
away. "I make it a rule never to bet material goods.
One's life is so much more interesting a stake."

"Are you saying I'm a coward for not going in the
Army?" Reggie snarled.

Richard was startled at the vehemence. Apparently

he had hit a nerve with his casual comment. "Not at all. I have heard many things about you, but never that you lacked bravery. There are any number of good reasons for avoiding the military that have nothing to do with courage."

Mollified, Reggie took a deep gulp of claret. "I wanted to join up," he confided, "but my dear uncle Wargrave would never permit it. He would pay my debts but never give me enough of the ready to buy a commission. And I didn't care to enlist as a common soldier." He stared into his glass, apparently brooding over how his life had gone wrong, then looked up suddenly, his eyes sharpening. "You are mighty fine tonight. Is there some entertainment in the neighborhood? It has been dashed dull around here."

"There is a ball at Wildehaven for Lord Radford's fiancée."

"Ah, yes. The pretty blond chit."

Richard remained silent, as any discussion of Caroline could rapidly lead to a fight if Reggie started making crude remarks.

Reggie took another drink. "If he had known I was in the neighborhood, Radford would have invited me from common courtesy. After all, we will be neighbors soon."

"You would know that better than I," Richard said. "I have never met the man."

"Devilish high in the instep." Reggie reached for the bottle and poured another glass as Richard bid him good night and left. By the time another bottle of claret had vanished down his throat, he was feeling belligerent about the ball. Damned bad manners of Radford to ignore him. Why, he was an earl, or almost. Outranked Radford. He would go anyway; Radford wouldn't have the audacity to throw him out. And it would be something to do in the endless boredom of country life.

Weaving slightly and bellowing for his valet, he went upstairs to change into evening dress.

After two hours of greeting guests at the entrance of the ballroom, Caroline felt as if her smile was chiseled in granite. She looked her best in a creamy silk dress with embroidered bands of forget-me-nots exactly matching her eyes. Betsy had contrived a simple tiara of tiny cream-colored roses for her hair, and Jason had sent a double strand of lustrous, perfectly matched pearls for her to wear. It was a generous gift, accompanied by a charming note, and it made her slightly sick.

Her nerves were in an appalling state and she had scarcely touched the sumptuous dinner preceding the ball. In the rush of greeting people, she had put aside the knowledge that she must confront her father this evening, but her hands were cold and her stomach queasy. Given a choice, she would have fled down the marble steps of Wildehaven with never a backward glance.

Instead, Jason and Lady Edgeware stood beside her and introduced the endless stream of relations and neighbors. All knew of the engagement but she would not be officially presented to the neighborhood until after supper. Jason looked wonderfully handsome, having given Wills, his long-suffering valet, free rein. That worthy was continually frustrated by his master's impatience; Radford frequently left his servant behind when he traveled, dressed himself in the early morning when any real man of fashion was still abed, and generally did not permit Wills full exercise of his sartorial genius.

Tonight, however, he was immaculately turned out in formal black evening dress, his cravat tied in an elaborate style of his own invention, the glint of a ruby at his throat. The Diabolical Baron to the life, Caroline thought. Virility radiated from him, plus that quality of controlled force that had so frightened her in the beginning. The thought that she might have to confront him as well as her father made her stomach give another lurch.

They were ready to retire to the ballroom when suddenly Richard was crossing the hall toward her. The quiet elegance of his evening dress announced to the knowledgeable that he joined other soldiers in favoring the tailor Scott. His jacket was not completely *à la mode,* since it could undoubtedly be put on without benefit of a valet, but there was no denying that the cut flattered his broad shoulders and compact strength. She looked at him, her soul in her eyes. He bowed and gave her a warm, private smile that melted her bones. "You look like Titania indeed," he said softly as he glanced at the roses in her hair. "Or Botticelli's *Spring.*"

She smiled her acknowledgment of the compliment, then said calmly, "It is good to see you, Captain Dalton. May I present Lady Edgeware and Lord Radford?"

Richard bowed to her ladyship, then shook hands with Jason. The two men looked at each other measuringly, the younger curious about Caroline's fiancé, the older with a vague feeling of recognition. Jason said, "I believe Caroline said you were staying at Wargrave Park. What do you think of the place?"

"Impressive but neglected."

"An accurate assessment. The place has not been properly managed in many years. I hope Reggie Davenport will get a decent agent or sell it to me when he inherits. It is criminal for good land and people to be mistreated as Wargrave Park has been."

"Davenport has been staying there for the last few weeks," Richard said in a carefully neutral tone.

Jason raised one eyebrow. "Hiding from some mischief in London, no doubt."

"You know each other of old?" Richard grinned at how quickly Radford had analyzed his cousin's unaccustomed presence in the country.

"Alas, yes. We have always acted on each other as fire and tinder."

"Which is which?" Richard asked with interest.

Jason smiled and decided he liked the fellow. "We always took turns—whoever speaks first is the fire; the listener goes up like tinder. Since my duties at the door are done, let me introduce you to some of the other guests. I gather Caroline and Mrs. Sterling are your only acquaintance locally?"

Jason nodded to Caroline before leading Richard into the ballroom. She watched them go, not knowing whether to be glad or alarmed that they had taken to each other. Her thoughts were interrupted by Lady Edgeware. The old lady had been observing the exchange with an inscrutable gaze, but she said merely, "Come along, child. Your dance card is full and it is time to reward all those gentlemen who have been waiting so patiently."

After several country dances, Jason claimed his fiancée for a waltz. The dance was more relaxed than their first one at Almack's, but there was hardly more conversation than on that occasion. Caroline's eyes searched the crowd for her father, finally locating him in the corner with a group of older men. He looked likely to stay there for a few minutes, so she turned her attention to the waltz, letting the lilt of it relax her. Jason also seemed content to dance in silence; it struck her forcibly that while they were now more comfortable together, they really had nothing to talk about. Their interests struck no sparks with each other.

As the dance neared its end, she looked across the room and saw Richard. He had been talking with the Chandlers and someone she vaguely recollected as Lord Randall, but he looked up as if feeling her regard. Their eyes locked across the width of the room, azure blue to calm hazel.

She suddenly remembered what Gina had said about Gideon: *It's like his arms are around me even when he is across the room.* She could feel warmth and strength flowing into her, preparing her for the coming interview. The music stopped and she looked up at Jason, saying, "I must talk to my father now."

Without knowing quite why, she added, "Why don't you dance with Aunt Jessica? She has been a little sad lately." Then she turned and threaded her way through the crowd without waiting for his response.

Jason watched her weave toward her father. Well, why *not* dance with Jessica? Even the highest stickler could hardly object to his dancing with a guest. The musicians had not yet struck up the next tune, so he quickly requested another waltz and went in search of Jessica. She was magnificent tonight in a silk gown of shimmering russet, her eyes perhaps too bright, her conversation mesmerizing her crowd of admirers. A young naval officer on leave was about to lead her out when Jason smoothly interposed, "I claim a host's right." Without giving her time to object, he carried her off.

If dancing with Caroline was like dancing with a cloud, dancing with Jessica was unmistakably dancing with a woman. They did not speak at first, both racked by the mixed pain and pleasure of their nearness. The dance was half done when she said, "I will be leaving tomorrow for Wiltshire."

"Must you go so soon?"

She met his eyes for the first time. "You know I must."

He was silent, loath to admit the wisdom of her action. He finally said, "Will I ever see you again?"

"I will come for the wedding. It would seem strange if I missed it."

"And after that?"

"I will not come again. I hope Caroline will visit me sometimes." Her voice cracked suddenly. "I could not bear to lose you both."

They continued to turn and glide, the moments running away like the sands of an hourglass. He said finally, "I will send you to the Sterlings in one of my carriages."

"That isn't necessary. The Letchworths said—"

"You will let me do this one last thing for you." His voice brooked no opposition, nor did she wish to pursue the point. Then the music ended, and they were separate again.

Chapter 14

Caroline easily detached her father from his cronies. He had been drinking and was in high gig, basking in the knowledge that he would soon be connected with the wealth around him. She carried him off to the small chamber by the ballroom where her pianoforte had been placed. Prompted by a feeling of unease, her stepmother had followed them in, firmly closing the door behind. She had never known her stepdaughter to voluntarily seek out her father; it could mean trouble.

Caroline was glad to see Lady Hanscombe; Louisa might not be an ally but she was fair-minded and might aid her stepdaughter's cause. Standing by the piano, Caroline rested one hand on the polished surface as if to draw courage from it. As she tried and failed to find the words she needed, her father said jovially, "You've done well for yourself, puss. There is not a finer gentleman in England than your future husband. Nor a more generous one," he added. The money that had already changed hands had cleared Sir Alfred's major debts, but the additional settlement money coming after the marriage would give him enough to be able to speculate again.

Caroline's voice was trembling and she couldn't

meet his eyes. "Papa, how serious is the money problem?"

His jolliness started to slide away, replaced by the first ugly signs of temper. "That's none of your concern. After you've married him, there will be no problems at all."

"I don't want to marry him."

"I'll have none of that missishness!" He made an attempt to be reasonable. His voice coaxing, he said, "It is natural for girls to be a mite skittish about marriage, but these vapors will pass soon enough."

Taking a deep breath, she said, "I am not the least vaporish. I want to marry someone else."

There was a sharp gasp from Lady Hanscombe. Sir Alfred stared at his daughter, too astonished even for anger. "What maggot is in your brain? Radford is the only man who has ever shown the least interest in you, and damned if I know why *he* has. You'll marry him and be grateful you're not left on the shelf."

She raised her head proudly. "Strange as it may seem to you, someone else is in love with me. I love him, and will marry him unless you can convince me that it is absolutely essential to the family that I wed Lord Radford."

Since her father seemed to have been rendered temporarily speechless, she added, "I have some money and will do what I can to help you establish my younger brothers and sisters."

"I'll forbid your sister's marriage to Fallsworthy!"

She shook her head. "I don't think you can. The settlements have been signed, the engagement publically announced. The Fallsworthy family love Gina and will support her. If you attempt to interfere, I think Gideon will get a special license and marry her on the spot."

Sir Alfred was in shock at the sight of his most bidd-able child countering him point by point. Grasping at a straw, he asked, "Who is it you want to marry? That fop Fitzwilliam? If he really wants you, I suppose it would be acceptable." It was well known that the Honorable George was heir to a viscountcy and had nearly as much money as his friend. And as a bonus, he would be a good deal more malleable than the un-comfortably acute Lord Radford.

"It is not George Fitzwilliam. It is no one you know."

His dreams of a rich marriage evaporating, he asked feebly, "Who, then?"

"His name is Richard Dalton. He was a captain in the Ninety-fifth Rifles. He has sold his commission and has been taking inventory at Wargrave Park."

"You would throw away Radford for a penniless ex-soldier?"

"He is not penniless. He thinks he can get a small es-tate on the south coast."

He shook his head, unable to believe his daughter compared a country squire's manor with the vast Kin-caid properties.

"I'll bandy no more words with you. You'll marry Radford and that is the end of it."

"No."

"What did you say?"

She lifted her chin defiantly. "I said *no!*"

The tension in the air was nearly tangible as the stocky man glared at the slim young woman, his hands unconsciously clenching into fists. Lively music from the ballroom sounded with grotesque cheerful-ness. Lady Hanscombe, silent till now, spoke in an at-tempt to defuse the situation.

"She is of age and we cannot stop her if she is determined, Alfred. And since that trading ship of yours made it back to London, our finances are not uncomfortable. We should investigate the young man to see he is what he claims, but I talked with him earlier this evening and he is pleasant enough. While it is not a great match, there would be no disgrace in it."

Sir Alfred shifted his angry glare to his wife. When he looked back at Caroline, he found her staring at him with huge accusing blue eyes.

"You mean . . . you have had the money and made no move to release me? After I had *begged* you to spare me from a marriage I didn't want? Have you never cared, even a little, about what happens to me?"

She was crying, raw pain in her voice. Over the years she had neither expected nor received much from her father, but to find his selfishness so great he would consign her to emotional desolation was too much to bear. That Jason had turned out to be a good man was beside the point—the pain was in knowing her father would have sold her to a malignant troll had the price been right.

Unable to refute the censure in her eyes and voice, he took two quick steps toward his daughter and grabbed her by the shoulders. Shaking her violently, he shouted in her face, "If you don't marry him, I will never be rich! You will do as I bid you!"

Tears coursing down her face, she still found the voice to whisper, "No!"

The precarious hold on his temper snapped. Drawing back his right arm, he slapped her across the face with the full strength of his thick shoulders. The violence of the blow spun her away from his grip and sent her slight body crashing to the floor.

She lay motionless by the piano while her stepmother knelt at her side and Sir Alfred's horrified rasps of breath filled the room. The chit had provoked him, but he shouldn't have hit her. Fragile as she was, being knocked against the heavy mahogany instrument might have hurt her badly, even killed her. And if killing his own child was not dreadful enough, there were two men in this house who wanted to marry her, and either one might feel a need for vengeance. . . .

Caroline shifted slightly and looked at Louisa with unfocused eyes. "Mama . . . ?"

Lady Hanscombe supported her as she struggled to a sitting position. Her father's gold signet ring had made a flaring welt on her cheekbone and the whole left side of her face showed red and angry. There would be heavy bruising soon; now the scent of crushed roses from her flowery headdress lent an incongruously sweet scent to the air.

Concern in her voice, Louisa asked, "How do you feel, child?"

Caroline moved her head slowly from side to side, then said, "I am all right, Mama. Please help me up." Her father's blow had destroyed what love and duty she had always tried to give him. In the wake of their passing she felt a freedom and power entirely new to her.

When she was upright, she looked her father directly in the eye. "It is no use, Papa. You can hurt me, but you can no longer command me." He made a confused motion with his hand while she continued in the same small clear voice, "They say that love casts out fear. Because I love and am loved now, I am not afraid of you anymore, and you can never compel me again."

He stared at her, then turned abruptly and left the room, unable to face his wife and daughter. As the door banged behind him, Lady Hanscombe pressed her gently to the piano bench and examined the welt on Caroline's face. "This will not scar, but you won't be fit for public view very soon. I will help you to your room, then tell Lady Edgeware you were taken ill and must miss the rest of the ball."

"No, Mama. I want you to ask Lord Radford to come to me here. The sooner I break this engagement, the better for all us. And then"—her face softened—"I must see Richard."

"Are you sure, Caroline? You must be badly shaken. There will be time enough tomorrow."

She shook her head. "No, it must be done now. It is bad enough I am jilting Jason. I would at least spare him the humiliation of having personally announced the marriage to all his friends and relatives."

When her stepmother still looked dubious, she said, "If you will not summon him, I will walk out there and get him myself. If anyone asks what happened, I shall tell them the exact truth."

Louisa shook her head in admiration. "You have grown a great deal, child. Will that captain of yours make you happy?"

"Yes, Mama."

"By the way, the money you thought you had—your inheritance from your mother—has been lost through poor investments."

Caroline looked mildly surprised. "I wasn't thinking of that—you had said it was not enough to signify. The money I meant is from a music publisher in London who bought some of my compositions. You needn't worry," she added hastily, "they will not have my name on them."

Lady Hanscombe looked more impressed than

upset. "You mean someone actually gave you money for your tunes? Perhaps music does have some value. Best not tell your father, though. It would just make him angrier."

She sighed, then said, "Try not to think too harshly of your father. He has not done well by you, but he is not an evil man. He just . . . does not concern himself with other people."

"I do not hate him."

Louisa found herself uncomfortable in the face of the pity in the deep blue eyes. After all, she had chosen Alfred Hanscombe freely, knowing his faults. Why should this chit be sorry for her? She gave Caroline an awkward pat and turned to the door. "I will find Lord Radford and bring him to you."

Jason saw Reginald Davenport's entrance from across the ballroom. His brows knit in a slight frown; then he shrugged philosophically. Davenport was going to be his neighbor soon, so they might as well learn to be civil to each other. He was wearing evening dress but had a faint air of dishevelment that probably meant he had been drinking. Quantities of alcohol that would lay most men under the table made Reggie quarrelsome and very, very dangerous; all of his notorious deeds had come when he was under the influence. Still, he didn't make a habit of causing trouble in respectable society, so Jason decided to give him the benefit of the doubt.

He intercepted his uninvited guest near the door, saying pleasantly, "Good evening, Davenport. I hadn't realized you were in the neighborhood or I would have had a card sent. How have you been keeping?"

"Well enough," Reggie shrugged. "The estate

should be settled by the end of the year, but waiting is a confounded nuisance."

"Have you thought any more about the disposition of the main property?"

Reggie's mouth twisted in a slight sneer. "Playing carrion crow, Radford? I warn you, there will be no bargains. I've more than half a mind to keep the place and run it myself."

Jason stiffened but with effort resisted the bait. A host's duties should not include fighting with guests, even uninvited ones. Instead he said, "No doubt it would be a good discipline for you; you have always shown a singular lack of that."

Reggie's eyes narrowed but he did not reply in kind, perhaps remembering he was nominally a gentleman. "I understand congratulations are in order. I met your bride-to-be. She is very lovely."

"Yes, she is. I am a fortunate man."

Reggie's eyes raked the ballroom, stopping when they reached Jessica. Her stunning auburn beauty was the focus of a group of admirers. "Who is the red-headed Incomparable? I would surely have remembered her if we had met."

Jason clamped down his automatic surge of jealousy; besides the fact he had no right, he was sure Jess was more than capable of fending off unwelcome advances. "That is my fiancée's aunt, Mrs. Sterling. Her husband died several years ago and she has not gone much into society."

Reggie raised his eyebrows approvingly. "A fine family to marry into. Perhaps I'll make a play for the widow. Or does Miss Hanscombe have any younger sisters?"

"None out of the schoolroom," was the dry reply. "Have you a yen to set up a nursery?"

"But of course! The succession, you know."

"It sounds like becoming a man of property will change you all out of recognition."

Reggie flashed a sudden genuine smile. "And high time, as you are so carefully not saying."

Their conversation was interrupted by Lady Hanscombe. After a low-voiced exchange, Jason turned to Reggie and said, "If you will excuse me, I must leave. I'm sure you are acquainted with most of the other guests." Then he turned and followed her through the crowd.

He stepped through the music-room door, then stopped in shock. "Caroline! What has happened?"

She had stood at his entrance, raising her eyes to his. "I had a discussion with my father."

Jason's voice was low and hard. "If he did that, you will be an orphan before the night is over."

Caroline raised one hand quickly. "Truly, it is of no importance. Indeed, you may feel like duplicating his action before I am done."

He lifted one eyebrow forbiddingly and said in a chilly tone, "Oh? What do you wish to discuss?"

She hesitated, groping for the words she needed. He was in so many ways a stranger to her, his darkly handsome face cool and remote. This man had effectively bought and paid for her; would he accept her desire to rescind the bargain? The calm she felt after confronting her father started to shred away. She turned her back on Jason and sat at the pianoforte, her right hand stroking the keys.

What flowed from her fingers was the theme of the sonata to Richard. As the calm crystalline notes surrounded her, she felt once more the sense of peace she found only with him. As she played, Jason circled the instrument and was standing opposite her. As the last notes faded into silence, he said quietly, "What is it, Caroline?"

She lifted her head and looked directly into his dark eyes. "I do not wish to marry you. And"—she drew a steadying breath—"I do not think you truly wish to marry me."

His face was so still that she felt a sudden thread of alarm, yet all he said was, "Why not?"

"I am in love with someone else."

An odd light came into his eyes and his voice was laced with veiled excitement as he said, "That is the whole reason? It is not because of anything I have done?"

She was puzzled. "What have you done but treat me with honor and generosity? It is a poor return I make, but I would not condemn us both to a loveless existence."

She was half-fearful of giving him the opportunity to declare a passion, but he made no attempt to do so. Instead, he said formally, "I must of course accede to your wishes. And," he said, a broad smile breaking out, "I wish you very happy."

She was a little disconcerted by how very well he was taking the news. She looked at him with narrowed eyes, then gave a sudden gasp of shock as pieces fell into place. The strange tension between Jason and Jessica, her aunt's abrupt desire to leave Wildehaven, the early love affair Jess had once alluded to . . . "I know why you don't wish to be my husband," she exclaimed. "You want to become my *uncle*!"

He laughed, suddenly looking years younger than

she had ever seen him. "You have the right of it. I fell in love with your maddening aunt fourteen years ago, and never recovered."

Caroline drummed her fingers on the piano bench as she thought. "But she knew I was not in love with you. Indeed, she kept me from going into a decline when you offered for me."

Jason looked amused. "What a blow to my *amour propre!* Was the prospect so very terrible?"

She had the grace to blush. "It was not you, but my own foolishness. You have a . . . forceful personality, and the prospect of marrying you was an alarming one."

She shook her head in wonder; that frightened weeping child seemed half a lifetime behind her. "She should have known that I would be delighted to step aside in her behalf."

"Well, there was the settlement money that your family needed." As Caroline's eyes darkened, he waved one hand negligently. "I am sure your father has spent what was already transferred, but he need not return it. Had I not engaged myself to you, I should never have found my glorious vixen again. And apart from the money, your aunt had the idea you had fallen in love with me."

As Caroline stared in blank astonishment, he added, "Something about hearing you sing love songs one night. She said you could not have sounded thus were you not in love."

"Oh-h-h," she said, enlightened. "But you were not the one I sang them for."

"So it seems. Tell me," he said curiously, "who is the lucky man?"

She answered with a dreamy smile, "Richard Dalton."

"Indeed! It becomes clear that much transpired in my absence. He seems a good fellow, but can he support you?"

She laughed. "You are sounding like an uncle already! I am sure he can, but I would go with him if he were a tinker with no more than a wagon."

He shook his head in wonder. "George was right—women are romantics. I sincerely hope Dalton can do better than that. I feel some responsibility for you, and will talk with him. I think your father has forfeited the right," he added, with a pointed glare at her bruised face.

She had been weighing whether to ask a question that had nagged at her, and now she plunged in. "Tell me, Jason. Why did you offer for me?"

He hesitated, reluctant to tell her she had been the subject of a tasteless wager. A gently bred girl was unlikely to take kindly to the idea.

"The truth, now," she prompted.

"George and I had a wager," he said, deciding honesty was the order of the day. "I bet him I could persuade a randomly chosen girl to marry me within six months." As she stared at him in disbelief, he added, "Your name was drawn out of the several dozen judged suitable."

His worry over her reaction ended when she dissolved into laughter. Shaking with mirth, she said, "I once told Jessica I thought you must have drawn my name out of a hat, but I never dreamed I was so close to the truth!"

"Actually, it was a nut bowl."

His literal-mindedness set her off again, and after a moment he joined her.

When they had sobered up, he said thoughtfully, "Do you know, I think we might not have done so very badly together had there been no one else in the picture."

She gave him an enchanting smile and offered him her hand. "I think perhaps you are right. But I know we shall both be happiest as things stand now."

He squeezed her hand very gently and smiled. "Yes. Now you must want to see your soon-to-be-intended." He thought for a moment, then said, "You will want more privacy than this room affords. Indeed, we are fortunate no one has yet invaded with tonight's conquest. Go out this door and left down the corridor. The stair at the end will take you to the armor room. That should be quiet tonight.

"But I warn you," he said firmly, "I shall allow you only a few minutes alone before I bring your aunt. Your credit will have quite enough to contend with over jilting me."

She looked suddenly anxious. "I am sorry it might reflect badly on you, when you have been so very kind to me."

He made a magnanimous gesture. "I have been remarkably well-behaved lately; it is time I did something for the gabble-mongers. I will find your captain now and send him up to you."

She rose and went to him, standing on her toes to plant a feather-light kiss on his cheek. "Thank you," she whispered, then slipped out the back door.

He touched a bemused finger to his cheek. She was more like her aunt than he had realized. . . .

* * *

Reginald Davenport prowled the ballroom rest-
lessly. He had forgotten the tedium of Polite Society:
He usually socialized with hard-drinking sportsmen
like himself. There was a certain amusement in watching horrified mamas shield their lambs from him; if he
had a daughter, *he* wouldn't let her near a man like
himself. Who would know better than he how dangerous a rake could be?

What revolted him were the rapacious women
thrusting themselves or their bashful daughters in his
direction. It was well known that he was about to inherit a title and a large, albeit encumbered estate. Their
aggressiveness gave him an inkling why Radford was
so devilish toplofty—it was a defense against the toadeaters.

It wasn't the sort of party where serious drinking
was possible. Bored, he decided to indulge his catlike
curiosity in a little exploration. He wandered out a
door in the corner of the room and found himself in a
quiet passage with stairs rising in front of him. Since
the corridor held few attractions, he started to climb.

Richard was standing at the edge of the crowd, his
eyes searching for Caroline, when he found his host at
his side. Radford had a mysterious gleam in his eyes as
he said, "My former fiancée would like to speak with
you."

"Former . . . ?" Richard spoke cautiously but his
heart was beginning to beat faster. "Has she spoken to
you?"

"She has told me in the nicest possible way that I
have no place in her future. For some unaccountable
reason, she prefers you." The words were wry but the
tone amused.

Richard drew in a quick breath before he asked, "Are you going to take a horsewhip to me?"

"That would be too fatiguing. Besides, while I am naturally devastated, I believe I shall survive the blow." Jason's eyes went to the dance floor, where Jessica was whirling with an older gentleman. His gaze was possessive as it rested on her laughing face, tendrils of red hair curling around it like a sunrise.

Richard smiled. "I think I understand. Have we been enacting a comedy of errors?"

"So it would seem," Jason laughed. He put his hand on Richard's shoulder and gave it a friendly squeeze. "I wish you both very happy."

"Thank you. May I say that if Jessica Sterling will accept you, you are the second-luckiest man in England?"

"I would dispute the *second*." He looked at her again and said softly, "I met and lost her when I was twenty-one, and I never thought I would be this happy again."

He turned back to his guest and said, "Go out the door in the corner and up the stairs to the left. She is waiting for you. Jess and I will give you ten or fifteen minutes to"—he paused delicately—"discuss your plans."

Richard smiled, then made his way expertly through the crowd. Jason stared after him, again feeling that nagging sense of familiarity. It did not occur to him to mention Caroline's injured face.

When the dance ended, he once more snatched Jessica from under the nose of the smitten naval officer; that young man considered challenging his host to a duel but was unable to decide if it would be correct behavior before the pair had moved away. He shrugged philosophically; when one spends most of one's time at sea, all love affairs are apt to be unrequited.

Beyond saying her assistance was needed, Jason did not speak to Jessica until they had left the ballroom and were climbing the stairs to the armor room. When they reached the landing, she planted herself firmly and said, "What am I needed for?"

A step below her, Jason found her lips were irresistibly at the same level as his own. Rather than answer, he leaned forward, cupping her face in his hands, and proceeded to kiss her with great thoroughness.

Laughing and irritated at the same time, Jessica broke away when he came up for air. "Have you run mad? What if someone should find us here? And"—here her breath wavered as his arms slipped around her and he drew her against him,—"this is too cruel a thing to do. Please, every time you touch me it gets harder to let you go."

"That is exactly my intention," he murmured, his lips moving down her neck and heading in the direction of her splendid décolletage.

"Jason, stop this minute! What about Caroline?"

He transferred his attention to her ear, then said between light nibbling kisses, "This is all a direct result of Caroline. Your adorable niece has decided that we should not suit and requested an end to our engagement."

"*What!*" She jerked away from him. "Jason, has she found out about us and determined to play the martyr?"

Since her hand was the most convenient part of her, he lifted it and ran his tongue from her palm down her wrist. She shivered and tried to pull away, but his grip was secure. "Jason! She loves you . . ."

He grinned at her, his mind temporarily off lechery. "On the contrary. She informed me that her heart belongs to another."

"Who?"

"Your friend Captain Dalton."

"She's in love with Richard?"

"Yes, and singularly good judgment she is showing. Don't you approve of him?"

"Of course I do! He is a wonderful man, kind and amusing and as musical as she is. And very handsome as well." Jessica was pleased to see her last remark drew a slight scowl from her beloved. "He is perfect for her."

"If he is so perfect, why did you not see it earlier, my darling pea-goose? The romance must have developed under your very nose."

She looked at him blankly. "It never occurred to me a woman could fall in love with someone else while you were about."

He gave a great shout of laughter and wrapped her in a bear hug, rocking her slightly from side to side. After a few moments he said, "My darling, darling girl. You are going to marry me this time, you know. You can't complain I haven't said I love you, and if you suffer an attack of nobility on someone else's behalf, I shall tie you to a horse and carry you off to Scotland! I'm told there are men there who will perform a wedding even if the bride is bound and gagged. Which I shall do if necessary."

"Really?" she said with interest. "What if it is the bridegroom who is bound and gagged?"

He silenced her with another kiss. After some moments had passed, he said, "Shall we get married on Wednesday? That will give me time to procure a special license and to bring Linda here. I assume you wish her to be present."

The brilliant look she gave him confirmed the fact. "I'm glad you realize you are marrying a package— the two of us come together."

A purr and a pressure on his leg made him look down. Infallible feline instinct had brought Wellesley to the scene to leave orange hairs on Jason's immaculate black pantaloons. "Actually, I was under the impression the package included three of you."

Jessica followed his eyes and laughed. While she bent to scratch the cat's head, he asked, "Will Linda approve of me?"

She straightened with a chuckle. "I should think so—she has been after me to remarry for the last year. Her only requirement is that the man be able to buy her a pony."

"I think that can be arranged." He was putting his arms around her again when a scream sounded from the armor room above them. Jason turned his head sharply, his ear now catching the metallic sounds he had overlooked while concentrating on Jessica. He stiffened and said tersely, "Swords." He raced up the remaining stairs, Jessica a bare half-step behind him.

The armor room had several lamps lit when Caroline reached it, but most of its great length was illuminated by the full moon. Suits of armor gleamed like silvery ghosts and the weapons mounted on the walls and cases shone from the shadows more like fairy ornaments than instruments of death.

As she waited for Richard, she dreamily danced to

the sounds of overheard music, her arms held out and her dress swirling softly round her ankles. Her only contribution to the ball arrangements had been ensuring a good orchestra. Though her feet moved to the waltz from below, her mind was weaving a new piece of music, a paean of joy tentatively titled "Wedding March."

A sound from the door caused her to run across the room, almost colliding with the unpleasant man from Wargrave Park. She gasped while he reached out a hand to steady her. He looked down in appreciation and said, "What a warm welcome, sweeting! Dare I hope it was for me?"

"*No!* That is, I was expecting someone else." She moved away from him but he followed, staying uncomfortably close. She backed up nervously until a glass case displaying daggers blocked her retreat. He was so close she couldn't move away. There was an unpleasant smell of alcohol on his breath as he lifted his hand, lightly touching her injured cheek.

"You seem to be having an exciting night, sweeting. Is this from your so-respectable fiancé, or do you have another lover."

She shrank back against the case, trying to decide what to do. Reggie was as tall as Jason, with a raffish vitality that seemed infinitely more threatening. The shadow-filled room was suddenly too isolated; she abruptly appreciated why young girls were hedged about with chaperons. It was to protect them from men like this.

She steadied her voice and said, "I am waiting for my fiancé. If you will excuse me. . . ." She tried to slip past him but he put out one arm, trapping her against the display case.

Reggie raked his eyes over her insolently. She was really a taking little thing. Her sweet young breasts were half-uncovered by the dress, with a hint of other curves under the shimmering silk. She had been unconsciously sensuous when he watched her dancing and he was sure the look of angelic innocence hid a passionate nature. And she belonged to Radford. . . .

Reggie's own life had been lived at the edge of society, with no solid position or fortune of his own. He had always resented Jason—his arrogance, his wealth, his calm sense of superiority. How delightful to taste something of the insufferable Radford's. Besides, he thought the chit had probably been spreading her favors around or she wouldn't look so much as if she had just gotten out of bed. Perhaps she had.

Bending over, he claimed her mouth. She was a delightful little armful; as she struggled against him, he moved forward, pinning her against the cabinet with the weight of his powerful body. Her struggles were arousing and he moved one hand down to grasp her soft breast while he parted her lips with his tongue. He was enjoying himself so much that he didn't notice company had arrived until he was ripped from behind and torn away from Caroline.

Reggie's frustrated lust turned to a rage that redoubled when he saw his assailant was not Radford but Dalton, the placid nonentity who had been underfoot at Wargrave. What right had this peasant to interfere with him? He was the Earl of Wargrave! As he collided with the wall, the hand he threw out for balance touched the hilt of a mounted sword. After thousands of hours of practice and several duels, it came as naturally to his hand as the hammer to the carpenter. With a roar of fury he pulled the sword from its mount and lunged at his attacker.

Dodging a thrust aimed at his heart, Richard came down on his damaged right leg at a twisting angle that made it give way under him. He fell to the floor as Caroline screamed his name and the relentless blade followed him. Cat-quick, he turned the fall into a tumbling roll that carried him to temporary safety.

Amazingly, by the time he regained his feet he had peeled off his coat and located the nearest sword. Hurling the coat away as he wrenched the weapon from the wall, he was barely able to put up a guard before his cousin was on him again.

"Caro, get back!" he called out. She withdrew slowly, gripped by an irrational fear that if she turned away, Richard would be killed.

Reggie's murderous rage had nothing in common with the formality of a duel—he was in a fighting frenzy, beyond judgment or sportsmanship. Moreover, his boasts of fencing skill were clearly founded on truth. His sword was a whirling dervish of lethal brilliance. The fight should have been over in seconds— except that Richard's blade moved with equal brilliance, parrying every thrust and creating an impenetrable defense. His weapon was the rapier of an earlier century, longer and heavier than the smallsword of his opponent, and the extra length helped counter his opponent's greater reach.

Outraged at seeing Caroline's injured face and her struggle with Reggie, Richard fought with controlled virtuosity, icy cold in contrast to his cousin's mindless rage. Half a head shorter and years younger than his furious opponent, he looked like a boyish David facing down Goliath.

When Reggie swept forward in a devastating lunge that should have ended the fight on the spot, Richard retaliated with a masterful parry that locked their blades together, their corded muscles straining while they were held motionless face-to-face for a few moments of illusory peace.

Richard said between gasping breaths, "You wanted to know what makes me angry? Now you have found out. I would have stopped you from hurting any woman, but because it was Caroline, I should kill you."

"Are you the lover the ice maiden awaited? How delightful! Then we must be fighting about who will have the privilege of first cuckolding Radford."

The suggestive laugh that accompanied the remark was the final straw—Richard exploded in an angry rush of thrusts and feints that slashed his cousin's right forearm and forced him into a standing suit of fifteenth-century armor. It fell with a resounding crash, the helmet and gauntlets bouncing noisily away.

Caroline whirled and ran to the door, hoping to find someone who could stop the battle before it was too late. Her flight drove her into Jason's broad chest as he rushed in with Jessica right behind him. "Please," she gasped, "stop them!"

Jason's experienced eye took the scene in at a glance. Anyone interfering would destroy the precarious balance between the two duelists and run the risk of death himself. He put an arm around Caroline to restrain her, reaching his other arm out to block Jessica's precipitate entrance to the room. "Nothing can be done," he said. "Stay back here out of the way."

When Caroline frantically tried to tear away, he

shook her and said fiercely, "Control yourself! If you distract your captain, you may be the death of him."

As the three of them watched frozen in their position by the door, Jason found himself detachedly admiring the skill of the antagonists. It was like an exotic dance, the flickering blades darting and retreating in graceful patterns that concealed the lethal consequences of a moment's error. He had seen Davenport fight at one of the fashionable fencing salons and knew him to be one of the finest swordsmen in England. But Dalton was at least his match, and was slowly driving him back across the room.

Reggie's rage was fading as he fought desperately to survive, knowing instinctively that the deadly menace in his opponent's eyes had been seen by few other men, and those few were now dead. He had forgotten that the mild-mannered man he had provoked was a warrior, honed by years of fighting. The casual malice of Reggie's remark about Caroline had unleashed a demon of ferocity, and the death he had flirted with for years was on him. His blood and strength were ebbing from the slash on his arm, and the hilt of the sword was getting slippery.

He gathered his fading strength into one last desperate attack, one he knew doomed to failure. With a snakelike movement too fast for the eye to follow, Dalton broke his attack and administered a wrenching blow that twisted the smallsword from his grip and left his right wrist and hand numb. The rapier's blade was at Reggie's throat, as cold and steely gray as the merciless eyes that looked down its length. Reggie thought, with brief wistfulness, of the life that might have been his had he chosen differently, and prepared to die.

The berserker rage that had driven Richard for the last half of the fight burned out when he was within a second of slitting his cousin's throat. Anger had been simmering inside him since he had heard why his parents left England. But that crime had been ably avenged by his father, and had nothing to do with this man whose pale blue eyes were watching him steadily and without fear. Nor could any sword touch the grandfather who had disowned his own son.

The fury triggered by Reggie's actions had its roots far in the past. While his cousin would doubtless come to a bad end, he did not deserve to die for what he had done tonight. But though Richard could not kill him in cold blood, neither could he give Wargrave into his hands.

As Richard's newfound clarity of vision swept away his ghosts, he released the anger that had driven him and accepted the future he had tried to refuse. It was not chance that had brought him to Wargrave, and he could no longer deny the responsibilities laid on him.

His breath came in great wrenching gasps from the exertion of the battle, but his voice resonated through the room as he said, "There are two important things you don't know about me. One is that my father was a fencing master, and would never have let his son disgrace his teaching. And the other"—he drew a deep breath before he made the step from which there would be no turning back—"He was Julius Davenport."

The room had the same tense silence that falls when a bomb is ticking its way to explosion. Radford softly exclaimed, "Of course!" as one of the women inhaled sharply in shock.

Richard held his cousin's eye until, suddenly and inexplicably, Reggie burst into laughter. Richard withdrew the sword so there would be no accidental impaling, then dropped the point to the floor when it became clear that Reggie's amusement was genuine, not a ploy.

When his mirth subsided, he said, "If you had gotten angry earlier, cousin, I might have recognized you as a Davenport. You have the family temper."

Richard's voice was dry as he said, "Perhaps you can judge from the results why I prefer to hang on to it."

"Very true. I have always assumed someone would eventually murder me, but I never thought it would be over a stolen kiss."

Richard's voice was flinty. "And the marks on her face?"

"Not made by me. It is my policy to persuade ladies by the power of my kisses. Beating them senseless is poor sport."

Still watching his cousin, Richard asked, "Is he telling the truth, Caroline?"

"Yes."

He was sure Radford would not have struck her: it must have been her father. Disturbed by the odd note in her voice, he glanced sharply over, then turned back to Reggie to settle things quickly. "Must I watch my back as long as you are alive?"

Reggie looked offended. "Of course not. It would not be at all the thing to attempt to murder the head of the family."

At Richard's pained expression, he said, "Like it or not, that is what the Earl of Wargrave is. That is what *you* are, my lord cousin. Besides, a stab in the back is not my style, and I have serious doubts about my ability to best you in a fair fight. Did your father ever run a shooting gallery?"

At Richard's nod, he sighed and said, "Then there is no help for it. I shall not be able to kill you. Besides, if I tried and failed, you would almost certainly cut off my allowance."

Richard shook his head in disbelief, too drained to deal with his cousin's frivolities. "You'd best get that arm taken care of." He untied his loosened cravat for a bandage, only to have Jessica take it from him.

"I'll bind it up—I have had plenty of experience. Brace yourself, Mr. Davenport, I think this is going to hurt *a lot.*"

Reggie's dark face had a look of comic resignation as she started to remove his jacket preparatory to bandaging his arm. Clearly she was making no particular effort to minimize the pain.

Richard turned and slowly walked to the doorway where Jason and Caroline still stood. He was limping heavily, his bad leg wrenched by the fall when Reggie first attacked him. Jason spoke up first, clapping a hand on his left shoulder. "You looked familiar, and I should have known you sooner. Your father would sometimes give me rides on his horse when he found me wandering around the home wood. I was only five when he left, but I have always remembered him fondly."

Richard smiled briefly at the tribute, but his eyes were fixed on Caroline. She had had a difficult evening—starting as the reluctant guest of honor and going on to be bullied, beaten, and mauled. She had broken an engagement, been terrified that her beloved would be killed, and now found that that same lover was not who she thought. Confused, angry, and hurt,

for the first time in her life Caroline Hanscombe smol-
dered.

"Caro?" Richard asked tentatively.

"There is no need for explanations, *my lord*," she
said with awful precision. "A man of your rank need
not think anything of making a May game of foolish
girls. There is little other sport in the country at this
season."

Richard glanced at Jason and said, "If you will excuse us, I must talk to my fiancée or this engagement
may be over before it begins."

"Quite right, *my lord*," she said through gritted
teeth. "I have broken one engagement this evening
and am quite capable of breaking another."

The expression on her face was grim when he led
her toward the far corner of the room—but she did not
have to be forced to accompany him.

Jason looked after the pair curiously and asked, "Do
you think he can talk her around?"

Her nursing chores over, Jessica came to his side and
said, "I have no doubt whatsoever. She just needs to be
reassured a bit—she has had too many shocks
tonight." She glanced at Reggie and said, "Can you
make it back to Wargrave Park, or shall we make up a
bed for you here?"

"I shall be quite all right. I have returned home in far
worse case than this. Radford, is there an exit I can use
without alarming your guests unduly?"

Jason nodded. "Down the stairs and around to the
left. At the end of the passage is a door that will let you
out near the stables. You are sure you are all right?"

"I am sorry to crush your hopes, but I shall be perfectly sound in three days."

"You've a wicked tongue on you, Davenport."

Reggie's sallow face was self-mocking. "It will be the death of me yet. But not tonight." With that, he turned and disappeared down the staircase.

Jessica shook her head after he left. "What an impossible man! Still, I'm glad Richard didn't kill him."

"Quite right. It might have ruined the party still going on beneath our feet. I propose we finish the evening with no announcements whatsoever. Our mystified guests can learn what happened from the *Gazette*."

He reached out his arms and pulled her close. She gave a sigh of contentment and let her head rest against his shoulder for a moment while he stroked her back and dropped a light kiss on the top of her head. He felt like a settled married man. He felt wonderful.

Jessica stepped back and shot an inscrutable green glance up through her lashes, then concentrated on straightening a nonexistent wrinkle in Jason's neckcloth. Her voice was muffled as she said, "I would like to ask you something before we go back downstairs."

"Yes?"

"Well, in spite of my rather lurid reputation, I have actually behaved with considerable propriety. The most *outré* thing I have ever done was kiss a man I wasn't married to."

"And who might that have been?" he asked with a dangerous gleam.

"You, of course!" She was still fiddling with his cravat, unable to meet his eyes. "I have always had a secret wish to do something wanton and profligate. If we are to be married in five days, I will have lost my opportunity forever. So-o-o . . ." She stopped.

"Yes?" he prompted.

"So"—she gave him a glance that was half-mischief and half-shyness—"Do you think that tonight . . . ?"

He shouted with laughter as he caught her meaning, then lifted her clear off the floor and whirled her around twice before depositing her down again. "You will keep me young forever, my dear minx."

He kissed her with a tenderness that rapidly escalated into passion, and whispered huskily, "It will be my very great pleasure to give you your wish tonight, my love. And every other night, as long as we both shall live. Shall we go downstairs now and see if we can convince our guests to leave early?"

She embraced him approvingly, only to be interrupted by a strangled squawk from the door. They both looked up, but Jason made no move to release her. "Good evening, George. Is the party going well?"

George Fitzwilliam was watching them with inarticulate fascination. Finally he sputtered, "Lady Edgeware sent me to discover where you had gotten to. Said there were rackety goings-on up here."

Jason smiled. "She must have heard the armor go over. Will you be the first to congratulate me? Mrs. Sterling has just agreed to make me the happiest of men."

"But . . . but . . . what about Miss Hanscombe?"

"She has made other arrangements." Jason's eyes flickered toward the far corner of the room; then he took Jessica's arm and headed toward the stairs. "May I congratulate you on your new team of horses?"

Never too quick on the uptake, it took a moment for George to realize that he had won their wager. His eyes brightened and he said with reverence, "You mean they are mine? The finest team of horses in England?"

"The second finest," Jason corrected. "A team of matched blacks I have bred and trained are now ready to take their place in society. Shall we return to our guests, my dear?"

Richard steered Caroline to a window seat in the far corner of the armor room. The flood of moonlight was bright enough to read by, but bleached the scene to an unearthly coolness.

"Will you not even look at me, Caro?" He took her chin in his hand and gently turned her face toward him. The huge blue eyes were filled with tears she was trying to suppress.

"How many other lies have you told me, my lord?" Her voice was a nearly inaudible whisper.

"None, not now, not in the past, and never in the future. And will you please stop calling me 'my lord'?"

"But that is what you are. An earl. One of the great men of England, with an ancient title and properties across the whole country. 'A small estate on the south coast,' indeed!"

He ran his fingers through his thick brown hair with a sigh of exhaustion, then stood and rested one hand on the window frame as he looked at the silver-gilt fields. The swordfight and the emotions released by it had driven him to the very limit of his physical and mental resources, and the lines of his body spoke of defeat rather than victory. Great patches of sweat caused the white shirt to cling to his body, the breadth of his shoulders emphasizing his lean hips and waist. She had never seen him look so powerful, or so vulnerable.

He said in a quiet voice, "Learning I was heir to an earldom was as much a surprise to me two months ago as it was to you tonight. I wanted none of it. I was twenty years old when I first became responsible for other men's lives. Younger than you are now. For seven years I carried that responsibility, sending them out and knowing many would die of my decisions. Seven long years. And half the men I commanded are dead now, slaughtered in a Belgian field. I know it was not my fault—we were doing our jobs, and we did them well. But after that, I had had enough of responsibility."

He turned his head to face her now, his hazel eyes a dark shadowed gray. "When I came here, it was because I had no will for any other action. Then I saw you, and knew what it was to live again. You have such a rare talent of joy and beauty. . . . I wanted to give you whatever would make you happiest. The moon and stars were beyond me, but I thought to find a place where you could be free to create. That is all I ever wished for you—to love me, and to make music."

He looked away again, unable to meet her eyes. "I never wanted Wargrave. It will take years of hard work to make it profitable again. Years of riding around England, learning about agriculture and law, settling disputes, caring for those in my charge. I know I can do it, and that I must.

"But the quiet life I longed to have with you is impossible now. The life of peace and love and music—you can never have it with me. A countess also has responsibilities that cannot be shirked. Even if you can forgive me my inheritance, you would be losing so much—the peace and privacy you crave, the time to create, to record the melodies of your imagination."

He faced her once more, his deep voice bleak with longing. "And the worst of being an earl is that it will

obscure that I am a man. Radford, Jessica, my cousin—
they all look at me with different eyes now. I can bear it
from others, but not from you. Can you not remember
that I am Richard? And that I love you?"

She felt a tightness in her chest almost beyond bear-
ing. Praying that this time she would find the right
words, she stood and went to him. Placing her palms
flat on his chest she felt the hard pulsing warmth of his
body. "If you can learn to be an earl, I can learn to be a
countess," she said softly. "I do not need an ivory
tower—great art comes from living life fully, and I
know my life with you will be richer than any other
path I might find."

Her eyes searched his, trying to look beyond the il-
lusions of moonlight. "I never truly thought you had
lied to me. I was angry to cover my tears. You have always been so strong, so assured, everything I am not. I
could not believe you needed me as much as I need
you."

He pulled her to him as a drowning man seeks
breath, drawing her to his heart. She felt once more the
sense of peace and safety she had always found in his
arms, but now was added the joy of knowing she also
sheltered him. The frightening events of the night
dropped from her consciousness and she was aware
only of him as they touched, mouth to mouth, body to
body, and soul to soul.

It was long minutes before he spoke, and humor had
returned to his voice. "Do you know, love, music is not
the only thing you have a genius for. I think it is your
ability to lose yourself utterly in what you do."

Caroline closed her eyes and laid her head against
his chest with a smile of utter contentment. "I will
never be so lost that you cannot find me. And no mat-

ter how busy we both may be, we will always find time for love and music."

Deliciously scandalized rumors hovered around the September marriage of Caroline Hanscombe to the Earl of Wargrave. It was said she threw over her first fiancé for a better title, that Radford and Wargrave fought a duel that nearly killed them both, that Radford was so heartbroken he had married the aunt to stay close to the niece.

Mothers of hopeful daughters complained that the new earl had been snapped up before they had a proper chance at him. Girls who had made their come-outs with Caroline remarked bitterly that it made no sense for such an insipid little thing to receive offers from no fewer than two peers of the realm. The vicar of Wargrave who married them was delighted that his wife had a new grandson, and he himself had secured a superlative organist for his church.

But the most breathless gossip occurred when the bride was given away not by her father, as was proper, but by her uncle and former fiancée, Lord Radford. The avidly curious attempted to discover why from Radford's companion, the Honorable George Fitzwilliam, but that gentleman would only say, "It was fitting."

The Duke of York Military Hospital was dismal, a drab monolith dedicated to the treatment of seriously wounded soldiers. Jocelyn wondered with black humor if the objective was to be so depressing that patients would do their best to recover quickly.

Steeling herself, she marched up the wide steps, her footman close behind. Hugh Morgan was tall, with dark curls and a melodious Welsh voice. He was a pleasant addition to the household, but today concern for his brother shadowed his eyes.

The building was crowded with casualties, and it took time to find Rhys Morgan's ward. Jocelyn experienced sights and smells that knotted her stomach, while Hugh's country complexion acquired a greenish-white tinge.

Rhys Morgan lay in a corner cot of perhaps forty jammed into a room too small for its population. Some patients sat on their beds or talked in small groups, but most lay in stoic silence. The bare walls created an unrestful clamor, and a miasma of illness and death hung heavy in the air.

Hugh scanned the room. "Rhys, lad!" he instinctively started to push past Jocelyn, then glanced back apologetically. With a nod, she released him to his brother.

The wounded man had been staring at the ceiling, but he looked up as his name was called. Though the face was startlingly like his brother's, Rhys Morgan wore an expression of blank despair that was only partly lifted as Hugh rushed up and grabbed his hand, Welsh words pouring forth.

The raw feeling in Hugh's face made Jocelyn uncomfortable. As she shifted her gaze away, her eyes were caught and held at the bottom of Rhys's bed. Where there should have been two legs under the covers, there was only one. The left had been amputated just below the knee.

She swallowed before approaching to touch Hugh's arm. He turned with a guilty start. "I'm sorry, my lady. I forgot myself."

She gave a smile that included both of them. "No apologies are necessary. Corporal Morgan, may I introduce myself? I am Lady Jocelyn Kendal, and I have the honor of being your brother's employer."

Rhys propped himself up against the wall behind his cot, alarmed at the vision of elegance before him. With a bob of his head, he stammered, "My pleasure, ma'am."

Hugh hissed, "Call her 'my lady,' you looby."

A wave of color rose under the fair Celtic skin as the soldier attempted to apologize. Wanting to alleviate his embarrassment, Jocelyn said, "It's of no importance, Corporal. Tell me, are you two twins?"

"Nay, I'm a year the elder," Rhys replied. "But we've oft been taken as twins."

"You are very alike," Jocelyn remarked.

"Not any more," Rhys said bitterly as he glanced at the flat bedding where his leg should have been.

Jocelyn colored, embarrassed to have reminded him of his loss. Deciding the brothers would be better off without her inhibiting presence, she said, "I'll find my friend now and leave you to visit. When I'm finished, I'll return here, Morgan."

Hugh looked uncertain. "I should go with you, my lady."

"Nonsense, what could happen to me in a military hospital?" she replied. "Corporal Morgan, do you know where the officers are quartered?"

He straightened when she asked for help. "The floor above, ma'am. My lady."

"Thank you. I shall see you both later." Jocelyn left the room, conscious of the stares that followed her. Impossible not to remember that while she had been living in comfort in London, these men had been getting blown to pieces for their country.

Climbing a staircase to the next level, she found a long, empty corridor with individual doors instead of open wards. As she hesitated, a thickset man of middle years strode purposefully from a nearby room. Guessing he was a physician, she said, "I'm looking for Captain Richard Dalton of the Ninety-fifth Rifles. Is he in this section?"

"Down the hall." The doctor waved his hand vaguely behind him, then marched off before she could get more specific directions.

Resigned to trial and error, Jocelyn opened the first door. A nauseating stench sent her into a hurried retreat. Aunt Laura, who had done her share of nursing in Spain, had once described gangrene, but the reality was far more sickening than Jocelyn had imagined. Luckily, the still figure on the bed was not the man she sought.

The next doors opened to empty beds or men too badly injured to notice her intrusion. No Captain Dalton. More and more unnerved, she opened the last door on the corridor. Several figures stood around a table with a man lying on it. A scalpel flashed, followed by a blood-freezing scream of agony.

Jocelyn slammed the door shut and ran blindly into the

open space at the end of the corridor. She'd thought it would be simple to locate a friend. Instead, she was finding the worst suffering she'd ever seen in her life.

Eyes clouded with tears, she didn't even see the man until she slammed into a hard body. There was a clatter of falling wood, then a strong hand grabbed her arm. Jocelyn gasped, on the verge of a hysterical scream.

"Sorry to be in your way," a quiet voice said. "Do you think you could hand me my other crutch?"

Blinking back her tears, Jocelyn bent to pick up the crutch that had skidded across the floor. She straightened to hand it over, and was profoundly relieved to see the man she sought. "Captain Dalton! I'm so glad to see you up and about."

Richard Dalton was a brown-haired young man of medium height, with hazel eyes much like her own. Though his face was drawn with fatigue and pain, his quick smile was warm. "This is an unexpected pleasure, Lady Jocelyn. What brings you to this wretched place?"

"You did, after Aunt Laura learned you were here." She glanced ruefully at the crutches. "I didn't intend to put you back into a hospital bed."

"It takes a good deal more than a collision with a beautiful woman to do me an injury," he assured her. "I can say without reservation that running into you is the most enjoyment I've had in weeks."

Richard's flirtatious teasing helped restore her ragged nerves. Though there had been nothing romantic between them, they had always enjoyed each other's company. Probably the lack of romance had made them friends. "Aunt Laura sends her apologies that she could not accompany me today, but she will call on you day after tomorrow."

"I shall look forward to it." He shifted awkwardly on his crutches. "Would you mind terribly if I sit down? I've been upright for as long as I can manage at the moment."

"Of course," she said, embarrassed. "I'll never make an angel of mercy, I fear. I seem to causing nothing but problems."

"Boredom is one of a hospital's worst problems, and you're alleviating that nicely." The captain swung over to one of several chairs and card tables set beside a window to create a lounge area. He gestured her to the chair opposite him as he lowered himself with a wince.

Jocelyn examined the drab walls and furnishings, and the windows that faced another depressing wing of the hospital. Not a place designed to aid convalescence. "Will you be staying here long?"

His smile faded. "It may be a while. The surgeons periodically poke around for bits of shell and bone they might have missed. We had one long argument about amputation, which I won, but now they are trying to convince me that I'll never walk without crutches again. Naturally I have no intention of believing them."

"In any such disagreement, my money is on you."

"Thank you." Bleakness showed in his eyes. "I'm fortunate compared to many of my fellow patients."

"Aunt Laura mentioned Major Lancaster in particular," Jocelyn said, remembering the letter. "Is there news of him I can take to her?"

"Nothing good. He has grave spinal injuries, and is paralyzed from the waist down." Richard leaned against the high back of his chair, his face much older than his years. "He can barely eat, and it's an open question whether he will die of starvation, pain, or the opium they've been giving him to make living bearable. The physicians don't understand why he isn't dead already, but they agree it's only a matter of time."

"I'm sorry. I know the words are inadequate, but any words would be," Jocelyn said with compassion. "He's a particular friend of yours?"

"From the first day I joined the regiment, when he took me in hand to turn me into a real officer." Richard's gaze was on the past, and the days and years that had gone into weaving a friendship. "Even in dying, he's an example to us all. Completely calm, except for his concern for his younger sister's future. She's a governess and well situated for now, but when he's gone, she'll be alone in the world, with nothing and no one to fall back on." He gave his head a slight shake. "Sorry. I shouldn't be depressing you with the story of someone you've never even met."

Jocelyn started to say that he had no need to apologize, then froze as an idea struck. She needed to marry before her twenty-fifth birthday, now only weeks away, in order to retain her fortune according to the terms of her father's will. The mortally wounded major wanted security for his sister. Unlike Sir Harold Winterson, there would be no question of "marital rights" since the poor man was on his deathbed. In return for his name, she could settle an annuity on the sister that would keep her in comfort for life. It was a perfect meeting of needs: she would retain her fortune, and he would be able to die in peace.

"Richard, I've just had a most bizarre inspiration that might solve a problem of mine while helping Major Lancaster." Quickly she sketched in the requirements of her father's will, then explained the solution that had occurred to her.

To her relief, the captain listened to Jocelyn's proposal with no sign of revulsion. "Your proposition is unusual, but so is your situation," he said thoughtfully. "David might well be interested. It would be a great comfort for him if Sally is provided for. Shall I introduce you to him if he's awake?"

"That would be wonderful." Jocelyn rose, hoping the major wasn't asleep. If she had time to think about her idea, she might not be brave enough to go through with it.

Richard pulled himself onto his crutches and led her to one of the rooms she'd glanced in earlier, where the patient had appeared unconscious. After opening the door for Jocelyn, he swung across the room to the bed.

As Jocelyn studied the emaciated figure on the bed, it was hard to believe that a man so thin and motionless could still be living. Major Lancaster appeared to be in his late thirties, with dark hair and pale skin stretched across high cheekbones to form a face of stark planes and angles.

The captain said softly, "David?"

Major Lancaster opened his eyes at the sound of his friend's voice. "Richard . . ." The voice was no more than a low whisper of acknowledgment.

The captain glanced at Jocelyn. "There's a lady here who'd like to meet you."

"Anything to oblige a lady," Lancaster said, a thread of humor in the low voice. "And I've nothing pressing on my schedule."

"Lady Jocelyn Kendal, allow me to present Major David Lancaster of the Ninety-fifth Rifles." Richard beckoned her to his side.

"Major Lancaster." She moved into the injured man's line of sight and got her first clear look at him. A jolt of surprise went through her. Though his body was broken, his eyes were very much alive. Vividly green, they showed pain, but also intelligent awareness. Even, amazingly, humor.

He scanned her with frank appreciation. "So this is the legendary Lady Jocelyn. It's a pleasure to meet you. Every man in the regiment took pains to tell me what I'd missed by spending the winter with the Spanish army."

"The pleasure is mine, Major." Jocelyn realized his eyes

were striking not only for the unusual shade of transparent green, but because the pupils were tiny pinpoints, making the irises even more startling. Opium. She'd seen eyes like that in society ladies who were overfond of laudanum.

She had intended to make her proposal without delay, but as she stood by the wreck of what had been a warrior, her throat closed and left her silent. To look into Major Lancaster's green eyes and say that she was here to make a bargain in anticipation of his death was impossible.

Correctly interpreting her strained expression, Richard Dalton said, "Lady Jocelyn has a most unusual proposition, one I think you'll find interesting. I shall leave you two to discuss it." He shifted his crutches to a more comfortable position, then left.

Jocelyn took a deep breath, grateful that Richard had broken the ice. Where to start? Not wanting to overtire the major, she said succinctly, "My father died several years ago and left me a substantial inheritance, on the condition I marry by age twenty-five. I shall reach that age in a few weeks and am still unwed. Richard mentioned your situation, and it occurred to me that we might make a bargain of mutual benefit. If . . . if you'll marry me, I shall settle an income on your sister to ensure her future security."

When she finished, absolute silence reigned, broken only by the distant sounds of street traffic. It took all of Jocelyn's control not to flinch under Lancaster's startled gaze. Yet when he spoke, his voice showed only curiosity, not anger at the bald implication of his imminent death. "I have trouble believing you can't find a husband in the usual fashion. Are the men of London mad, blind, or both?"

"The man I want has shown an unflattering lack of interest in me," Jocelyn admitted, feeling that nothing less than honestly would do. "Perhaps he may someday change his mind. I hope so. In the meantime, I don't want to marry only for the sake of an inheritance, then regret it the rest of my life. Do you understand?" Her last words were a plea; it was suddenly important that he accept her actions as reasonable.

"It would be utter folly to marry the wrong man because of a ridiculous will," he agreed. His eyes closed, leaving his face alarmingly corpselike. She watched anxiously, hoping she hadn't overstrained him.

His eyes flickered open. "How much of an annuity are you proposing?"

Jocelyn hadn't thought that far. After a swift assessment of her income and the costs of living, she asked hesitantly, "Would five hundred pounds a year be acceptable?"

His brows rose. "That would be very generous. Enough for Sally to live a life of leisure if she wished, though I can't imagine her idle. Perhaps she'd start a school."

He fell silent, the pain lines in his face emphasized as he thought. Uneasily Jocelyn said, "No doubt you'll want some time to consider this."

"No," he said emphatically, his voice stronger. "There is . . . no time to waste."

The words chilled her. For an endless moment, their gazes locked. Jocelyn saw no fear about his impending death, only stark honesty, and hard won peace. With every breath he drew, this man humbled her.

Carefully shaping each word, Lancaster said, "Lady Jocelyn, would you do me the honor of becoming my wife?" A faint, wry smile curved his lips. "Though I have nothing to offer you but my name, for your purposes that will suffice."

His ability to joke under these circumstances almost

undid Jocelyn's self-control. Choking back her feelings, she laid her hand over his. It was bone-thin, almost skeletal, but the pulse of life was still present. "The honor would be mine, Major Lancaster."

"David," he said. "After all, we are about to wed."

"David," she repeated. It was a good, solid name that suited him.

His brows drew together in concentration. "We shall obviously have to be married here. I'm afraid that you'll have to arrange for the special license, but if you have a man of business, he should be able to obtain one by tomorrow."

"I'll have my lawyer take care of it. He can also draw up the settlement for your sister. Her name is Sally Lancaster?"

"Sarah Jane Lancaster." He closed his eyes again. "Your lawyer must also draw up a quitclaim for me to sign, relinquishing all customary claims against your property."

Surprised, she asked, "Is that necessary?"

"Legally your property would become mine on marriage, and on my death half would go to my heir, Sally. Since the purpose of this exercise is for you to retain your fortune, we don't want that to happen."

"Heavens, I hadn't thought of that." What if she'd made this strange proposal to a man less scrupulous than Major Lancaster? It might have meant disaster.

Voice almost inaudible, he said, "If your lawyer is worth his hire, he would have protected your interests."

Recognizing that he was at the limits of his strength, Jocelyn said, "I should be able to have the license and settlements by tomorrow. Will this same time be agreeable to you?" As she studied the spare figure under the blanket, she wondered if he would still be alive in another twenty-four hours.

Uncannily reading her mind, he said, "Don't worry, I shall still be here."

She gave his hand a gentle squeeze, then released it. "Thank you, David. I shall see you tomorrow then."

A little dazed by the speed of events, she left the room, quietly closing the door behind her. Richard was seated in the lounge area at the end of the hall, so she joined him, gesturing for him not to stand for her. "Major Lancaster has agreed. The ceremony will be tomorrow. Thank you, Richard. You . . . you've allowed me to take a measure of control over my life."

"I'm glad I could help two friends at once," he said quietly. "Perhaps providence was taking a hand."

"I'd like to think so." With a slightly crooked smile, she bade him farewell.

Wondering if David looked as shaken as Lady Jocelyn, Richard pulled himself onto his crutches and made his way to his friend's room. "I gather all is well?" he asked as he entered.

David's eyes opened. Though he was gray with exhaustion, there was a smile on his face. "Very much so. Will you stand witness for me?"

"Of course." Richard settled in the chair beside the bed. "Do you need me to do anything else for the wedding?"

"Could you take the ring from my little finger and keep it for the ceremony?" He pushed his right hand over the dingy sheets. "I think it's small enough to fit her."

Richard carefully removed the ring. It came off David's bony finger easily.

"My efficient bride will arrange everything," the major said with a spark of amusement. "Thank you for bringing us together."

"The marriage of convenience is a time-honored tradition, though I've never heard of one quite like this," Richard said thoughtfully. "But everyone benefits."

"There are other men here whose families could use the money more than Sally, but I am selfish enough to be glad she will be provided for. A woman without family is only a step away from potential disaster. An accident or illness could push her into abject poverty. Now that won't happen." David exhaled roughly. "Time for more laudanum. Over there, on the table . . ."

Richard poured a dose of the medicine, then held the spoon so David could swallow. "Your sister is not entirely without family."

"She'd starve to death before she would ask help of one of our brothers. Can't say that I blame her. I'd do the same." David's eyes drifted shut. "Now she'll never . . . have to ask help of anyone."

Thinking his friend asleep, Richard hoisted himself onto his crutches, but before he could leave, David murmured, "I would have helped her even without the annuity. I rather like the idea of being married to Lady Jocelyn, even if it's only for a few days." His voice faded to a bare whisper. "Something to look forward to . . ."

Richard left the room with satisfaction, grateful that Lady Jocelyn was bringing some pleasure into David's last days. The only person likely to object to the arrangement was Sally Lancaster, who guarded her brother like a mother cat with her only kitten. At least the income would give her something to think about after he died.